Two Children Behind a Wall

To my darling sons, Alexander and Constantin.
You are the rays that light my life.
Day after day, through unashamed pain,
I call out your names. Source of my life.

However cruel our destiny, whatever injustice we face,
the strength of my love for you endures forever,
Inextinguishable and invincible.

TWO CHILDREN BEHIND A WALL

Catherine Laylle

ARROW

First published in the UK by Arrow in 1997

First published in France by Editions Fixot in 1996

1 3 5 7 9 10 8 6 4 2

First published in the United Kingdom in 1997 by Arrow,
Random House, 20 Vauxhall Bridge Road, London SW1V 2SA

Random House Australia (Pty) Limited
16 Dalmore Drive, Scoresby, Victoria 3179, Australia

Random House New Zealand Limited
18 Poland Road, Glenfield, Auckland 10, New Zealand

Random House South Africa (Pty) Limited
Endulini, 5a Jubilee Road, Parktown 2193, South Africa

Random House UK Limited Reg. No. 954009

A CIP catalogue record for this book
is available from the British Library

Papers used by Random House UK Limited
are natural, recyclable products made from wood grown in
sustainable forests. The manufacturing processes conform to
the environmental regulations of the country of origin

ISBN 0 09 925504 9

Printed and bound in Great Britain by
Cox & Wyman Ltd, Reading, Berkshire

Europe: our homeland

This is why we are channelling all our energy into creating an integrated Europe, because Europe includes our own homeland, because Europe – in a broader sense – is our homeland and because it is only by taking this step that we can give our children the chance to live in peace and happiness.

Konrad Adenauer
Leader of the Christian Democratic Union and Chancellor of West Germany 1949-63
Speech at Recklinghausen, 1 September 1957

Chapter 1
Cri de Coeur

My heart is filled.
It is filled with nothing but pain.

My little angels, from 1992, you lived in London
with your mummy and visited your daddy in
Germany on your holidays – until this one last trip
from which you never came back. Your father
abducted you and since that day in July 1994, your
mother has never been able to speak to you freely
again.

This is my last scene of our life together.

In our London home the three of us were packing in
Alexander and Constantin's bedroom. A few hours later
my sons would be leaving for their summer holiday in
Germany to stay with their father. Little did we know
then that this would be the end of our happy and peaceful existence. Little did we know that this would be the
very last day we would be free to talk, free to cuddle, and
free to love.

'You won't touch anything, Mummy? Promise. I have
cleared my desk and arranged my toys the way I want
them for when I get back.'

Alexander was always so meticulous. His collection of
tube tickets was neatly held together with a rubber band
in one drawer, his stamps in another and on the shelf
above, small boxes containing his secret treasures and
souvenirs were tidily stacked. Everything had its special
place and no one, not even his younger brother
Constantin, was allowed to disturb the private domain of

his desk. In the large cupboard, his Lego was laid out very precisely, like a theatre. On one shelf, he had arranged his medieval knights, shields and spears in hand, ready to venture forth on their next crusade. On the shelf beneath, pirate ships encircled a lone island, ready for imminent attack. The display was so carefully planned that the models looked almost real.

My Alexander: part a serious boy and yet still part a demanding baby. By nature he was less level-headed and even-tempered than Constantin. He was full of mischief, often given to embroidering the truth with his vivid imagination; he could be capricious sometimes, torn between the real world and fantasy.

But fate would throw him prematurely into adulthood. His father and I had separated when he was six and a half and since then we have lived in different countries. His daddy stayed in Germany and the three of us moved back to London where he had been born. Living without a man around, he gradually assumed that role for himself. I never imposed it on him. In my eyes he was still so tiny and vulnerable. But he cherished this new status, and at times he would become conscientious and protective of me. Today was such a day.

'Do we still have time? We won't miss the plane?'

'There's plenty of time. We don't have to leave for another hour.'

'And Mummy, don't forget to buy the exercise books I need for the beginning of term. Here's the list from school.'

He spoke to me in French, as he always did, French being his and Constantin's mother tongue. Both children had always attended French schools but they were also fluent in German, and would automatically speak to their father in it. It was wonderful to hear them switching so easily from one language to the other. Alexander was particularly gifted and his English too was perfect now. English offered many fun expressions which he loved to intermingle, sometimes with a Rastafarian accent which

2

he imitated well and which always made Constantin and me laugh.

Both my sons were the perfect image of the new Europe. Brought up in London, with a German father, a French mother, they had, and still have, three passports and are trilingual. In a future Europe this background would surely give them tremendous advantages. I was thrilled that they had this chance and terribly proud that both of them could rise to the challenge. Even given the opportunity, not all children are so adept at languages!

As I was packing their last items, I fell into thinking how lonely the next six weeks would be without them. I knew how much I would miss their cheerful voices, the constant to-ing and fro-ing and rampaging about the house. Without them the house was always so silent: no one to greet me with a shower of kisses in the mornings. This is the harsh price of a broken marriage: schooldays with Mummy and most of the holidays with Daddy. But watching Alexander pack his rucksack, I realised that he was already half-way into his German forest.

'I think I've packed everything – my magnifying glass, my swimsuit, my goggles and a few toys.'

Alexander loved going to Germany, finding the woods and the birdlife; examining the insects under his magnifying glass. Alexander is an explorer and his lively interest and curiosity were always a delight to watch. Verden had become a second retreat, offering him an assortment of mysteries to discover. He had two lives, one there, one here in London, and each offered its thrills – even though he was occasionally torn between them.

Alexander is, I think, the more complex of my two sons. Not so much a difficult child but rather apprehensive and restless. He was a funny mix of tender emotion and anxiety; a will to please and obstinacy. Somehow, I was always slightly worried about him and wondered whether he would eventually be at peace with himself. Alexander saw life as full of complexities and paradox.

Constantin, on the other hand, was the balanced, steadfast and reliable one. No mother could have an easier, more enchanting child. Constantin was a sheer delight to bring up. In seven years, I'd scolded him only once. He was incredibly loving, squeaking with delight as I got home, kissing and cuddling endlessly. He was even-tempered – almost never moody. At school he was exceptionally competent and top of his class: did his homework without protest, was good at sport and popular with his schoolmates. Constantin had a calm, cheerful, robust disposition. He was independent and utterly self-confident – two traits Alexander lacked – and he struggled not to feel overshadowed by his younger brother.

Alexander and Constantin were so different, yet so compatible. One observed the world with solicitude, the other with serenity. One was already longing for peaceful country walks, the other looking forward to his return to London.

'Mummy when are we coming back?'

Constantin had not packed a thing. Packing was boring, and besides, a holiday in the countryside did not hold the same fascination for him. It was just something that could not be bypassed, but soon he'd be back with his Mummy and on holiday with her.

'Where are we going to go? To Valerie's, like last summer?'

'I am not saying. It's a surprise.'

'Oh, Mummy!'

'If I tell you, it won't be a surprise.'

I had arranged a trip to the theme park, Alton Towers. The thought of their excited little faces as they discovered what the surprise was made me smile in anticipation. Little did I know that this was never to be. Little did I know that day – 6 July 1994 – what a tragic turn our lives were about to take.

Had I had the slightest inkling of what was going to be inflicted on them, I would never have let them go. I would have protected them, protected their peace and, above all, their freedom. I never realised, never imagined . . . and because I was so naive their lives have become a monstrous charade.

How can I ever explain to them the injustice of the law, the injustice of life, when it is they who are paying the ultimate price? How can I ever make them understand that they have become the victims of a bitter intra-European dispute when it is so far removed from their reality – two small, vulnerable boys who have no idea about justice or politics? How can I ever make them realise that they have been used as two malleable toys, that they have been denied their own mother, in order to make a point?

All day and all night, I dwell on the images of my children, the boys they were and the dark shadows of the two little prisoners they have become. I can feel their warmth close to my body, remembering how we used to read our ritual bedtime stories snuggling together in my bed. How many nights have I heard Constantin's calls, which woke me with a start, cold perspiration dripping on my face. Sometimes he felt so close I could almost feel him touching me. At other times his voice was far away, lost in a fog. These calls were the most agonising because they were calls of despair.

With Alexander, I could only ever sense his silence and his fear. I only saw him confused and angry, a black cloud around him. I know that it is Alexander who is suffering more. It is he who is carrying the weight of remorse and guilt on his tiny shoulders. But there is no guilt to carry. It is not of his doing. He is only a tool. Alexander is the older, the more emotionally vulnerable, and this is why he was the one who was most used. If only I could take him in my arms, take away the pain and the enormous burden. If only I could speak to him, comfort him . . .

'Mummy, let me carry the suitcase, it's too heavy for you.'

How protective of me he was that day . . . Maybe in his young mind he is protecting me even now. Alexander was leaving. Constantin was just chugging along behind. He sat behind me in the car, his arms around my shoulders, his cheek against mine.

'When did you say we were coming back?' Constantin asked.

'In six weeks, Tini.'

In the two and a half years we had been in London, they had made this trip many times, at Easter, at Christmas and in the summer. Yet this time Constantin was set to endure it calmly while Alexander was marching blindly on, driven inexorably by fate.

At the airport, the stewardess came to pick them up, attaching a BA folder around their necks containing their passports and plane tickets.

'Mummy, will you put the old one in my cupboard, please.' This was another of Alexander's collections. 'The others are in the cupboard on the right.'

Alexander always needed reference points and organisation. This side of his character touched me. Tini, bolstered by his self-assurance, didn't need any extra organisation around him. Life was already in crystalline order in his head.

Their departure to Germany was symbolic. I remember every detail, every word we said, every expression on their little faces. This was my last image of their freedom, the last time I could truly share my emotions with them and they with me, before an impenetrable wall would cruelly separate them from the world and from me, their mother.

Alexander was so grown-up that day, so solicitous in his responsibility of elder brother. He dutifully took Constantin by the hand and gave me their last instruction:

'And don't forget to buy the Lego.'

This was another ritual of ours. A present would always be waiting for them on their return and this morning they had each marked an 'A' and a 'C' next to the Lego they had chosen in the brightly coloured catalogue.

'Mummy, you won't be sad without us. We will be back soon, remember.'

6

I felt tearful as Alexander hugged and kissed me good-bye, but I smiled.

'Of course I will be a bit sad, but as you say, it won't be long and you will have fun in Verden and on the island of Juist.'

Constantin was sad that day. He hardly spoke, but kissed me desperately instead. His arms were still tight around my neck when the stewardess interrupted us:

'Come on, time to leave.'

Tini extricated himself from my arms. I stood up from kneeling on the floor and he just walked away led by Alexander, without turning back. Constantin never showed his intimate feelings, but I had never seen him so dispirited. It was precisely because he did not turn round that I realised how deeply upset he was. Now, looking back, I know he had a premonition, even before I did.

Alexander turned round, waving, blowing kisses at me and calling: 'Bye-bye, Mummy. Be good.'

And there they were, two very small boys, each with his rucksack on his back, disappearing amidst the crowd of adults into the transit area. They looked so vulnerable. Suddenly, I had an overwhelming desire to stop them and I almost called out:

'Stop. Don't go. You can't go!'

Yet I told myself that it was irrational. In no time, they would be back and we would be off on our holiday together. Besides, their father would have been hysterical on the telephone:

'Are you mad? Why aren't the boys here? I need them as much as you.'

Was it a premonition? My younger son was experiencing the same, strange feeling. But, like Constantin, I could not show my emotions in public. Like him, I complied with the form, head high, ready to face reality. I said nothing but could not contain the tears in my eyes as I watched him walk away, proud and strong. Even from the back of his fragile little neck, I could tell that my Tini was biting his lip and sighing resolutely.

Alexander stopped at the last corner and blew a final kiss, then suddenly they both vanished, swallowed into the crowd of travellers.

This was my last image of them.

They were stepping into a trap their father had set. My little birds would be transformed into puppets on a string, commanded by their father's hands. They would be taught to fear their mother, to wipe all thoughts of her from their minds. Caught in this never-ending nightmare, I am no longer the woman I was: I have lost my sense of self-preservation and can no longer hide my feelings. I am in despair. Privacy no longer has any importance. I don't care who witnesses my emotions. All I care about is justice for my sons.

I am their mother. I am the one who gave birth to them, carried them inside my womb, feeling them grow inside my body as an intrinsic part of me. I could feel their kicks grow stronger by the day, already sensing their different identities. I fed them, cuddled them, calmed their fears . . . Since the day I gave birth to them my life has been devoted to them. How can I go on living when a part of me has been torn away?

But I will never abandon them. I will never be dragged into self-pity and resignation. I will stay strong and composed, otherwise I will never be able to release them.

My own mother wrote to them: 'The years pass, and we pray that God will reunite us before we vanish from this earth. Hope is the last thing to die.'

Hope has also become my only solace, my only resource. This is the story of a mother whose life relies on hope. A mother who cannot even talk to her sons, who has been wiped out of their existence. I do not know when they will be free again or when they will be able to read this book, but deep in their hearts they must know that I have not abandoned them, as I know they have not abandoned me. A mother cannot be rubbed out like a spelling mistake.

How deep and unquestioning a child's love is! No one

can love so freely and so unreservedly, yet only a mother's love is boundless. This is what 'they' are trying to eradicate. The only way this can happen is through systematic manipulation. Because my children have always loved me, and because I am their mother.

'They' are a small-minded, bigoted, close-knit community in the heart of Europe, in a small provincial town in Lower Saxony in Germany. 'They' are by no means typical of Germans in general, let me hasten to add. 'They' would not have mattered at all had they not categorised me as a 'foreign mother' – for them an unpardonable sin. Their xenophobia, which encouraged my husband to abduct my children when I had custody of them and then refuse me all access, should alarm every citizen of the European Union.

The story I have to tell is an outrageous one. Confronted by a wall of nationalism, corruption and legal loopholes, I have used every avenue available to me: the media, embassies, European institutions . . . I have fought in England, France, Germany and even Holland. There seems to be no one left to help me support the human rights of a mother and her children. Within the European Union we are trying to create, I have been treated as a pariah. A German province has ostracised me, as though the present era of European co-operation did not exist, and the local German courts have refused to hear me.

I will not, cannot, remain silent before such a barbaric injustice. My only concession is not to name them, because above all I want this book to be published in Germany where my sons are living, a land which forms a part of the tapestry of Europe, a land which must review its system of justice in cases of child abduction.

We are citizens of Europe, citizens of a democratic society, and I want to see my children grow up in this free world. No one should be allowed to deny us the freedom to love and speak. No one should be allowed to separate a mother from her children in the name of a nationality.

I want the mothers of Europe to hear my call.

Alexander and Constantin are my sons. They were only nine and seven when they were abducted and they are unaware of what has been done to them. Even their photographs of me have been destroyed, their mother tongue has been forgotten and London erased from their minds. These are the lengths to which they have been manipulated, the extent of the wickedness perpetrated on them.

This book is like a bottle tossed into the sea. It will float away and, some day, reach my children. Only then will they finally know the true facts and understand how in spite of the justice and decency in which I naively believed, we are being kept forcibly apart. Only then will they realise how cruelly and unnecessarily we were separated and how this book is the only way I have left to communicate my undying love for them.

Chapter 2
Your Mother's Story

In the way that adopted children crave to know their origins and who their natural parents are, you too will want to know. A wall of silence and lies now surrounds you, and the remains of your mother's image must be blurred and confused. This is why I must tell you about myself and the other world – your world, your heritage. The world you also belong to and which has been mercilessly screened from you.

So here is my story – our story.

I was born in Baden-Baden, Germany in the French occupation zone where my father was posted after the war. My sister, Véronique, who is nearly eight years older than me, went to kindergarten and learnt to speak German fluently, but I was only a year old when my parents returned to Paris.

My father is French. He was born in Pau, in the Pyrenees. His mother died when he was only ten and his father sent him to a Jesuit school where discipline was very strict. Pupils were not even allowed to talk in the corridors.

He became a career officer in the French Navy and between 1934 and the Second World War he travelled around the world. When I was a little girl I used to love him telling me about all the French and British colonies he visited and the balls which were organised to receive the officers. At the outbreak of the war he was sent to what was then French Indo-China. For his achievement against the Thai fleet (controlled by Japan) in January 1941 he was awarded the Croix de Guerre and the Légion d'hon-

11

neur, the highest awards for bravery that France can bestow on her citizens. In 1944 he was made a prisoner of war by the Japanese but he would never tell us anything about this period. When the war ended on 14 August 1945 and he was freed, he went to look for my mother, whom he had met in Saigon a few years earlier.

My mother, Babusia, as the boys called her, is Russian born. She comes from an old aristocratic Saint Petersburg family who fled Russia after the 1917 Revolution. Her father, a naval career officer, fought against the Bolsheviks as an artillery officer in Admiral Kolchak's army in Siberia. When the army dispersed, his regiment retreated to Harbin in China, where my mother spent her early childhood.

Harbin was a town built by the Russians, on the Manchurian branch of the Trans Siberian railway. But after the 'Chinese Generals' Wars' and the Japanese invasion of Manchuria in 1932, her family fled again, first to Peking and then to Shanghai. My mother married her first husband, and my sister, Véronique, was born in Saigon.

Being such a mixture of nationalities and cultures, I always felt a citizen of the world. I was also soon exposed to living in different countries, as my father was transferred abroad by the American oil company he had joined in 1958. We lived in Gabon in French Equatorial Africa, for two years and when I was twelve we moved to London. Here, I went to the French Lycée in South Kensington, then I went to university at the School of Slavonic and East European Studies, part of King's College, London University.

I loved the Lycée and have many wonderful memories of my schooldays there. It is very international but has a strong, underlying French influence and method of instruction which has, no doubt, shaped my Cartesian way of thinking. However, my Russian inheritance and the English environment also deeply influenced my character, making me both rational and emotional, determined yet forbearing.

I had an old-fashioned and stricter upbringing than my school friends, who belonged to a much older and more organised world. I longed for my own freedom – to choose things for myself. Even then, I remember thinking: 'When I have children I'll let them be independent and self-reliant, so their own personalities can flourish.'

Knowing now that the exact opposite is being done to them fills me with horror. They were accustomed to think freely and be respected and all of a sudden their world is narrow and restricted. I'm tortured by this thought because, from very early on in my life, I have realised that the most important thing in life is freedom. In Western Europe we take this for granted.

My Aunt Natasha, who had been a journalist in Shanghai, returned to Russia in 1948, following Stalin's active propaganda campaign to attract the children of *émigrés* back. For the next twenty years she was cut off from my mother. It was only in 1961, when the 'iron curtain' was partially lifted in the Khrushchev years, that they were finally reunited. I was eight, but I remember that day and the impression communist Russia left on me. I could never forget, either, how several years later my Russian friend cried on my shoulder because she would never be free to visit me abroad. Today it is my own little two boys who are behind an iron curtain and I, their mother, cannot reach out to them.

I sit alone in silence and pain in the empty flat which once resounded with their laughter and happiness, trying to tell them more about myself, careful that nothing I say will be used as evidence against me. Even through this book I cannot communicate freely with my own flesh and blood.

London.

London is where my happiest memories belong.

On my 24th birthday, on 26 January 1977, my parents announced that they would soon be returning to Paris as my father was retiring. They understood that I was enjoy-

13

ing life in London but were worried at leaving me. What I needed, they felt, was a husband. Here our views differed. I still had romantic notions of marriage and dreamed of meeting the perfect man. My mother saw the world in much more practical terms:

'Katia, you live in a fantasy world. You will never find the man of your dreams. Reality is just not like that.'

There was no one I particularly liked amongst the men I knew. My heart still belonged to Robin, my first adolescent love. He was American and I had spent years writing passionate letters to him (although they were only sporadically answered). But when he eventually came back to England he had fallen in love with someone else. Although I had some admirers, my heart was still broken by that first romantic disappointment.

While I was at university, I entered the world of finance: the work I was doing fascinated me far more than any romance. Merrill Lynch was an excellent company and I felt appreciated and valued. I also enjoyed the excitement of the financial markets: each day was different and challenging. It demanded strong nerves and quick reactions. It involved politics, economics and public relations, and I enjoyed them all. The nature of this unconventional business created a terrifically charged office atmosphere and I felt very much part of this male-dominated environment. I was particularly fascinated by the up and coming commodities markets, with their erratic price movements and their mysterious novelty. The challenge of making it in a man's world excited me far too much for me to contemplate settling down to the demands of married life. Not at that point, at least.

But life is always unpredictable, and in no time, Robert appeared. I met him in the City through a friend. He was working in the same business, commodity broking, and was relatively successful with a promising future as a partner in a private metal trading venture.

Twelve years my senior, he was going through a crisis in his life, battling through a complicated divorce. Robert was tall, dark and extremely charming, and his great sense of humour, unaffected ways and social ease had caught my attention.

'Of course, he's divorced. But at his age, most men are not free . . . He has experience and you need a mature man.' My mother could relax. Robert would offer her daughter security and there was no need to worry about me any longer.

Robert's demand for marriage was expressive of his particular disposition. We went out to a Greek restaurant in Bayswater, which at the time was a favourite place of ours. We had dinner and Robert drank a whole bottle of wine to sum up the courage:

'Well, I suppose I can pop the question now. Will you marry me?'

It came out of the blue and I was taken aback. We hadn't been together for long and he'd just got his divorce. The following day, we were due to have dinner at my parents' house, and in the morning I called my mother from work to tell her what Robert had asked me. When I got home, there was champagne on the table and a list of guests had been prepared.

But it wasn't far into our marriage when I realised we had little in common. At first, Robert tried to change me as I later tried to change him, but of course neither of us succeeded, and in time we drew further apart, both locked in our different cultural moulds. Robert soon returned to his energetic and wild social life and I felt increasingly disoriented. His friends were older and much more worldly than me. I would just tag along feeling out of place and insecure.

Robert and I simply could not create a life together. We had been drawn together through a misreading of what we thought we needed.

After spending months organising the decoration of the house we'd bought, everything was finally ready. Robert was on yet another business trip and I found myself separating his things from mine as I moved in alone. I knew then that the gap between our two worlds could not be bridged.

Whereas Robert was able to escape, I was left behind to face reality. The time had come to do something.

I wrote a long explanatory letter which I presented to him as we went out to dinner. I knew this was the only way he would hear me out. Although I was capable of managing clients and their investments, I felt incapable of conveying my innermost thoughts. Robert read the letter in silence, folded it and calmly put it in his jacket pocket. He was composed:

'OK, how much do you want and where will you sleep tonight?'

I couldn't believe it. Who was this man? I had understood so little about him. His restrained reaction was far removed from the reality of the event for me.

I have never seen Robert since. Our divorce was quick and uncomplicated, neither of us seeking unnecessary bitterness. We had simply made an error. He had wrongly celebrated the end of his divorce and I the end of romanticism.

Somehow I never doubted the soundness of my decision, but I felt confused and guilt-ridden. Our marriage had been a failure and I had to reconcile myself to that.

'If you were silly enough to leave Robert, don't expect us to support you,' my mother announced, after my explanatory lunch with her.

My mother still saw her role as a directive one, with me as a little girl. 'Katia, the perfect union you still go on about is only in the movies. I've told you before – and now you've left a perfectly nice husband.'

I was disappointed by her reaction and could not understand her down-to-earth wisdom. Half businesswoman, half dreamy child, I was incapable of abandoning my naive belief that somewhere out there existed a Prince Charming. My father, though, reacted in his usual gentle way: 'Catherine, at least you had the courage to do what you thought was right. That is something to be respected.'

I am my father's only child (my sister's father had been killed by the Japanese in the war) and – like most young people with their parents – I had not realised at the time that he respected and loved me very much. My father was extremely fair-minded and very principled but rather reserved and self-effacing. The education of us children had been entrusted to my mother and my father would rarely interfere. My memories of childhood hardly included him and I was rather intimidated by his conventional discipline.

This was the day I discovered my father. He no longer saw me as a child. My education was over and the time had come for a new relationship between adults. We talked a lot, about all sorts of things, from current affairs to personal ones, but too many years had to be made up for in a single lunch.

My father was born in 1912 and the gap between our two generations had yet to be properly filled. My parents were now living in Paris and I was too busy with my job for such an opportunity to occur – until a disaster would irretrievably unite us.

The emotional failure led me to be totally engrossed in my work and within a year of my separation from Robert, I became a successful broker at E.F. Hutton. My life was shaping itself after all and I relished my independence and success. I was comfortable in an environment of instant decisions, constant movement and practical colleagues. My best friend, Leonard, had recently joined the firm and my office days were infinitely more gratifying than my weekends. ·

That is, until one summer's day, when I unexpectedly fell in love.

A series of coincidences created a curious encounter that would change my life. The future father of my children would uncannily take the same road as I did.

I had decided to take a short break. My job was very demanding and I was tired; I seemed to work endlessly. I would stay in the office until the close of the US markets, come in early for the opening of the London ones, read the news, write sugar reports, analyse charts and trade, a telephone at each ear. In the past year my business had grown substantially and I now had my own assistant.

These were the years when price volatility was enormous and several of my clients used to 'day trade' in the gold, silver, stock index and currency markets. I had a few very large clients who demanded constant attention; others for whom I managed accounts. When the markets got busy, the stress was high. Being a woman in a world almost exclusively male, I could not allow myself to fail, and ended up working twice as hard as the men did.

August was traditionally a quiet month and I set off in my newly acquired car. This had been a small, admittedly immature, extravagance which I had spoiled myself with to reflect my new success. I had built up some savings in the bank and felt I had worked hard enough to deserve it.

A holiday plan with friends had fallen through at the last minute and I decided to drive down to the South of France. This change of mind was the first coincidence in the chain of events that would bring Hans-Peter and me together. Why did I decide to go to that part of France, stay at that particular hotel in Beaulieu? My original plan had been to holiday in the States.

I spent my time contentedly, reading beside the hotel swimming pool, relaxing and enjoying my unscheduled days. One of the books I read was *Lady Chatterley's Lover* – an unusual choice for me and I can't recall if I found it dated or daring! It was probably a combination, but the views of D.H. Lawrence on the complexities of women were memorable.

After several days of peace and quiet, I was getting bored with my books and the men who hovered hopefully around any single women. The inactivity started weighing on me. The following day, 15 August, my brother-in-law was to celebrate his birthday:

'Why don't you come to La Baule to visit us?' my sister asked me over the telephone. I agreed instantly, packed my bags, checked out of the hotel at around four o'clock and set off towards Brittany.

Night was falling on the deserted motorway. Luckily, I found a hotel close to Bordeaux. The next day, without any precise timetable, I was back on the road and eventually stopped to fill the car up. I decided to walk into the petrol station to have some coffee.

As I stood drinking the watery coffee, a tall, boyish-looking man wearing Bermuda shorts walked past me and stopped at the counter to buy some sweets. I looked at him mechanically and he smiled – a broad, childlike smile, which lit up his face. Automatically I smiled back. He looked very young. He took his sweets and headed out of the station.

I finished my coffee and walked outside to my car. Just as I stepped out, a navy blue Volkswagen Beetle drove right in front of me. The same youthful man was at the wheel, now smiling broadly at me. A man sitting beside him looked up and I guessed he had just been told: 'Hey, that's the girl I saw inside . . .'

I was amused and secretly flattered by this impromptu success, though it had little significance. As their car drove away, I noticed the D for Deutschland above the registration plate.

After another hour's drive along the motorway, I turned west towards Nantes on the *route nationale*. The August traffic was thick with endless lorries one never seemed able to overtake. I switched on the radio, with nothing particular on my mind, concentrating on the music.

Two hours later the traffic was still awful. But because I was on holiday, it didn't matter. As I drove through yet another village blankly looking at the houses lining the road, my eyes suddenly widened in astonishment: they were there! The two Germans of the motorway were having a drink on the terrace of a café. They waved as I whizzed by.

The road stretched on. After another hour, I wanted a break. Parking my car, I walked into a small café and sat down at a table by the window. As I drank the *café au lait*, staring aimlessly at the ribbon of cars threading by, my eyes were suddenly jolted as I caught sight of the navy blue Beetle.

This was definitely fate. Somehow, the peculiarity and the blondness of this man resembled someone. It had struck me at the petrol station. He'd reminded me of Camelia who had been my best friend until she died tragically when we were twenty.

Camelia was very beautiful and looked like Jane Fonda. I remember so well the first day she arrived in our class at the Lycée. She looked different, more beautiful, more interesting, more delicate than any of the other students and everyone looked up at her in silent admiration.

Her life had been difficult. Her German father had fled Germany at the rise of the Nazis and became active in the Resistance movement operating from Romania. He married a Romanian; Camelia was born in 1953 under the communist regime. Life became increasingly hard for her parents until eventually they managed to escape to France, later settling in England.

Camelia was much brighter and more mature than we were. I worshipped her and was proud to be her best friend. Until the car crash took her life away, we were inseparable. She died on 23 December 1973.

My world collapsed and it took me over two years to reconcile myself with the injustice of God. Adolescent friendships are often intense and absolute. When she died, a part of me went with her. I could not accept that God had taken her life away at twenty but had allowed Hitler and Stalin to live.

Sitting behind the window of the café, seeing this blond man again for a third time, I thought of all this. There was no doubt that the material and spiritual aspects of life were often contradictory, but both existed and neither could be discounted. Such coincidences did not just happen. I considered.

What should I do? Catherine, this is quite ludicrous. A

stranger passes by and you think it's fate.' My mind was confused.

But what if . . . What if this was written and I simply ignore it?

I finished my coffee and half consciously, half in a dream, hurried out to join the trail of cars.

Looking back, I think I saw it as a sort of game. I was placing a bet on fate: if I bump into him again, it was meant to be. If I don't it was just a fluke!

Yet, deep down, I already knew that I would find him. It was just a question of overtaking the few cars which separated us.

Soon enough, the Beetle with its D was in front of me, the back of his blond head on the left, his companion waving his arm as he recognised my car. Our little game lasted for a while across Nantes. At the traffic lights, smiles were exchanged. At times they were in front, at times I was. Coincidentally, we were following the same road signs. It was fun.

Finally, we found ourselves on a dual carriageway. Automatically, I accelerated.

Playing hide and seek with two strangers on French roads is quite ridiculous, I thought to myself as I disappeared at high speed.

My car was much faster than theirs and as I glanced in the mirror I saw their little Beetle dissolving in miniature. It was shaking, nearly out of breath in its vain attempt to catch up with me. It was silly, but I felt rather sorry for it. I slowed down.

The game could have ended there, but they overtook me and signalled, turning into a parking bay. I told myself that the joke was a bit over the top now, but I followed them to the roadside and stopped. What a funny situation. I hesitated; the two young men had already stepped out of their car and were approaching mine.

They spoke good English. Wasn't it amazing we should meet three times like this? It transpired that they too were heading for La Baule. As I gave them my business card on

21

the back of which I scribbled my sister's telephone number, I thought: Catherine, you are making a mistake. Why on earth did you let them have your office number? This is so unlike you. They may not belong to the same world as you. What will you do with them? The blond man looks so young and naive. He's probably still a student on a camping holiday.

But it was precisely the youthfulness of this twenty-seven-year-old man with his cheerful and enthusiastic manner which had put me off guard. And it would be only a fun holiday encounter, to be forgotten once I was back in London.

His name was Hans-Peter Volkmann and within four days he had fallen in love with me. His love was youthful, platonic and exuberant and it sparked a maternal chord in me. Hans-Peter was a wonderful breath of fresh air, an escape from the demands of everyday life.

On the first evening, I fell asleep thinking of him. The following evening we parted reluctantly, and on the third day we kissed in the car like a couple of students. He left for Germany on the fourth day. Three hours after waving me goodbye from the little Beetle, he telephoned. He called again that evening and the next day. I returned to London. He called there, too and then at the office. At the end of the week, he decided to visit me in London.

At the time I did not notice the forcefulness of his demands. I only saw how much Hans-Peter was in love with me, and found myself falling under his spell.

However, on the Friday he was due to come I was beset with doubts. This had just been a light holiday romance. Did I really like him? Want to see him again? In my own environment?

But it was too late to stop him coming. I could hardly send him back to Koblenz as soon as he stepped off the plane! Instead, I asked some other friends to dinner that evening to give me time to think and neutralise the situation a little.

He arrived at the airport gate with his broad smile and I immediately forgot my anxieties. On the way home he talked excitedly about his medical studies, his military service in Koblenz, the last time he had been in London and how much he loved it . . . His English was excellent. That was lucky, as none of us spoke any German.

He kissed me as if we had known each other for ever, taking my hand in his, and settling in among my friends. Nothing seemed to disconcert him. Hans-Peter had walked into my life and I found myself encouraging him to stay.

The only one who observed us with a critical eye was my friend Leonard, but he was too polite and too perceptive to say anything. He was happy that his friend was happy and in love. This was reason enough to restrain judgement. Although I sensed his reserve, he was aware that it would have been pointless to criticise at this stage.

I had become so wary of men that subconsciously I had selected a child – whom I would later discover to be capricious, jealous and possessive, a man who needed constant attention and would manipulate others to achieve his ends. Yet for a long time I thought this was an expression of his love.

If only I could talk to Hans-Peter today, I would tell him how misguided he was. Some men are so terrified of loneliness and of leaving their mother's protection that they think marriage will compensate for both.

Hans-Peter wanted a mother, not a wife. He has now returned to her and I believe deeply that she is the one to blame for most of his inability to grow up.

Hans-Peter's mother wanted her son back and, in regaining him she has stolen both of mine.

Chapter 3
The Blindness of Love

Alexander, Constantin, you were children of love, brought by Destiny. Both born on Sundays, both born in May, both born under the rays of a sunny day.

After our weekend together, Hans-Peter went back to Germany on the Sunday evening. I could sense that my friends didn't relate to him – perhaps they found him too demonstrative. His continuous need to kiss me in public to prove that I was his, and his alone, seemed cloying to them.

But I felt that Hans-Peter had temporarily transported me into a world of youthful fantasy. Now I returned to the adult world and my daily responsibilities for clients, the news updates and market analysis. However, as soon as he had reached Koblenz, Hans-Peter began inundating me over the phone with declarations of his love and demands for mine. At times, he would ring when I was in the middle of trading, concentrating on the erratic price movements appearing on the Reuters screen, one line connected to the US Exchange, the other to a client. He would become childishly impatient, and I would succumb to his pleas and ask my assistant to take over:

'Hello, Catherine? It's me.'

'I really can't talk to you now. The gold market is in chaos and I have a client on the other line.'

'Do you still love me?'

'Of course I do. But Hans-Peter, my client is waiting. I'll call you back when the market closes.'

'I must talk to you now . . .'

Hans-Peter could not accept my daytime priorities and although I was often irritated by his brash intrusions, his loving voice would soon win me over. It was flattering to feel so wanted. Hans-Peter was like a ray of sunshine. He brought a carefree, cheerful radiance into my life.

By the following Friday, when Hans-Peter resurfaced in London, I was regressing to childhood. He would splash me in the bath, joyfully hug me, stretch out on the sofa, eat sandwiches between meals and turn my life into chaos. This was no diversion any more. These turbulent and youthful retreats became a part of my regular life. Blissfully unaware, I was already caught in a web.

Hans-Peter's calls were so frequent that it became a sort of joke in the office.

'Cat, it's Hans-Peter!' my assistant would call out, ready to take over.

Shirley could attend to the client. She was efficient and able. Hans-Peter was calling from abroad; I could not make him wait on the line. His reprimands and pleadings made me feel alternately moved and guilty. Hans-Peter just could not accept a professional reason. Our love had to come first and he managed to make me feel ashamed that, as a woman, I should be giving precedence to business responsibilities. I would find myself apologising, even though it was he who was interrupting.

Soon, my life had totally changed. I would come home in the evenings and, instead of accepting a friend's invitation out, I would wait for his calls. I would think of him as I was falling asleep and wait impatiently for the weekend. My life was becoming entirely dedicated to him. He managed to arouse in me strong feelings of devotion, mixed with a sense of guilt, and he came to control me.

On the fourth weekend, I flew to meet him in Koblenz. His flat startled me a little: it was completely soulless – white walls, thin, colourless curtains, plain furniture and not a single painting to warm its impersonal mood. It was in such contrast to the homes I felt comfortable in, with their thick fabrics and warm colours. But what disconcerted me most was his untidiness – paper thrown everywhere; bank statements scattered between book pages and overflowing drawers.

· Hans-Peter was like an uncared-for child, who needed his mother's pampering and constant attention. Had I had any sense then, I would have fled, but I was drawn to his warm, carefree personality. Hans-Peter was intelligent and well read and I enjoyed his inquisitive and enthusiastic character.

However, even though I was already too in love to heed these warning signs, meeting his mother should have raised the alarm. Gundel, who had come to inspect the foreigner her son was involved with, was a tall, blonde, severe-looking woman. We had nothing in common and, as she spoke very little English, our conversation was limited to banalities. She scrutinised me with an unmistakable expression of distrust which made me retreat into polite reserve.

I belonged to an international metropolis which she considered overpowering and threatening. The gap between her secure provincial world with its structured order and my world was an unbridgeable one. Soon her attention centred on her beloved son, whom she had not seen in a month. They seemed so absorbed in the privacy of their conversation that Hans-Peter hardly bothered to translate. I had no choice but to offer only a strained smile. After all, it was Hans-Peter I was in love with, not his mother.

Hans-Peter seemed totally unconcerned about the disparity between the two women in his life and I felt reassured by this. He was on the verge of finishing his military service and would soon flee the maternal nest. I did not realise then that this appearance of nonchalance was more to do with self-absorbed uninterest in others, than tolerance.

Hans-Peter had mentioned the possibility of moving to London once he was released from the Bundeswehr, the

German army. Although I cannot recall having any say in it, in June 1983 he and two suitcases appeared in my flat. Within a month, he told me he'd obtained a two-year research grant from Germany. From the little knowledge I had of the medical profession this seemed amazing, and impressive. Being selected from hundreds of other applicants clearly suggested that Hans-Peter was very capable and had excellent career prospects. If he was disorganised and chaotic, this was obviously because he was a promising scientist constantly lost in his thoughts!

Living with this absent-minded professor, I had no choice but to be the practical one. In principle, I had no objection to being the breadwinner. My career was established so it seemed natural for our joint life to depend on my income to start with. I presumed Hans-Peter didn't earn much, on a grant, but in time he would take on more financial responsibilities. Medicine requires many years of training.

We started seeing less and less of my friends. Hans-Peter would tell me how much he would rather be alone with me than invite people over. In the name of love, Hans-Peter was isolating me and, in the name of love, he convinced me that we didn't need the outside world.

During our first year together, I did not know how Hans-Peter spent his days. He seemed to return home early and sleep a lot in the early evenings, asking me to call him from the office at 7p.m. to wake him up. He hardly ever spoke about his research work, gave evasive answers and preferred talking about us and our perfect love.

This vaguely bothered me, but I assumed it was only a stage; once he was in a proper career, he would be more responsible. After all, the few times Hans-Peter mentioned his future plans, they were filled with ambition and high prospects. Some days he would talk about becoming a famous professor; at other times he saw himself running a high-profile medical general practice. He had not yet decided what direction he would take – but whatever it was, it would have a successful outcome. He knew nothing about the financial world, and I was ignorant about the paths to success in his field.

Very soon, Hans-Peter mentioned having children.

'It would be so cute!' he mused, cuddling me.

I could not disagree but the timing was precarious. Hans-Peter was not established and we were reliant on my income, which was not so lavish as when we first met.

Sugar was my speciality and I tended to be fairly accurate in my forecasts. In the summer of 1983 I predicted a rally out of the previous year's sideways price trend and advised my clients to invest in sugar. I was spot on. Very few had expected this move and I was rewarded with reverent recognition. Brokers from our Bahrain and Beirut offices were calling me the new 'sugar guru', seeking my advice and daily predictions. Should they buy now, or wait for a price correction first? I wrote morning reports and was glued to my screens and charts.

This unexpected and sudden success caused me to be over-confident and bold. My clients were delighted and impressed at my performance. Such moves seldom occur and are difficult to anticipate. I felt that if I was such an inspired sugar trader, I too ought to share in the good fortune. So I started buying one contract of sugar, then another, and as the market continued up I bought more.

There were, however, several problems. The first one was that by the time I got into the market I had already missed much of the upmove. Even in a 'bull' market, prices do not rise consistently but have occasional setbacks, or 'corrections' as they are known. These are often caused by some investors liquidating their positions, i.e. selling, in order to cash in their profits. The greater the number of sellers, the sharper the price decline.

When a particular market experiences a 'bullish' trend investors will rush to participate in the new profit opportunities. This invariably causes greater price volatility and this was what was happening to the sugar market. The price rise which had begun slowly had attracted more and more participants, many of whom were speculators looking for a quick return. As more people bought, prices started shooting up. However, this created great market nervousness, as any dip would be interpreted as a possible reversal of the trend. Still glued to my charts, I was recalculating my upside objective daily, before the downward correction could occur.

The problem was that this correction took place three days too early. And it was sharp – involving a string of six consecutive 'limit down' days. This meant that the maximum daily price 'limit' move set by the New York Sugar Exchange was reached immediately on the opening, and the market would close – no one was allowed to sell until the following day. If the market opened 'limit down' again one was simply stuck in a collapsing market, waiting for the day when trading would finally resume. Sugar traders, clients and I were trapped for an agonising week, unable to liquidate our positions while the losses mounted.

I tried to explain to Hans-Peter what was happening but he wasn't interested or sympathetic.

'You have problems? Well, what do you expect with your type of job? It's just sheer gambling' – and he would change the subject or switch on the television.

In the meantime, I spent sleepless nights, worried to death about how to control the losses. Leonard and I tried to work out ways to improve the situation. He would listen to my angst and carry some of its load on his shoulders.

I tried to hedge my position by selling in the cash market, which has no daily limit moves when trading is suspended. But even this did not help. On the third day, the cash market remained static while the futures were still 'limit down'. The following three days, the cash prices actually went up! I was now losing on both sides.

In the space of a few days, I saw all my profits disappear. By the time I was able to get out, I had incurred a huge loss. Unlike my clients who had adequate funds to cushion the loss or who could 'ride' out the correction, I had lost much more than I could afford. From then on, most of my income was taken up repaying my debt.

Hans-Peter considered the problem to be exclusively mine, so he dismissed it and criticised my working in this business. Only today do I realise that Hans-Peter did not object to the job itself but to the very fact that I was working. Only today do I understand that it was not a question of it being my problem rather than his, but that there *was* a problem. In Hans-Peter's world problems simply do not exist. He belongs to a *heile*, perfect and untouched, world and this is his only reality. The rest does not exist so long as he does not look at it.

In those early days, however, I had grasped little other than my immediate predicament and I became disillusioned with the brokerage business. This job had been my passion and a source of great professional satisfaction. How many times had I spent eleven-hour days in the office, radiating happiness? Hans-Peter was right: commodities futures was sheer speculation. Only two days after I liquidated my position, prices rallied to their initial levels. The only players who seemed to profit were the unethical brokers who lived from 'churning' their clients' accounts in order to earn more commissions, or the actual insiders who had proper market information.

Hans-Peter however, had other preoccupations:

'Catherine, you know, at thirty-one it's high time you had children. Trust me, I'm a doctor. Late pregnancies carry risks. And just imagine how cute our baby would be.'

Hans-Peter had a high opinion of his physical appearance: in fact he was very vain. Admittedly, he was handsome but his eternal need to glance at himself and readjust his blond fringe falling to the side of his forehead was probably the result of his mother's endless praise of his looks.

Of course our children would be cute – but shouldn't Hans-Peter concentrate on getting a job for the next year if he wanted to assume the responsibilities of a father? Instinctively, I knew he was not mature enough for such a step, and I was right. But my maternal instincts were awakening. I found it increasingly difficult to remain uninterested in the idea, especially with Hans-Peter telling me how fulfilling it would be.

By spring 1984, less than a year after Hans-Peter had arrived on my doorstep with his amorous and insatiable passion, he finally convinced me:

'I love you, for sure. I need you. We should have children. Why not get married?'

After all, when two people are in love, marriage is a normal step. But before we had children, my finances had to improve or Hans-Peter had to ensure he had a job.

I thought I was in control. On the surface I was. Leonard was to be my best man. We would rush out from the office at lunchtime to visit hotels, choose the rooms for the reception, the menus for the dinner, the flower arrangements for the church . . . Both perfectionists, we went over every detail with a fine toothcomb: was the menu balanced? Would everyone like the choices of food? How would we seat the guests? There were so many considerations to take into account to blend the disparate groups, and we enjoyed the challenge. Hans-Peter steered clear of our deliberations, but was happy to see the event shaping around him.

As the day drew closer, I was overwhelmed with pre-marital nerves and, like every bride, I managed to lose three kilos in a few days! The Volkmann clan was landing in London in ever-increasing numbers and needed immediate assistance. I was running to pick one lot up, drop another, draw maps and plan sightseeing routes while Hans-Peter, still locked away in his separate world, remained impervious to it all.

Most of Hans-Peter's Verden and Bremen relations were totally disorientated, alarmed by the traffic and unable to find their way around. There was the aunt who hardly spoke English, the mother who needed constant attention, the sister who was arguing, the brother who went his separate way, uncles, cousins . . . Except for Hans-Peter's holiday friend, everyone was family.

The contrast between this overpowering clan and my own friends and family was striking. Even their physical appearance differentiated them. The men were all over six feet tall and Hans-Peter's sister, Antje, was two heads taller than my father and brother-in-law. I felt small and brittle. The wedding portrait snapped in front of the Russian Orthodox Church in Ennismore Gardens would capture the oddness of this assortment: his tall and extravagantly large family and the four diminutive adult members of mine.

Besides my parents and my sister's family, I had no other relations, but my circle of friends was very large and Hans-Peter's lack of friends surprised me. But our wedding was beautiful with its inspiring ceremony at the Orthodox Church in the warm June sunshine, the wonderful reception . . . I felt loved and happy, yet disquieted by Hans-Peter's pride in the woman he was marrying: the perfect Catherine who loves him and gives in to all his capricious demands.

As I listened to Leonard's elegant and witty speech, recounting how he and I had arranged the entire wedding between our client calls, I thought about Hans-Peter's aloof ways with a mixture of loving indulgence and latent unease.

I had hung on to the belief that Hans-Peter would cut the umbilical cord. His family would shortly go home and he and I would create our own independent world. Our Orthodox wedding, with its ritual of the crowns being held over our heads, symbolised exactly this.

Hans-Peter was different from his family. He was the only one who spoke fluent English, had worked in the USA and in England and seemed fascinated by the cultural mix of London. At one stage, we had visited my aunt in Moscow and he'd been so captivated by Russia that he intended to learn the language. Of course, the bond with his family was strong and I respected this, but he expressed open-minded opinions and his outlook seemed to be very different from theirs.

I thought I was marrying Hans-Peter. How desperately wrong I was! I didn't marry Hans-Peter – I took on an entire, matriarchal dynasty that would engulf me in its grip and control our lives. Hans-Peter himself is probably its unconscious victim. His mother, his sister and their small-minded mentality are manipulating him today and I do not believe he even realises it.

If only he would allow me to talk to him now, maybe he would bring himself to question his actions and this intolerance of foreigners he never shared before. But Hans-Peter has run back to his mother, and in so doing has become a remorseless xenophobe.

When Alexander and Constantin were born, their father did not jump up and declare: 'You are German and nothing else!' On the contrary, he wanted them to be trilingual, multicultural, baptised Russian Orthodox, as a mark of their Russian blood, and to attend French schools. He is now denying them all he had wished for them, all he had praised as an extraordinary advantage for their future. He is now demanding that they should be German.

Today, Hans-Peter can have nothing left of the exploring creature he once was, ready to enlarge his vision. He has become scared of open-mindedness, scared of the former image he had of himself. He has allowed himself to be dragged into intolerance. He has allowed his family to erect a wall to separate him and our children from their mother.

Our children are as much mine as his and at such young ages they need a mother's love at least as much as the attention of a father – maybe even more. This deprivation will scar them for life.

How can any law support the robbing of two children from their mother and the denial of their basic human right to see her? This tragedy is an attack on the ideal that

Germany has been trying to foster for the last forty-five years: the concept of a united Europe. Because the German judicial system has not been reformed in line with this move towards Europe, the Volkmanns, with their local power within the independent *Land* (state) of Lower Saxony, have been able to flout basic human rights and undermine European ideology.

Hans-Peter has used our children. He has tried to erase from their memory their natural birth right: maternal love.

Chapter 4
Responsibilities

*Alexander, you were my first. From the very instant
I laid eyes on you, I realised how unfulfilled my life
had been.*

We had been married less than three months when I discovered I was pregnant. At the very moment I expressed my suspicion, Hans-Peter rushed out to buy a pregnancy test. He hurried back in a state of great excitement.

'Here, we must find out. It would be so wonderful . . .'

He sat and stared at the coloured dots to see whether the chemical reaction would show positive.

He was ecstatic.

'Be careful now, you shouldn't move too quickly.'

'But Hans-Peter, I'm not sick. I've only just done the test!'

It was touching to see Hans-Peter's concern. He knelt in front of me, his hand on my stomach. His heir was inside and the womb carrying it had become his most precious treasure.

He kissed me enthusiastically and then rushed to call his mother and sister. I could hear the excitement in his voice, mixed with exuberant exclamations: 'wunderbar', 'fantastich'. Within a few minutes, his whole family had been informed of the happy news.

This revelation raises strong emotions in a woman, especially when it is her first child. I needed a little time to understand the meaning of our new existence. Soon, I would be a mother. A small being was beginning its life inside my body. I was trying to absorb the implications of this sudden and unexpected turn of events.

As I write these words today, I relive the strange feeling of disorientation I experienced then. Hans-Peter had come into, and taken over, my life and now he was dispossessing me of my own person. He had appropriated my womb. The baby was clearly an extension of Hans-Peter and Hans-Peter alone. I had simply become his childbearer, the surrogate mother carrying what was his. The endless battery of precautionary comments was stifling. I was bewildered and felt harassed by Hans-Peter's forceful intrusion.

Maternity leave was only six weeks and since Hans-Peter's hospital work would end in September, there was no question of my being able to take extra time off. I decided I would stay in the office until delivery day, to have as much time as possible with the baby later.

Hans-Peter phoned his mother all the time. I had no idea what they needed to discuss for hours on end. The baby? Future plans? Only they know. However, one day I did discover that Gundel had been regularly sending him money in secret. Hans-Peter never said how much and from then on he mostly talked to his mother when I was not about.

Our financial situation was not brilliant, but we were certainly not in any desperate need. My opinion was that we should keep our independence at all costs. Hans-Peter, however, dismissed my views and continued to accept his mother's handouts. His boisterous and carefree attitude now worried and irritated me. However, I hoped that when he had settled into a regular job he would share my attitude towards dependency. After all, he was still completing his specialist training and if he didn't object to his mother treating him like a child, why should it bother me? Youth is not eternal: one day Hans-Peter would grow up and maybe I would miss his cheerfulness then!

In the meantime, though, it was I who was assuming the responsibilities of our life together. Hans-Peter relied on my sense of order and my ability to lead two lives simultaneously: as career woman and mother-to-be. I had always been organised and accustomed to hard work, and as I managed well under pressure, Hans-Peter gradually discharged himself of practically all domestic duties, which sometimes exasperated me.

As the months went by, my work gradually became less central in my life. I had put on well over two stones in weight, tired easily and work became a serious strain.

Being pregnant was a new and strange sensation. The baby was a part of me. Day and night I could feel him, sometimes with little unexpected kicks in the ribs which would make me hiccup just as I was telephoning an order through to the exchange.

It was wonderful to feel the baby grow and to experience the blossoming of my maternal instinct. I thought about what he would be like, what sort of a mother I would be, and how our life would be changed.

At times, I minded looking large and tired. At other times I was transported into the blissful world of motherhood and impulsive love. But I was always conscious that a new being would soon come into this imperfect world and a strange anguish would grip me: *Please God, make him strong and healthy. Protect him from pain and distress. Let him find happiness and peace*, I prayed.

The baby was due towards the end of May 1985 and I was still in the office on Friday the 24th. The next evening, Hans-Peter drove me to Westminster Hospital. As soon as we reached the maternity ward, Hans-Peter took over. In his capacity as medical practitioner and in the name of his child, he had decided that an epidural was out of the question.

'It can be harmful for the baby. We really should not run this risk,' he announced.

I couldn't argue. He was a doctor and I reminded myself that generations of women had had children without the help of pain relief. Although I have a very slight build, I have a high pain threshold. I can tolerate having my teeth drilled without an injection and usually ask not to have one. Having a baby would test my courage, but I did not particularly wish to show any suffering.

'What do you mean? Of course I won't leave the room.'

'But Hans-Peter . . . A woman giving birth is not a pleasant sight.'

'Don't be stupid. It's just the way you've been brought up. I'm the father and I'm a doctor. It's absolutely natural for me to be there.'

Well, I suppose he's right, I thought to myself. My education has made me too shy and self-conscious. Although in the privacy of my home, I was natural and unreserved, I was very aware of my public appearance and even more of any display of emotions. Growing up in England had moulded me this way and I could not simply change overnight. I was torn between remorse and annoyance, and the pain had already become too acute for me to argue. Hans-Peter stayed.

No contractions occurred after my waters broke, so I was put on an infusion. People say one forgets the agony. I won't. There seemed nothing left around me besides this excruciating pain. The nurse, who had a dinner engagement, kept increasing the doses of the drip to accelerate matters. This led to practically uninterrupted contractions and I couldn't even find the strength to beg her to stop. It seemed endless. I wanted to die.

Nine hours later, Alexander finally appeared. He was a big, sturdy baby weighing 3.4 kilos. I had fought between the implacable nurse and Hans-Peter's gesticulations. We were both shattered. Later Hans-Peter was reproachful:

'And you didn't even react when the baby was put in your arms!'

In fact, I couldn't even properly remember what happened. Half conscious, everything seemed a blur. I remember Hans-Peter's emotional voice, though:

'Oh, what a beautiful baby. He's so big, so well formed . . .'

My body had given up on me and my mind was still suspended in a trance. Hans-Peter was enraptured with his new son. I fell asleep with the disquieting impression that Hans-Peter had not been there for me. He had only been concerned with protecting his property.

The next day I felt better and was holding happiness in both hands. A tiny being was lying next to me in his cot. I looked down to examine him, hardly daring to touch his minute hands. In the space of an instant, I was completely convinced he was the most beautiful baby in the world. Maternal instinct is an extraordinary phenomenon which seizes you suddenly and completely. Only yesterday I was a pregnant woman: today I am a proud and protective mother.

I stood looking at him:

'You are so beautiful! My baby!'

That afternoon, he was no longer mine. Hans-Peter arrived with flowers in hand, his mother behind him. He had contacted the whole clan to announce the news and Gundel had taken the first flight to London and settled into our flat.

I had not known this was planned and presumed she had come for a couple of days. It was natural enough for a grandmother to rush in but I was surprised that I hadn't even been given breathing space.

'Oh, Catherine! You are so fat!'

As I was susceptible to the fact that I had gained so much weight, reminding me was rather unnecessary. But, as I found out later, this was Gundel's idea of being 'honest'.

Gundel and Hans-Peter rushed towards the cot and I was no longer invited to partake in their conversation, which continued in German with exclamations from Gundel:

'*Er sieht genau wie du, mein Junge*, your nose, your eyes . . .' except for what to her was one unfortunate detail: 'Well of course, he's dark like Catherine . . .'

Rejected and still exhausted from the birth, I found solace in silence. After all, Gundel's favourite child had just given her a grandson. Her reactions were understandable. I should be tolerant and patient.

But it was exactly this lack of reaction and my eternal will to please which would become the source of my terrible fate and that of my sons. That day, had I felt stronger, I should have stood up and insisted to Hans-Peter: 'look, this is *our* son. Not your mother's. Don't let her boss you around. Don't let her control our lives.'

But would Hans-Peter have listened to me? I doubt it. He seemed to belong to his mother and when she was around they were an indissoluble entity. Recently, I have spent many days, many months dwelling on the past, asking myself why I was so restrained and why I had allowed mother and son to command my life. I blame myself for my lack of insight, yet I know this is not entirely fair.

At that time, I understood little and was too ready to keep the peace by compromising. Relations with mothers-in-law are often uneasy. Gundel was particularly besotted by her son and so we were competitors for his attention and affection. I was the woman who 'stole' her son from her, keeping him in a foreign land. Gundel had no doubt seen me as a threat. With the additional language barrier that prevented us from establishing the affinity which can easily bond two women, I was unable to express my own fears.

But language was not the only barrier that separated us. Gundel simply did not like me. I wonder, though, whether I realised it then and whether I had formulated in my mind what really needed to be said: 'Gundel, please cut the umbilical cord. Let go of your son and let him become a father.'

Hans-Peter was Gundel's property and his newborn son the extension of her rights. She couldn't accept that a child eventually becomes his own person and needs to be set free. She had hung on to her children and retained control over them, probably frightened that her life would become empty without them. Hans-Peter, her favourite and the weakest, had remained entirely hers: he had never grown up, and still relied on her. Alexander was meant for her – never for me.

After a week in hospital, with Hans-Peter and Gundel
paying daily visits, it was time for my baby and me to
come home. They arrived, in my car, eager to claim their
priceless possession. Gundel held her arms out, ready to
take Alexander from me. It was then that I uttered my first
NO.

'Oh, of course. I simply wanted to help,' she said,
retreating immediately and withdrawing her hands.

My instinct to protect my baby had made me react
automatically. But inexorably, Gundel and Hans-Peter
took over my life and postnatal depression set in. Even my
flat felt alien. Things had been moved around and it smelt
different. Gundel's presence was everywhere and I no
longer felt it was my home. She slept in the sitting room,
strategically positioned between Alexander and our bedroom.

Gundel sent me to rest: I looked tired and pale and
should take advantage of her presence to recuperate.
There was no need to worry, she and Hans-Peter would
take care of the baby. He was a doctor and she had been
a nurse during the war. Alexander was in excellent hands.
I was a businesswoman and could therefore not be competent. The only requirement was that I should breast-
feed the baby.

'Breast-feeding is essential. It's the only way to ensure a
child's healthy development. Alexander deserves a good
start in life.'

Nature gave me tiny breasts and my inadequate milk
production drove Gundel to despair, but she would not
give in. She bought a pump and, by hook or by crook, she
was going to extract her grandson's requirements! I felt
completely demeaned and my sense of insufficiency was
accentuated by Gundel's sighs:

'The poor child hasn't had enough milk to satisfy him.'

Tired, frustrated and depressed, I was quite unable to
stand up to her demands. She would feed Alexander and

41

her reproachful stare at the half-empty bottle threw me into gloom and a sense of incompetence. Shocked by this violent intrusion I felt absorbed into a vacuum.

My friends who came to visit could not fail but notice. 'Catherine, what's going on? Your mother-in-law has taken over!'

Gundel's stay in London seemed an eternity. Rather than defend me, Hans-Peter was entirely swamped by his mother's behaviour; they spoke German together, and I couldn't join in.

Alexander cried a lot and had trouble getting to sleep but, at my slightest movement, mother or son would rush to pick him up first. Doctor and nurse could attend to his needs; I had better regain my strength to increase my milk production.

When Gundel finally returned to Germany, there were less than three weeks before I had to go back to work. Kept from my baby, my day now became dedicated to him. But the hours were short, as Hans-Peter returned very early from the hospital. I wondered how he could carry out his research study but he never wanted to discuss it. Later I discovered that he used to slip out from the hospital through a back door. Like a boy playing truant, Hans-Peter rushed home to play with his baby. Whether Alexander were asleep or not, Hans-Peter would pick him up, hold him in the air as if he were a doll and roll with him on the bed.

'Hans-Peter, please. He's much too small for that. You're being too rough and he won't be able to go back to sleep.'

My remonstrances were ignored and Hans-Peter would continue to amuse himself, unperturbed. But, once he decided he was bored, he would put Alexander down, oblivious to his cries. Then it was up to me to soothe him back to sleep.

Mornings were my heaven, finally alone with my Alexander. These are my happiest memories of our early months together. We used to sit on the sofa facing the large window which gave directly on to the communal garden. A large chestnut tree was in full blossom, beautiful in the warm June sunshine.

Alexander was mine, and I could sense how comfortable he felt in my arms. When he cried, I would immediately pick him up and hold him tight and he was instantly comforted. I could feel the warmth of his little body, snuggling up to mine. This was his home, this was where he belonged and he needed to feel the security of it enveloping him. People say that babies recognise the smell and the voice of their mother from the time they have been inside her. Alexander certainly did! His little gurgles of happiness made me wonder how deeply he had missed me in the past weeks.

He did everything with me when he was not sleeping and even then I would not leave him in a different room from me. I took my bath with him beside me in his cot, I prepared the food holding him in my arms, I talked to him all the time – sometimes in English, but mostly in French. He was my little angel, the most beautiful baby in the world, so warm and cuddly.

Alexander was born with tiny muscles in his arms and legs. I was fascinated and extremely proud. All the other babies in the hospital had pudgy limbs. He was different and very special! He was adorable with his darkish tan; brown eyes like his mummy, but shaped like those of his daddy with his square face and well-shaped nose.

'No one will ever harm you. Your Mummy will always be there to protect you. You'll see, your life will be different. You will not be raised so that anyone can walk all over you!'

These were the times when I would freely talk of my love and the fears which were surfacing in me. My love for Hans-Peter had been tempered and I was beginning to have doubts about our relationship.

At night Hans-Peter was totally uncooperative and always pretended he could not hear Alexander's cries. Most men do not realise what physical and emotional stress the first months can be for a woman. I could not really blame Hans-Peter – he was working and I wasn't. However, when I did return to the office and had to deal with the long hours, I resented Hans-Peter's excuses.

I tried to organise my day to spend as much time with Alexander as possible. Since I was mostly working on the US markets, I was able to leave home as late as twelve o'clock, my assistant holding the fort.

The mornings still belonged to us, and they were sheer delight. Day by day Alexander was developing into a little bundle of cheerful babbles and chirps. He started to grab things, sit in his baby chair and loudly express his joy, a dimple appearing on his right cheek. At noon, the Portuguese nanny would take over until his daddy's return.

At first, I found it hard to reconnect with the futures markets, world events and statistics, but slowly I settled into my new life, being a mummy in the morning and a career woman in the afternoon. There was little choice. Hans-Peter's grant would run out in September.

'What will you do now?' I queried.

'I'm not sure. You know, I think it would be difficult for me to become a doctor in this country.'

'What do you mean?'

'Well, I want to become a specialist and since I haven't been trained through the National Health Service, it won't be possible.'

'But I thought this was the reason why you got yourself a grant in a teaching hospital in London?'

'You just don't know the system! I haven't done my training here and it will be practically impossible to open a practice.'

I was aware of the problems in the National Health Service and how difficult it was for doctors and nurses. This was often in the national press. I could not argue with Hans-Peter's views.

'OK, but what do you intend to do then?' I asked.

'Go into the pharmaceutical industry. In any case, one

earns much more money. I'm thinking of applying for a job in research or in marketing.'

I was taken aback. Hans-Peter had always said that medicine was his vocation, and now he was considering the business world of marketing! I presumed his experience at the London teaching hospital must have disappointed him. This was why he had been so detached and evasive. At least he realised it now and with his medical training and a PhD I had no doubt he would find a good position.

Days went by. Hans-Peter mentioned nothing. Weeks went by and I began to worry. I did not want to pressure him as I knew how frustrating job hunting can be, but his silence was disturbing. The only interview I remember was in south London and I wonder now whether Hans-Peter actually ever looked for work in England.

Finaly he announced, 'Hoechst is offering me a marketing job here and they want me to fly to Frankfurt to meet the big boss.'

Two days later Hans-Peter returned from Frankfurt looking sheepish and ill at ease.

'So, how did it go?'

'Well, I was offered a job in Frankfurt in marketing.'

'What do you mean? I thought the offer was for their London branch?'

'Yes, but . . . It would only be for two years and the salary is much better in Germany.'

Hans-Peter was still standing and I could sense some embarrassment. He started pacing nervously around the sitting room waiting for my reaction. I was thinking aloud:

'Of course, getting a contract with head office is always a good idea and a better assurance of promotion . . .'

I hardly had time to finish my sentence when Hans-Peter threw himself at me, enthusiastically kissing me.

'So you agree! That's fantastic!'

This was typical of Hans-Peter – extracting a positive answer before I had even expressed my views. He had his desires and nothing would deter him from getting what he wanted. He would pre-empt people's words and twist them to suit himself. Hans-Peter was so happy. He was hugging and kissing me. Already he was making plans and I could not stop his flow of enthusiasm.

So many things were disturbing me about Hans-Peter after only two years of marriage: his mess, his selfishness, his irresponsibility, his overpowering possessiveness. But no one is perfect. I must have been irritating too, with my meticulousness and perfectionism.

The more I understand Hans-Peter now, the more I wonder. Had he contacted Frankfurt directly? For months, he had been quiet about his search. I can't remember much correspondence either. If Hoechst-Frankfurt had known about a London contract, why had they offered him something?

But at the time, the thought that my husband might be lying and that he was enacting a unilateral plan never occurred to me. On the contrary, I was optimistic and supportive. His career was my main concern. Two years was nothing if it meant establishing the basis for his future. Furthermore, this could offer me an immediate way out of my financial situation. I could sell my flat and pay off my debts. By the time we returned, the flat would be too small, in any case. Leaving London and abandoning my work did not thrill me, but it would allow me to dedicate all my time to Alexander.

On the other hand, I knew Frankfurt would be difficult for me. I could not speak a word of German and knew no one there. Hans-Peter did not have these problems when he came to London, as he spoke English so could easily integrate himself, and meet people through work.

'The office will keep my job open until we come back . . .'

'*Ja, ja*. Frankfurt wants me to start on January the 3rd.'

'So soon.'

My life was again running ahead of me. I felt there was nothing I could do to determine its course any more.

46

It was bitter cold and grey on our arrival in Frankfurt. Modern, impersonal tower blocks rose imposingly against the wintry sky, and occasional pedestrians, wrapped in their thick coats, hurried along the half-deserted streets. My first impression of 'Bankfurt' was disheartening.

Every flat we were shown seemed sterile. Unable to understand what the estate agent was saying and irritated by Hans-Peter's oblivious enthusiasm and expediency, I chose the flat which seemed to be in the most central part of the town, next to the attractive Palm Garten. I felt as if I were in a movie, that this reality was not mine, that I would never actually live here.

We returned to London and I sold my flat. The last of my London roots had disappeared. After the loading of the removal van, I walked back into the empty sitting room, with its high ceilings, cornices, warm-coloured curtains . . . and a strange sensation overtook me. Everything had happened so quickly that there had been no time to think. A chapter was ending and the unknown future was alarming. I was overcome with apprehension. As I closed the door I thought: *Catherine, you're closing the door on your freedom.* I was giving up my friends, my career and, above all, London, the soul of my existence. So many memories belonged here. Instead of feeling excited, I felt hesitant.

Hans-Peter was already in the car and raving to go. He hooted impatiently, interrupting my thoughts. As usual, I controlled my emotions: *Don't think about it, Catherine. Go and join your husband. We'll soon be back . . .*

That day, as I ran down the stairs saying goodbye to London and all it held of me, I clung on to the belief that we would be back as Hans-Peter had promised. I should not feel sorry for myself.

'So, are you coming?'

Hans-Peter's tone of voice was already different, nearly commanding. He was leaving a place which had become irrelevant to him, though he had settled into it with such vitality and conviction. My heart was cold that day. If only Hans-Peter had said 'Don't be sad. We'll soon be back.'

But he could not say these words because, I am now convinced, he would have known them to have been a lie.

My heart and soul belonged to London. Leaving it was as if half my life were being torn away from me. But I was a young mother following my husband to the country of his choice for a limited period. There was nothing tragic in that. In fact I learned to appreciate Germany, to speak its language and understand its ways.

Germany was not, is not, the focus of this drama. The fortress in which my sons are held could have been built in any country. The German legal system was simply the mechanism that made it possible.

Chapter 5
Endings and Beginnings

*Constantin, you were all and everything to me. After
you, there could be no more. Without you, I am no
more.*

We arrived in Frankfurt on 29 December 1985. Hans-
Peter unlocked the door and an empty, unwelcoming
apartment stared back at us. We unpacked the cot and I
gently laid Alexander in it. He was fast asleep and only
the flickering of his eyelids indicated that he was dreaming. I could hear Hans-Peter's voice echoing along the
empty corridor. He was already on the telephone to his
mother and I couldn't understand what they were talking
about.

I felt abandoned and dispirited.

'If you weren't with me, Alexander, I'd be very lonely,'
I whispered, gently stroking the back of his head. He
looked so beautiful and so vulnerable.

Hans-Peter walked into the room, interrupting my
thoughts: 'My sister and her husband are coming to spend
New Year's Eve with us.'

'Already?'

'Of course.'

Antje and her husband arrived two days later. They
were both loud and irrepressible. There was no room for
privacy. Antje was quite an overwhelming person. She
was six foot one, broad-shouldered, and fair-skinned. Her
hair was so very short it looked like a punk haircut.

She was a lawyer and so was her husband. When they
talked with Hans-Peter in the sitting room it sounded

more like an argument than a conversation. I was forgotten, isolated in my new kitchen. From time to time I went to join them. Antje didn't notice me and, although her English was quite good, it was her husband who struggled with polite conversation to include me.

During dinner they continued their incessant conversation, while I was serving and clearing away the plates. Antje liked to have the last word, as if she were still contesting a case in court. Even without understanding, I noticed the way she interrupted the others. Hans-Peter was her elder brother, their mother's favourite, and I could sense that their relationship was based on a mixture of rivalry and sibling complicity. Hans-Peter and Antje did not talk but barked at each other; yet if someone intervened to defend one of them, they would both immediately say: 'It's none of your business.'

I eyed this unfeminine woman with mistrust. Her forceful, abrasive manner seemed so uncompromising that I could not see how our relationship could improve, even with time. She focused her attention exclusively on Hans-Peter, ignoring her husband, who kindly tried to translate when he could and, after the meal, helped me tidy up.

Ths first reception on New Year's Eve was a foretaste of the future. Antje soon divorced this man (who seemed to me the only considerate person in the clan) to marry another lawyer. Her new husband, Klaus, was a giant. Both he and Antje were eventually to play a decisive role in Hans-Peter's family life and legal crusade. It would be Antje, later employed at the Ministry of Justice in Lower Saxony, who would support Hans-Peter when he abducted our children while Klaus built up the legal case to support it.

I had already met most of the family: Hans-Peter's younger brother, Hans-Jorg, shared a dental practice with their father and would later become politically involved with the CDU (Christian Democrats) party. He, too, later married a lawyer, who practises in Bremen. Gundel, my mother-in-law, also came from a legal family. Her father was a judge who practised in Hanover during the Second World War and later, I believe, in the small town of Verden, the family stronghold. Gundel's younger brother was the parliamentary spokesman of the CDU party in Bremen and later its president, while Gundel's sister was married to a famous Bremen lawyer whose family had emigrated to Chile in the aftermath of the war.

The Volkmanns all seemed to make a living as lawyers, judges or politicians. I had never studied law, and I had no specific political affiliations; the family's political affinities and connections did not worry me at the time.

Unsuspecting, I would visit Wilfred and Ute, small landowners living near Verden. Wilfred was, and still is, a local judge, who I believe used to practise in the town of Celle. His wife Ute is devoutly religious. Together, they were later to aid and abet Hans-Peter to abduct my sons. Thanks to them, Hans-Peter would obtain an absurd psychologist's report to substantiate his claim on our sons in court.

It may sound far-fetched to group all these characters and motives together, but without understanding the links between them, their respective functions and roles, it would be difficult to imagine how, in our civilised Western society, a mother could have her children stolen from her and be deprived of all human and legal rights to see them, know them and show her love to them.

Life in Frankfurt was rather cheerless – for three months I saw almost no one but Hans-Peter and Alexander. Hans-Peter would set off in my car every morning to Hoechst and Alexander and I would spend the day together. We could never venture very far, as we were always on foot, but almost every day we took walks in the Palm Garten nearby. Although he was only eight months old, and too young to be real company, seeing Alexander develop was a real joy.

Hans-Peter used to return home early at 5.30 whistling a tune to announce his arrival, and I would throw myself at him, craving someone to communicate with. However, he would usually head straight for Alexander to play with him, whether Alexander was asleep or not, then he would nibble something from the refrigerator and settle down in front of the television. His work remained a mystery. As I had been a businesswoman myself, it would have been interesting to hear about his commercial environment, but he never wanted to discuss it.

Hans-Peter had few relationships in the outside world, besides his elusive work colleagues and the ever-present family. One person outside his family who did call him was the friend with whom he had been on holiday when I had met him. They used to spend hours on the telephone, eternally making plans (making plans seemed to be Hans-Peter's constant preoccupation) which were never carried out.

Fortunately my friends from London kept in regular contact with me. However, there was little I could tell them, besides Alexander's developments (but even the most involved mother realises, sooner or later, that such information is of limited interest to others). They kept me up to date with all the latest events and Leonard gave me regular run-downs on the market and the office gossip. These short moments soon became the highlight of my day. I missed them all so much and hearing their voices on the telephone made me question my life with Hans-Peter. I felt a growing sense of unfulfilment and being away from my environment and friends only emphasised this feeling.

Hans-Peter's mother phoned every day to enquire about her grandson and soon she paid us a visit. Gundel was not a restrained grandmother. She always knew better than her daughter-in-law and constantly commented on how I fed Alexander, changed him or acted with him. If Alexander cried, Gundel would order me not to go to him:

'Leave him, he's already too spoiled.'

Her tone was so authoritative that I would not dare move. Then she would suddenly get up and rush to him:

'The poor child, he can't be left like that . . .'

Was she just completely inconsistent or was it her way of controlling me? I could not tell and I decided it must be a combination of both.

When Hans-Peter was around, the two of them talked continually and although I could now recognise a few words of German I could not make much of their endless conversations. As soon as Alexander woke up from a nap, they rushed over to him. Gundel took the nappies from my hands, Hans-Peter his plate, after double-checking that the food was at the right temperature. Alexander was their precious treasure. He belonged to them. I had given birth to their heir and this was the extent of my role. I became a mere spectator in their handling of the most important part of my life: my son. Feeling barely tolerated, friendless and debilitated, I did not know how to deal with this deteriorating situation.

When we went out, in my car, Hans-Peter would drive, Gundel beside him, Alexander and me in the back. We drove where they wanted, stopped where they wanted and returned home when they decided they had had enough. I could not participate in their conversation, which in any case was hard to make out from the back seat. My only consolation was to steal moments with Alexander.

One evening in March 1986, Hans-Peter announced that Hoechst was sending us to the States where he would attend a three-month training programme. If he was being sent on such an expensive introductory tour, it obviously meant that his career was taking shape and that his boss appreciated him. This was wonderful. I was very pleased for him and looked forward to an interval away from his family.

It was great to be in New Jersey, in an environment where I could communicate with people. Alexander was still too young to walk but the two of us bowled out, visiting tourist sights, forests, shopping malls. People were friendly, warm and welcoming. I was alive again and summer was coming!

Several weeks after we arrived Hans-Peter was sent across the US to meet other Hoechst representatives and Alexander and I accompanied him. The business trip turned out to be more of a holiday tour than a commercial one: three days in San Francisco, a two-day relaxed drive along the coastal road to Los Angeles, three days at Disneyland, five in Disney World, Florida and two in Philadelphia. Hans-Peter contented himself with a one-day presence in the local offices and off we went again.

After fifteen days of holidaying (with Alexander ecstatic over the Disney characters) we returned to New Jersey. Hans-Peter unenthusiastically went back to work, coming home at five to head for the tennis courts. I was very worried. I knew little about this industrial sector but couldn't imagine that the rules would be so different from the financial world I had known. Hans-Peter had just joined his company and it seemed to me this was the time when he particularly needed to impress his colleagues. For the first time, I realised how unmotivated and unsettled Hans-Peter was. Even if he was not career orientated, I could not help feeling that he should at least assume the minimum of professional responsibilities for his family's sake.

Life in the US in general was a breath of fresh air to me. We were on neutral territory, away from the clinging family, with no one to interfere in our lives. The thought of returning to Frankfurt and my in-laws was daunting. What about Hans-Peter pursuing a position in the States? When Alexander was older I could easily help our finances by returning to work for E.F. Hutton, which had its head office in New York. I tried out my idea, choosing my words carefully:

'You see in Germany it would be impossible for me to work. I can't speak the language and haven't any business contacts. Here, there would be no problems.'

'You don't need to work!'

'My savings are running out, your salary isn't yet

enough for us all and before we return to London . . .'

Hans-Peter was adamant. We wouldn't stay in the US. He would miss his family. It was too far from home.

'But I'm away from my family, if we live in Frankfurt,' I ventured.

'No further than when you were living in London. In fact, France is much more accessible from Germany, as you don't have to cross the Channel. Don't worry, we'll move to Wiesbaden. You'll see, it's much nicer there!'

Hans-Peter no longer wished to discuss the subject.

And so we packed up and left America. As the plane landed in Frankfurt, I was overcome with sadness. I felt as if I were being handcuffed, pulled back into a cage. I walked disconsolately through the airport crowd with Alexander tightly locked in my arms, our cheeks together. I was haunted by the idea that we would never be free from the tight control of our extended family.

We reached our flat and as soon as I had fed Alexander and put him to bed, I let myself collapse on my bed in despair. I cried tears of frustration, of utter powerlessness. The way Hans-Peter had dismissed all discussion had made me realise his resolve: I would never be allowed to work again. Hans-Peter was, I believe, subconsciously jealous of my achievements, my friends and my interests in which he was not the centre of attention. He loved me possessively, and wanted to wipe out anything that might rival his position in my life.

'Catherine, I love you so much. I need you and you make me so happy being here.'

It was up to me to make him happy. 'Just two years. You'll see how quickly the time will go,' he had said, holding me in his arms in the London flat. What if he never wanted to go back? What if he really wanted my only role in life to be to serve his personal demands? When we got married, he knew I had a job and enjoyed my career. He knew London was my chosen and cherished home. He had led me to understand that he loved it too . . . At the time there had never been any indication that he disapproved of me working, or that we would not live in London.

Had he only moved in with me because it was convenient for the two years' training he wanted to do abroad? Had he married me to give a child to his mother and then brought all his toys back to her in Germany? I shivered and I was ashamed to even let myself have such a thought. No, of course this couldn't be true! I told myself I was being unfair.

'Catherine, don't you love me?' Hans-Peter pleaded.

But what did love mean? His idea of love and my idea seemed to have little in common. I had always believed love consisted of tenderness, like-mindedness and mutual respect. Hans-Peter was so different from the man I had met in France. Or perhaps he was just the same and it was I who had made the mistake in thinking he was someone he wasn't. I found myself mothering two children – and one of them was over thirty and suffocating me!

My London friends ventured a comment:

'You're simply unhappy with Hans-Peter. He isn't the man you thought he was.'

They were right, but 'unhappiness' can be such a confusing emotion and often difficult to admit. I blamed my environment, this cold, unwelcoming town, my inability to communicate, Gundel's interference and the social desert in which Hans-Peter was keeping me. I felt alone and discarded. I began dreaming of freedom: the freedom to be myself again.

Wiesbaden, to the west of Frankfurt is a pretty town still carrying the vestiges of its elegant past. I enjoyed walking in its peaceful streets, admiring the unspoiled houses and imagining the splendours of what had once been a fashionable spa. The Kurpark was beautifully kept and welcoming. A Russian Orthodox church perched on the hilltop above it; I learned, curiously, that a great aunt of mine had been married there. The Russian side of my family had always had a close affinity with Germany and several of my great-uncles had studied in its universities.

During my strolls with Alexander, little old ladies would invitingly smile and talk to us. People seemed kind and friendly here. It was only when Alexander and I ventured into the commercial centre of the town that I realised that these polite ways did not always prevail. In the 1980s, Wiesbaden still belonged to the American zone and there was a large army base outside the town. Some of the local population seemed to resent the fact that foreigners were still 'occupying' their homeland. Admittedly American GIs were not always well behaved, stumbling out of beer-houses loud and drunk on their Saturday night outings, and this was not looked upon kindly in this orderly Kur town.

At that time I mostly spoke in English to Alexander and when people overheard me they presumed I was a 'Yank'. On a few occasions I was taken aback by snide comments made by passers-by. I had never experienced any sort of racial hostility and began to become aware that the implications of the past were far more complex than I had thought. It was as if I was suddenly looking at history through the other end of the telescope and I realised how narrow my vision had been.

I would have liked to discuss issues such as these, but there was no one to talk to. The elderly ladies I met on my walks were my only source of communication during my days with Alexander and the only constructive thing I could do was to practise my few words of German and expand my vocabulary.

The days passed with nothing to differentiate one from the next until one morning I discovered I was pregnant again. That evening Hans-Peter welcomed the news, kissing me lavishly.

'Another baby! Maybe this time it'll be a girl.'

He was overjoyed and immediately rushed to telephone his mother.

I had not planned this, and was rather taken aback. Alexander was only fifteen months old and the thought of another baby so soon frightened me: two small children, no help, a husband whose future seemed uncertain and his mother now congratulating him on his achievement.

Hans-Peter was delighted and, in his usual fashion, he grabbed me by the arm to place me next to him and feel the stomach which would again become the object of his devotion. Catherine was once more only the carrier of Hans-Peter's child.

Tenderness, care and attention are what a pregnant woman most longs for. Instead, Hans-Peter was taking control of me and I could already hear in my mind Gundel's voice telling him: 'I'm coming!'

At four months I almost lost Constantin. We were walking along the street when a sudden acute contraction forced me to sit on a bench. I was as white as a sheet and feeling dizzy. I was rushed to hospital, the doctors operated immediately and he was just saved.

I was still in hospital when Gundel arrived, smiling and very happy with herself, Alexander in one hand, Hans-Peter in the other. The doctors had ordered me to stay in bed for the rest of the pregnancy. There was no question of getting a nanny for Alexander; Gundel would take care of him!

My pregnancy was particularly difficult and I was taken back to hospital twelve times. The rest of my days were spent lying down. I longed for my mother to come, but with Gundel around, the space was already occupied.

I could no longer be with Alexander. Gundel would bathe him, feed him, take him for walks and completely monopolise him while the kitchen was mostly left to me. Both mother and son expected me to clear up.

When Gundel finally left, Antje appeared to help out, grudgingly, until I finally called for my mother to rescue me. I never liked to impose on others, nor complain about my private life, but as far as I was concerned, this was an emergency!

My mother was shocked to see me living under these conditions. Hans-Peter, so used to being waited on, did not change any of his habits in my mother's presence. He would come home, nibble on a sandwich while my mother was still preparing dinner and leave a trail of crumbs. He would then play with Alexander, overexcite him and then push him away when he decided he was bored.

My poor mother would run around after him: 'Hans-Peter, please, take a plate at least . . .'

But he simply ignored her entreaties. Hans-Peter had a habit of waving his hand dismissively as if to say 'Raus – Away with you.'

The tension between my mother and Hans-Peter intensified and I was caught in between: 'Catherine, I'm not his maid. Nor are you!'

In the evening, it was Hans-Peter who assailed me with complaints: 'Your mother's getting on my nerves. She's constantly interfering. When's she leaving?'

I couldn't make him understand that his mother had done the same. In fact, she imposed far more. At least my mother did not take Alexander away for herself, but was helping me – she did the shopping, the cooking and relieved me of household duties.

All I could do was hold on to the new life I could feel growing inside me. Although my pregnancy was difficult, I knew the baby would be fine. It was another boy and I tried to imagine how he would look – probably very like Alexander. The same cute face with its slanted eyes and sweet nose and, for the moment, no one could take him away from me! He felt more fragile, and was much calmer than Alexander had been inside me.

I enjoyed being alone with my unborn child in the hospital. I would spend my days there endlessly talking to him, reading and studying German out loud.

When it came to giving birth, I was luckier than I had been with Alexander. Hans-Peter was at work and the doctor who looked after me was a woman. Immediately she noticed how nervous I was.

'Why don't you have an epidural?' she asked after I explained how painful it had been the first time. 'You won't feel a thing and you'll enjoy the birth.'

'My husband doesn't want me to have one. He says it's risky for the baby.'

'Nonsense.' At once she called an anaesthetist.

'But my husband –'

She stayed beside me. Even when Hans-Peter arrived, she took no notice of his outstretched arms and gave the baby to me. Efficient and discerning, she had protected me, and this time I was not denied giving birth the way I wanted. It had only lasted two hours and I had felt nothing. Instead of suffering, I stayed conscious and enjoyed the ultimate experience of childbirth. Hans-Peter rushed to my side to admire his second son and embrace his wife. This was the picture I had longed for: mother and father united with their newborn baby and we shared this moment of bliss alone.

Spring had arrived in Wiesbaden and Constantin was born on a sunny day, on 17 May 1987. He was adorable, much smaller than Alexander had been, and looked very fragile. I was surprised at how different he was.

The next morning, Gundel and Hans-Peter brought Alexander to meet his new brother. I hadn't seen Alexander for two days. He was wearing new clothes which Gundel had brought him. He smelt like her as she had used her soap on him. I tried not to let myself be irritated by these little details and I took Alexander in my arms. 'So, what do you think?' I asked.

'He's so cute, Mummy.'

Alexander was shyly examining tiny Constantin, wide eyed, with a mixture of disbelief and excitement.

In June Hans-Peter suddenly abandoned his job at Hoechst, announcing that he did not enjoy the pharmaceutical industry after all. He was unemployed and his proposed solution was to move to Verden where the four of us would live in one room at his brother's house. As I had no savings left, I also had no independence.

Catherine, the autonomous woman, who once had made a living and owned a flat, had become a helpless wife who was totally dependent on her in-laws, the Volkmanns.

As I try to recount the failure of my marriage and my refusal to acknowledge this fact for a long time, I realise that I was gritting my teeth and clutching on to one last hope: Hans-Peter can't go on relying on other people – especially his mother. After all, he has two children and a wife and must realise that he cannot build his future on capricious whims. One doesn't just leave a job without another one or at least having a definite aim! He'll pull himself together and mature. It's just a phase.

Chapter 6
God and Verden

When Man talks too loudly about his religion and its morality one wonders what are the motives behind his desire to convert – the salvation of the soul or the suspension of freedom?

The only explanation I managed to extract from Hans-Peter was: 'Marketing isn't for me. In any case I hate flying and the job would involve too many trips abroad.'

I wondered why he hadn't considered this before joining. He went on: 'I've decided that I'd actually much rather have a general medical practice.'

There was not much I could say. Hans-Peter's mind was made up and he had already left his job. He had no specific plans, though, and before he could open a practice he still needed two years' hospital training. Furthermore, opening a practice required a lot of sacrifices and hard work to build up a list of patients. But Hans-Peter talked about it as if everything would just fall from the sky and be brought to him on a silver platter. My own resources had been depleted; the £40,000 that I had when we left London had been my savings from ten years' work and now there was practically nothing left.

It was July 1987. Alexander was two years old, Constantin nearly three months. Our furniture went into storage and, with a few suitcases, the four of us set off for the north, along the motorway. The Volkmanns' family home was in Verden, in the centre of Lower Saxony. The nearest town was Bremen from where, I once read, the Saxons who invaded England came in 449. Verden, on the river Aller, is a small provincial town with a population of about 25,000. It prides itself on its eighteenth-century cathedral, a large horse auction, a small equestrian museum and its own law court.

Gundel had arranged for us to live with Hans-Peter's brother Hans-Jorg, who lived alone in what had once been the family home. At the back, the house joined on to the dental practice which he shared with his father. The welcome Hans-Jorg gave us was lukewarm, to say the least. But I could understand why – after all, the arrival of his chaotic elder brother, with wife, toddler and baby in tow was hardly a pretty sight!

Hans-Jorg decided from the outset that we would not infringe on his life and that he would preciously guard his territory. Hans-Peter, the boys and I were allocated one room on the first floor. The white-walled room was sparsely furnished with two single beds, a small wardrobe and an old table. Old-fashioned turquoise tiles covered the walls of the shower room, which consisted of a small sink and a plastic shower cubicle. Opposite was Hans-Jorg's bedroom and bathroom. The other two bedrooms were cluttered with old furniture and junk that had accumulated over the years. Downstairs, his drawing room, library and study were kept in the most meticulous order and it was clear that they were out of bounds for us.

Hans-Peter's thirty-year-old cot was quickly brought down from the attic by Gundel who had impatiently been waiting for us to arrive. Immediately she began reminiscing on the happy memories of her first-born:

'You were so cute, so blond, *mein Junge*. Now your son will sleep here!'

It was summer and I should not have felt so cold. But I shivered as I realised the kind of life that lay ahead of me here: no music, no books, no photographs, no space . . . not even a tiny little corner where I could snuggle and feel comfortable. This was a barren island, firmly under Gundel's control.

It was grey outside and bleak inside. Gundel seemed to fill every room with her invasive presence, attending to the organisation of our lives. I could not fight it. There was nothing left for me to fight with, bound to a husband who had willingly imposed us upon his family.

Gundel and her husband lived only ten minutes away and every morning, she would drop in. She usually appeared when I was giving Constantin his bath:

'Catherine, you shouldn't use this soap. *Nein*, don't hold the baby this way . . .'

Then taking Alexander by the hand, she would vanish to do her shopping in the town, feed him lunch and spend most of the afternoon with him.

Hans-Peter's father, who seemed to have an extensive network of contacts, made a phone call to some general and immediately secured a position for his son in the Bundeswehr. It was not long before Hans-Peter was admiring himself in the mirror dressed in his uniform and driving off to the army, leaving his little family anchored safely on his mother's territory.

My life was becoming a series of daily complications and worries. I was at the mercy of others for the simple necessities of daily life. Everything involved difficulties, from the careful bathing of the children in Hans-Jorg's bathroom, to running behind Alexander to make sure he did not touch any of his uncle's belongings. Uncle Hans-Jorg was not very tolerant or keen on children and it was obvious that our presence was as much an ordeal for him as it was for me.

Helpless, I slowly withdrew into a shell. Alexander was continuously taken away and hidden from me and there was nothing I could do to prevent it. My sole consolation was little Constantin, to whom I instinctively turned for affection. He was mine and no one would ever take him away!

Unlike Alexander, Constantin was a peaceful and easy baby. He would wake up smiling, gurgle happily in his cot until he spotted me, when he would jump and squeal with joy. We would play on my bed and spend most of the mornings alone in our sterile room. I would invent stories for him and talk to him about the happy world we would have when we finally got our own home . . .

Hans-Peter usually returned well before five, delighted by the lack of demands his job imposed on him. His dream was now to become a colonel. However, Hans-Peter's vanity, and self-satisfaction was viewed critically, not only by me, but also by others. I noticed Hans-Jorg frown as he watched Hans-Peter take books from the shelves without putting them back. Hans-Peter seemed immune to any remarks his brother might make, and would merely shrug his shoulders. I also noticed that Hans-Jorg seemed to resent Gundel's blatant preference for Hans-Peter. Even in front of Hans-Jorg, she would slip money into Hans-Peter's trouser pocket, pampering her elder son and pandering to all of his whims.

The months went by. Suddenly, Gundel grew bored with Alexander:

'Catherine, I just can't take him with me every morning!'

I had never asked her to take care of Alexander. I said nothing. There was little point in poisoning our relationship further, and anyway, what mattered most was that I would be able to spend time with Alexander at last.

Life was restrictive and dull. Lunches and dinners with Hans-Jorg, Sundays at Gundel and Hans-Werner's and permanent encounters with the family members who would walk in or out of the house through the communicating doors leading to the practice. I had no privacy and felt as if I were being continuously checked up on.

'Hans-Peter, we just can't go on like this. We can't live in your brother's house, eat at your parents' and be financially dependent on them.'

Hans-Peter dismissed the conversation and walked off. I followed him out.

'Why do you want to stay in the army? Is it so important to become a colonel?' I asked.

'If ever there is a war, I won't be sent to the front if I'm a colonel!'

His answer stunned me. Where had the great plans he had talked about in London vanished to? He hadn't liked the pharmaceutical industry and now he was considering being an army doctor as long as he did not have to be in danger himself.

A short visit from my sister and her family that rainy August depressed me even more. I was an utterly different person from the vivacious, happy London career girl they had known. Here I was kowtowing to Hans-Peter's domineering family. No money, dependent, with a husband who had no ambition and could not care for his family.

'You can't live like this, Catherine. You must do something. I hardly recognise you!'

I summed up the courage to speak to Hans-Peter again: 'Ok, I'll look for a hospital job.'

Half-heartedly, he started to send a few applications to the hospitals which would not distance him from his mother.

'Hans-Peter, you should apply to big towns: Berlin, Hamburg or Munich.'

What I really meant to say was: a place where we could re-establish a social life and feel free again. Here I can't even telephone my family or my friends without feeling I'm imposing. Maybe I'll still be able to work and improve our finances. Hans-Peter, please, I'm suffocating here, alone with your family – but I did not dare say any of this. I was too intimidated by his moodiness and too weakened by my own depression.

I had been approached by someone I knew in London who wanted to break into the German market with a famous brand of office diaries. Convincing prospective clients to invest in the futures and options markets had been part of my daily routine when I was a broker. Convincing a store to order diaries should not have been insurmountable! Yet my self-confidence had been so crushed that I asked Hans-Peter to go with me, incapable of confronting the store buyer by myself.

Although I was aware of how far I had strayed from the

66

person I once was, I seemed unable to break the rhythm of my decline. I was permanently tired and would wake up in the mornings practically paralysed at the thought of facing another day. The road that lay ahead seemed dark and unrelenting. I felt a prisoner of my fate, being swept along, powerless to resist.

Hans-Peter had not even noticed and I, myself, was unaware that I was going through some sort of depression. The approach of winter did nothing to improve my prospects and in despair I called for help. However, my parents were abroad; my sister was busy. Had I been allowed to escape for a week or two, maybe our future would have been entirely different.

As it was, I was on a sinking ship with nothing but my two beautiful boys to hang on to. The three of us would retire into a world of fantasy and dreams. I spoke in French to them, and sometimes in English; even this was a release, as I could express myself without being endlessly corrected. My sons were my own source of hope but I longed for the company of an adult, a friend, a confidante.

It was on an autumn walk, seeking out the last ray of sunshine, that I met Ute Monkmann in a Verden street. I was pushing Constantin in his pram, holding Alexander by the hand, when a tall, dark woman, in her forties perhaps, came towards me with an engaging smile on her face:

'Are you Catherine, Hans-Peter Volkmann's wife?' she asked. I nodded.

'I'm Ute Monkmann. I heard Hans-Peter got married in England and that you've moved to Verden. And these are your children?'

A smile, a friendly face in this cold town and lonesome days . . .

'I expect you don't know anyone. Why don't you come over for tea at my place tomorrow?'

When I got home I told Hans-Jorg about my chance encounter.

'Oh, yes, Ute Monkmann. She spoke to you?' He nodded approvingly. 'They're very proper people. Her husband's a judge and she is an aristocrat, born a von Klemp.'

Obviously, this was some great achievement on my part!

Nobility impressed Hans-Jorg. In fact he was a passionate, if not an obsessed, genealogist, utterly absorbed in people's origins, names and inheritances. It transpired that the von Klemps were a small rural noble family. Hans-Jorg did extensive research after I met Ute and proudly announced some days later that thirteen generations ago they had been related!

Hans-Jorg's behaviour began to intrigue me. He entertained strange men in his house. They would suddenly appear, greet me politely and mysteriously disappear with Hans-Jorg. He belonged to a fraternity and I presumed that his guests were fellow members, but I never really paid much attention to them.

But Hans-Jorg's affected, arrogant demeanour, the rigid, disdainful manner in which he usually addressed me, confining himself to the bare minimum of civilities, were that day transformed into a strange restlessness and excitement. Clearly I would have to go for tea since it was such an honour to be invited by this family.

I realised that Hans-Jorg was hoping to be introduced to this 'proper' couple through me. I learned that Ute's brother-in-law was a school friend of Hans-Peter's sister, Antje, and also a lawyer. More lawyers!

After the invitation to tea, we met again, and once a week Hans-Peter and I would go to dinner. Hans-Peter too was very keen on this new association.

The one recurrent theme that emerged from the small talk of our afternoon conversations, in half-broken English and German, were Ute's religious beliefs. Her opinion was always related to God. If I felt lonely, I would find solace in God. If I was unhappy, I should think of God . . .

'Your belief will save you. God is our saviour!'

'Yes, but it is difficult for me to adapt here. I'm used to having a job, living in a town that has lots going on, being surrounded by friends. We had such a different life in London. Here nothing belongs to me, and I don't even have my own home.'

'You should pray and think positive thoughts. God will help you. Pray and you will see how your life will transform itself.'

I had been baptised Catholic, spent my early school years in a convent and eventually became Russian Orthodox, like my mother. I was attracted by the more spiritual and less structured dimension of the Orthodox teachings. Alexander and Constantin had also been baptised Russian Orthodox.

'Actually, there's a wonderful pastor in Bremen. He gives private seminars and I go to them twice a week. Perhaps you'd like to come with me?'

That Ute was pressing me to meet her pastor made me feel uncomfortable. I believe in God, but I had my own religion and certainly could never become a fanatic. Praying was one thing, but I could hardly expect God to re-establish my finances!

Imprisoned in this small town, I began to realise what a ghastly mistake I had made. I should never have sold my flat and removed my base in London. Instead I should have rented it out so that at least my children and I would have had a basic income. Now I could not even take a holiday with the boys without asking others for help.

I tried to share some of my feelings with Ute; I thought maybe she might be able to help me regain some self-esteem. However, I soon saw that I was asking too much of her. She had no understanding of my frustrations, and would answer any misgivings I had about life in Verden by saying:

'Here, the quality of life is excellent. The area's extremely green, with wonderful forests. There's an excellent market in Verden once a week, meetings at the church, and for the children it's much healthier to live away from towns.'

Ute, who presented herself as a friend, as time went on became an intrinsic part of this extraordinary coalition, which would strip me of motherhood. She would protect Hans-Peter, provide the powerful support of her husband, a local judge, and house him and my sons on their remote property. This would become the fortress where Alexander and Constantin were put under 'protection'.

At the end of December 1987, Hans-Peter finally got a job and we moved to Hamburg. I had hoped for Berlin, which I found a fascinating place. Berlin was a vibrant metropolis and the very moment I set foot in it for the first time, I had sensed its energising qualities. Artistic, intellectually avant-garde, Berlin is a city full of contradictions and has a special grandeur about it. Immersed in Eastern and Western cultures, it was then an island within the DDR; one really felt part of history.

Hamburg, though, seemed a good second choice with its famous port (its 'door to the world') and its Anglo-Saxon influence, seen in the white, London-like houses bordering the Alster lake. Living there would be pleasant and at last Hans-Peter and I could be on a more neutral territory, out of his family's pocket. I was convinced that there I could breathe again, re-establish a reasonable lifestyle and teach my sons something more than just the way to Gundel's and Ute's houses.

My vitality returned and I threw myself into the organisation of our move with enthusiasm and determination. Most people rented properties rather than bought them in Germany, and flats would usually be rented out on the very day the advertisement appeared in the papers. Being nearly two hours away and not knowing the geography of the town made flat-hunting difficult. One place was especially nice but Hans-Peter gave up easily: 'There's already an offer on it.'

'Well, make another one?'

We had no chance of grabbing it. Hans-Peter lacked the

70

dynamism and the incentive to do so. He stared blankly at me as if I had just asked him to move a mountain.

'But, Hans-Peter, my German isn't really good enough. You must call them back.'

For the past six months, we had been without a home and living out of a suitcase. I suddenly stood up and lifted the telephone. However good or bad my German, I was going to persuade the landlord – suddenly it seemed a matter of survival.

January 1988, Hamburg,

At last – our own space and privacy. I had become very active, unpacking, buying the essentials, getting the furniture out of storage – which needed as much dusting as I did! My mother could finally come and visit her daughter and grandsons in their own home. She stayed a couple of weeks and together we started getting to know the centre of Hamburg.

Our flat was in an old building, 'Altbau', in the university area of Hamburg, close to a museum and within walking distance of the centre and the banks of the Alster lake. Alexander first went to a kindergarten close by and as soon as Constantin was old enough, they both started at the French Lycée. Hans-Peter and I were keen that they should be raised multi-lingually. They were fortunate to be exposed to three languages and my mother even taught them a few words of Russian. Alexander and Constantin would be teenagers in the year 2000 and, with this background, we hoped the doors of Europe would be open to them.

I had left the deep countryside with enormous relief. In Hamburg I learned to understand and appreciate Germany and I made friends. I learned to speak German, and continued to bring up my children. Paradoxically, as my state of mind improved, I saw my love for Hans-Peter disintegrate further.

Hans-Peter still carried his mother's photograph in his jacket pocket, her money in his trouser pockets. He

71

seemed to survive only through this unhealthy bond.

January 1988 was a month during which I realised many dreams, but destroyed others. Hans-Peter had promised two years in Germany and then we would return to London. Now he was adamant:

'I'll never leave Germany', and 'You shall not work.'

Hans-Peter refused to acknowledge our precarious financial situation; as for our responsibility for two growing children and the happiness of his wife, these, in his mind, were even lesser considerations.

When I mustered the courage to point out that his sister Antje worked, although she had children who were even younger than ours, his only answer was, 'That's different!'

'Why?'

No reply.

Chapter 7
The Break-up

Alexander, Constantin, it will be here that your first childhood memories will belong. Your first days at school, your first friends, birthday parties and summer picnics will be at Hamburg, and although, Constantin, you were still too small by the time we left to remember, Alexander, you will have some memories . . .

Hamburg was less than two hours away from Verden, but it was home. Alexander, who was going to be three in May, was overjoyed when he discovered that Constantin and he had their own bedroom. The day we moved in, he ran around the flat, calling out from each room in excitement and I realised then how he too had missed his own private territory where he could be alone with his mummy, his daddy and his little brother.

We spent over four years in Hamburg. It was where Constantin learned to walk and talk, where Alexander will have his first childhood memories and where I established our life as a family. The boys and I developed our daily life routine of school, play and outings with friends. I entertained and soon spoke enough German to get by and allow me to make German friends.

Amongst these, there were two special ones. Amélie was my bosom friend and confidante. She was exceptionally warm, generous and loyal. We spent a lot of time together, often with our children who got on very well.

Joachim was my mentor and he became nearly as indispensable as Leonard had been in London. Exactly eleven years older than me, Joachim came from an aristocratic family who had fled Prussia when it fell into the hands of the communists. His life had been particularly difficult. His family had lost everything and his widowed mother had raised three children on her own. Joachim had also spent most of his childhood days in various hospitals and clinics after he contracted an acute and unusual rheumatoid illness which had left him slightly handicapped physically. Through the hardships of his illness and the influence of a Prussian education he had developed strong principles and an iron will. He was now a bantjer, but had never married.

We got on extremely well and I respected and admired Joachim's intelligence and rational mind. He had a particular quality about him which he shared with Leonard. He was logical and detached, yet at the same time extremely sensitive.

Through him I began to understand Germany and appreciate its history. Joachim would talk about it with love and passion, yet his interpretation was lucid and at times critical. What had confused and sometimes even shocked me in the behaviour of Hans-Peter's family became clearer, and I realised that their views were only representative of an isolated minority.

Germany is a young country. It had been created only in 1871, when eighteen sovereign states of various sizes, with their mixture of regional characteristics and entirely different forms of domestic policies, were drawn together under one constitution and one foreign policy. But Bismarck's Germany lacked a uniting philosophical framework and the aspirations of a nation-state. Bismarck's concern was above all with the creation and expansion of a greater Prussia. Much of his foreign policy, or 'Realpolitik', was orchestrated to restrain the latent incompatibilities of the states from erupting into war. For two hundred years Germany had been more the victim than the instigator of the wars in Europe, but after Bismarck Germany would lack moderation.

The light and dark side of Bismarck's achievements and the tragic two wars that ensued have deeply marked Germany's short history. The mistakes of the past, aggravated by the destruction of values and traditions in the course of the brutal intellectual *Gleichschaltung* of the Nazi period, left an enormous social void in the aftermath of the Second World War. But because demolition had been so complete, the German people could now begin all over again, while trying to reconcile themselves with a belligerent past.

However, some *Länder*, or states, remained inward looking and resistant to the new vision of Germany's role in Europe. Lower Saxony (created in November 1946 by the Allies), rural and provincial, was less resilient and adaptable to change, although even within this isolated environment my husband's family did appear especially conservative.

'What do you make of Gundel's father with a huge scar on the right cheek?' I asked Joachim.

'Oh, that comes from his fraternity days. Fencing was part of the ritual of acceptance as a member of the club. In fact, a scar was a symbol of courage. There are still many fraternities in Germany but most of them no longer abide by these strict rules. They're similar to those in American universities. The few which keep up the rigid, traditional codes of conduct are considered outdated and are often criticised.'

There were many comments of the Volkmann family that needed clarification.

Whilst Joachim's clear and objective explanations had helped me they increased my wariness about the character of the Volkmann family. But at least Hans-Peter was not an active member of his fraternity, and although he had changed a great deal since we returned to Germany, he had never expressed radical, conservative views.

At the time, I was more concerned by his continuous evasion of responsibility and his growing conceit. He was uninterested in his job, constantly avoided household duties and couldn't decide on career plans. He would swing between opening a practice, becoming a university professor or returning to the pharmaceutical industry.

Since we had been living in Hamburg our financial situation had not improved. Joachim would consistently pick up the tab at the restaurants where we ate together and my mother chipped in as well. She had been heartbroken when she saw me and offered to pay for a cleaning woman to help in the house once a week. But Hans-Peter continued to accept his mother's handouts, which she discreetly slid into his hand or trouser pocket during the regular, tedious visits we made to Verden on Sundays. He sold my car and bought an old diesel instead, yet he still objected to the idea of my working.

By autumn 1991 Hans-Peter's lax attitude worsened. Hans-Peter complained about his boss, his colleagues and the nature of his work. More unpaid bills piled up on his desk: he forbade me to touch them, dismissing me and locking the door of the dining room which he had turned into his study. We even received a summons.

'Hans-Peter, we can't go on this way. We must pay the bills!'

Without Hans-Peter's consent I finally decided to take a part-time job in an interior design shop. I thought it would restore my self-confidence. The children were now both attending the French Lycée and I felt I should actively strive to improve our autonomy, even if Hans-Peter disapproved.

My working full time was dismissed as 'criminal'. The boys could not be picked up from school by a babysitter! Instead Hans-Peter suggested applying to be on the Hamburg list for emergency night call, to improve our income.

A few days later, after a long telephone conversation with his mother, Hans-Peter announced: 'I got selected for the Hamburg area of Saint Georg. There are a lot of drug dealers and sleazy clubs around there but my mother said I don't have to do the night calls. She'll send me the

800 marks instead.'

During one of my rare trips to London, I confided in Leonard.

'Help him find a practice in London. It seems the only logical solution for both of you,' he said.

But Hans-Peter still refused to leave the fatherland; to him, his 'motherland'. Joachim, who had observed for months Hans-Peter's untidy ways, habitual laziness and total lack of discipline, tried to come to my rescue and suggested Berlin. For a moment there was hope, and Joachim drove us to the capital he knew and loved, in search of a suitable practice. Hans-Peter remained undecided. Finally, he declared that he would only consider a practice in Hamburg. Berlin was too far.

Then, in December 1991, Hans-Peter suddenly gave up his job at the hospital. As if a brick had fallen on my head, I woke up to the realisation that I no longer respected him. As abruptly as I had fallen in love, I fell out of love.

Hans-Peter's version was that he gave in his notice because he needed a year's experience in a general medical practice before being qualified to open his own.

For a few weeks, he looked in vain for a position in Hamburg, then like a spoiled child who has just broken his toy and wants to have it replaced, Hans-Peter rushed off to his parents.

This permanent recourse to his family for help exasperated me but Gundel's instant response incensed me even more. Hans-Peter later commented that I was obviously jealous. But how could I tell my husband, an adult, that as long as his parents succumbed to his whims he would never grow up?

His father, Hans-Werner, had picked up the phone and a position was instantly found for his son in a large practice in Verden. Hans-Peter was now back in his mother's nest where he had always belonged. He stayed there during the week and came to us at weekends. His compelling need to retreat to his mother and bring her his treasures was slowly succeeding. It had happened in small, calculated steps and I had not realised it. With the move from England back to Germany, then from the south to the north and now back to Verden, Hans-Peter had finally returned home. Now he only needed to convince us to join him. I knew that sooner or later he would play on my sympathy, and financial considerations would be part of the justification.

However, I had adapted to life in Hamburg. The children were settled at school and happy. They had friends and so did I – I had regained my self-confidence and had lost all respect for the man I no longer loved.

The weekdays without Hans-Peter were peaceful and enjoyable, and his presence during the weekends became increasingly disquieting. On Friday afternoons Hans-Peter would storm in, overexcite the boys, play with them one minute, tire of them the next, and create an incredible mess. The spoilt boy had come to play with his sons and on Monday he returned to his mother to take on the role of the child.

Hans-Peter's presence was weighing on me. I felt uncomfortable with him and no longer yielded to his pleadings:

'Catherine, I feel unloved. Tell me you love me.'

The truth was I didn't love him any more because I could not love a child who refused to become a man, who constantly called for my total blind devotion, sometimes phoning me as often as three times a day to be reassured of my love.

How could I make Hans-Peter understand that I had given him all I had, followed him everywhere, succumbed to all his whims and that there was nothing left for me to give? Yet I knew now that Hans-Peter could not change and, somewhere inside me, I felt very sad about it – for him, for me, but more for our children.

One evening, as the children slept, I sat at my desk in the silence and put my thoughts on paper. I went back step by step, through the years we had spent together, apologising and trying to explain why our love had turned to failure. I concluded:

'This is a sad love story. A love story between two people who were probably too different from the start, two people who were in different stages of their development and who had different needs. We never reached an equilibrium, we never lived in peace. I am too tired now – the fight has been too long, too intense. I need peace . . .'

I did not want to hurt Hans-Peter. I felt protective and wanted to preserve him. I thought he would understand and forgive me for having failed to love him in the way he wanted. But I should have stayed silent; I should have known that written words remain engraved for ever. What I meant as a confession, as an assumption of my responsibilities, Hans-Peter saw as an attack on his ego.

Three years earlier we had had a long discussion, but Hans-Peter had dismissed my words, pretending they had never been spoken. His *heile* (perfect, untouchable) world had to be preserved at all costs – even if it meant closing his eyes to the blunt reality. But this time my decision was made, and it was final. He could no longer appeal to me on grounds of pity.

Hans-Peter arrived for the weekend and I dragged him out to a restaurant: we needed to talk in peace away from the boys. He kept changing the subject. He was drawing up new plans for our future. I couldn't listen to his endless vain projects any longer. I had to explain rationally and put emotions aside. This was the only way of conveying my message without hurting him unduly. Besides, I could hardly admit: Hans-Peter, I can't bear your presence any more. This would not be fair. I was also responsible for having believed in this relationship. Even though he felt I had not loved him the way he demanded, I had loved him, but he had been incapable of loving me as a person.

'Hans-Peter, we can't go round in circles any more. For the past six years you've been trying to settle down in your life and in your job. For the past three years we've talked about it. Yet you still change your mind continu-

79

ously: London, Berlin, Hamburg and now you're in Verden. It's not right for the children. They need stability and so do I.'

Hans-Peter's lower lip started to tremble, his face flushed. He was despairing, yet he realised this was serious and that he must compose himself.

'So what will you do?'

'I want to separate. I'll probably return to London since I'll have to go back to work. My German is not fluent enough to get a proper position here. Besides, even if I could stay in Germany, I'd have to move to Frankfurt to get a job in my field. The boys can continue their French schooling at the Lycée in London and come to visit you during the holidays.'

'But . . .' Hans-Peter's *heile* world was slipping out of his hands and he did not know how to hold on to it.

'Hans-Peter, I won't take the children away from you. You can come to visit them in London too, if you wish. They are *our* children. They have nothing to do with our personal problems. Our marriage has failed and it would be useless to go on pretending. You too obviously feel uncomfortable in our relationship if you need to ask me all the time whether I still love you and tell me you feel unloved. It would be best for all of us, and the children need stability,' I tried to reassure him calmly.

Hans-Peter was silent. We returned to our flat and I desperately wanted to ask Isabella, our babysitter, to stay overnight. His silence worried me and the idea of sharing a bed with the man I was about to leave haunted me. I got undressed in the dark, put pyjamas on and slipped into bed hoping he would not notice my presence. But he did.

'Catherine, I love you.'

'Hans-Peter, we've just talked for three hours. Didn't you understand what I said?'

'Yes, yes. But I need you . . .'

'Hans-Peter, please, don't pretend our conversation never happened. It did. I explained everything: I'm leaving you.'

But Hans-Peter could not accept this. He wanted to put the clock back. I explained again but this time my voice was cold, nearly businesslike. I was exasperated. I explained again. He started begging and touching me.

'It's late. Let's talk about it tomorrow.'

It was two o'clock in the morning. I rolled over with my back to him and heard Hans-Peter sobbing loudly. As I fell asleep without any feeling of pity.

Hans-Peter left the next afternoon to go home to his mother and for two days there was silence. The boys and I returned to our normal daily routine. But by Wednesday, Hans-Peter was back on the telephone, as if nothing had happened. We had another long discussion that evening and I hoped that this time Hans-Peter would understand. The next morning he left early for Verden and on Friday he phoned to say he would be arriving at six.

'Hans-Peter, I don't really think this is a good idea. Let's just talk on the telephone.'

Hans-Peter started pleading with me.

'I need you. You can't leave me . . .'

I found myself explaining everything all over again, but after an hour of useless talk I finally hung up in frustration and anger. For a while I heard nothing more and I felt relieved.

The boys were calm without Hans-Peter's flustered and unsettling presence. They had been used to him being away during the week and did not query his absence. Our life settled down peacefully. Hans-Peter had never been keen on socialising, but now we invited their friends over in the afternoon and some evenings I would go out with my friends. Liberated from the weight of Hans-Peter's possessiveness, I started to enjoy Hamburg. Had it been possible for me to obtain a job in finance, I would have considered staying.

At least, that is, until I received the first call from God. It was Ute, telephoning to offer help and advice. She had heard through Hans-Peter that I wanted to leave him.

'Catherine, I just can't believe it. You're both such kind and wonderful people. You shouldn't make a rush decision like this. You're probably just going through a phase and should pray for God's guidance. What about going to see this pastor I told you about in Bremen? He would be able to help you both . . .'

'Ute, this is not a phase. It has been a preoccupation for the last three years. It is not a question relating to believing in God: our personalities are simply incompatible. And do tell Hans-Peter to call me if he wants to talk to me.'

'Oh, but Hans-Peter didn't ask me to call you. He doesn't even know about it. I just like you both so much and think it would be such a pity for you to part. I would like to talk to you as I'm sure I can help in bringing you back together. You know, God . . .'

I began to realise what was happening in Verden. Hans-Peter, the poor lost little boy, was crying for help and support. His tough wife, the City 'career' woman, was leaving him – a husband who adored her. Ute's beliefs would guide me back on the right road.

'Ute, thank you very much, but this is really not necessary.'

A few days later, Wilfred was on the telephone, trying to rescue the situation by interfering in our private lives. His approach was more down to earth:

'Catherine, I really understand what you're going through. You're just frustrated. Hans-Peter is still unsettled in his career. I know he is rather young and immature but this is exactly why you should be reasonable and lenient with him. You know, I also went through a crisis a few years ago when I fell in love with another woman. I even considered leaving Ute, but thank God I didn't . . .'

'But, I'm not in love with anybody else!'

'Yes, of course . . . I only mentioned my experience as an example in the sense that I had thought of breaking up my marriage. Catherine, you must think of Hans-Peter and the children too . . .'

82

'Thank you, Wilfred . . . Goodbye.'

I had remained polite with these people – too polite, since I felt their intervention was distasteful and obstructive. Hans-Peter had obviously spent his evenings in their house, crying and seeking their help. Had he shown them and his family my private letter to him?

Ute did not abandon her rescue mission. She called again. This time she suggested coming to see me in Hamburg. I was angry at Hans-Peter's exposure of my privacy and answered her curtly: 'Thank you, but I'd rather be alone. I've made up my mind and it is really not appropriate for you to come to Hamburg.'

A week or two of silence followed. I began to draw up my plans for the move to London: I needed to find a job, a flat and a place at the Lycée for the boys. This was a tall order: we were in the midst of the worst recession since the Big Crash of 1929. E.F. Hutton had been taken over, commodities were no longer the order of the day and I had not worked for six years. My London friends were sceptical about my possibilities of finding a job at the age of thirty-nine, given the current market conditions. But I was determined and had always been very energetic. it had taken me three years to make a decision and now that I had, nothing would stop me. Since I did not want to leave Hamburg until the end of the school year so that the children would have the least disruption possible, I had more than five months to organise the move. I felt I could do it.

But Hans-Peter only allowed me two and a half weeks during the February school break and I saw that he would not give me a second opportunity. He came to pick up Alexander and Constantin and take them to his mother in Verden. Walking down the stairs he sneered at me: 'You'll see, your friends won't be there for you after six years. You'll never get a job!'

Hans-Peter was wrong. All my friends rallied around me to help. Even my City contacts went out of their way to arrange interviews and introduce me to companies where there might be openings. It was very heartening. Suddenly I felt strong and self-confident and I must have radiated this energy, because I managed to get two offers in the bond brokerage business. The only problem was that they wanted me to start immediately and I was unwilling to move in the middle of the school term. Finally we agreed: I would start at the end of April. Now, I needed a flat and two places at the Lycée. I had less than a week.

By coincidence I bumped into my old headmaster who had come by to pick up his mail at half-term. He was delighted to see me after so many years and introduced me to the director of the primary classes. But he was unhelpful, totally unsympathetic to my problems:

'Mrs Volkmann, do you think I can find a space for your two boys, just like that, in the middle of the school year? Some people would offer me money but even that will not change matters.'

'Well, I certainly don't have any money to offer . . .'

Phone calls to the director of the Hamburg Lycée, mobilisation of all concerned – and a place for Alexander was secured at the Ecole Française in Brook Green. More phone calls, more running around and just two days before I was due back, a flat was found. I had managed! Exhausted, but in seventh heaven, I tried to prepare myself for the next big hurdle.

Hans-Peter and the boys were in the arrival lounge at Hamburg airport. The children rushed to greet me; Hans-Peter stood behind them with an anxious expression. He had hoped to see me return with my tail between my legs, admitting failure. The expression on my face obviously raised doubts. But Hans-Peter, being Hans-Peter, still hoped. He hoped in the car, he hoped as we drove home and finally, after the boys ran off to their bedrooms to open their London presents, he asked in English:

'So, how did it go?'

We were sitting in the kitchen, a very large and beautiful room, with original tiles and an authentic coal oven.

'Well, I found a job.'

'What type of job?'

'Bond broker.'

'So, it means you'll be working late and the boys will be alone with a sitter.'

'Not at all. The boys' school finishes just before four and the bond business works on continental hours. I'll be home by 5.30.'

'But have you got a place at the Lycée?'

'At the French school. It's a small, really cute school – in fact it will be a much easier transition for Alexander before going to the Lycée.'

'And what about Constantin then?'

'They will take him at the Lycée next year but for this term I've enrolled him in the Knightsbridge Kindergarten.'

'But that must be ridiculously expensive.'

'I've sold my watch to pay for it.'

'And where will you live?'

'I've found a flat within walking distance of the kindergarten.'

'And who'll take care of the children until you get home? She must be German. I want my sons to speak German with someone.'

'I'll find someone and after the summer holidays I thought Isabella might want to come to London. She's often mentioned wanting to go abroad after her A levels.

'Ah, Isabella,' Hans-Peter said pensively.

Isabella was a seventeen-year-old who came to babysit since we had moved to Hamburg. She had known Constantin as a baby. The boys loved her and she had developed a teenager's crush on Hans-Peter.

Hans-Peter was silent, slowly absorbing this information he had been so unprepared for. His last hope had just been crushed and he no longer knew how to react. I went on:

'But Hans-Peter, you have to promise me one thing: we must never, ever fight. That is the most horrible thing about separations. People sometimes become bitter with

85

each other and it's the children who pay the ultimate price.'

'I promise.'

I offered him my hand and we shook hands on it. Hans-Peter said goodbye to the boys and left for Verden.

A week later everything changed. Hans-Peter phoned. A decisive voice trembling with anger drily announced:

'So, if you've decided to move to London with the boys, we should draw up a contract. I've got a lawyer here in Verden and I suggest you get yourself one as well.'

There was not even the possibility of a conversation. In icy tones Hans-Peter said goodbye and hung up. He had been so bitter that he had not even been interested in hearing about the boys' day. What was he up to? I began to be a little nervous.

Joachim gave me the name of a lawyer and I went to see him the next day. Eight years of marriage, two children and I was answering to statistics:

'How much does your husband earn? You cannot be expected to support the children on your own. Your husband must give them and you financial support.'

I had found out in the meantime that the practice where Hans-Peter had been employed in Verden had offered him a partnership but he had refused, and had gone back to work for the Bundeswehr.

My lawyer thought that Hans-Peter could be trying to demonstrate smaller earnings so as to avoid paying alimony. He said, 'You came into the marriage with money, a car, you gave up your career and are now eight years older. We'll have to fight this. I don't like your husband's attitude.'

The tone of my lawyer frightened me. I did not want to face Hans-Peter's temper. I wanted everything to remain civilised, as he had promised. Joachim advised me:

'Catherine, don't be an idiot. You've made this mistake once before, after your first marriage. But you were young and fell on your feet. Now you have children and responsibilities towards them.'

But, as usual in situations like this, I listened to no one – only to my desire to avoid confrontation at all costs. A letter was sent by my lawyer in answer to Hans-Peter's offer of £350 maintenance a month for the two children. it stressed the fact that if Hans-Peter earned little it was only due to his unwillingness to work. He was a qualified doctor, with a PhD, and had even had the possibility of wellpaid night calls which he had immediately turned down . . . The next day, Hans-Peter stormed into our Hamburg flat.

'What the hell are you doing to me? You're walking out of my life, taking my children and now your lawyer is implying I'm lazy and not offering them enough support.' He leant against the oven. His face was red and his whole body was shaking with rage. I felt frightened. Then he put his hands in his empty trouser pockets, turned them inside out and yelled:

'Look. *Ich habe kein Geld!*' (I have no money.)

Just at the moment Alexander, who had heard his father's voice down the corridor, walked into the kitchen followed by Constantin. At the sight of his father standing facing them and screaming furiously, he rushed out like a terrified little dog to seek refuge in his bedroom. Constantin ran behind him. I was horrified – even more horrified when I saw that Hans-Peter hadn't even noticed and continued screaming:

'I'm nothing. I have nothing – nothing.'

I was speechless.

Finally he stormed out, running down the stairs of the building, still screaming that he had no money. His reaction was intimidating but the anger that was brewing inside me was such that I managed to reply frostily: 'Your problem is that you never want to do any work.'

This was the last image I have of our life together. The breakdown of eight years of marriage had ended on a bitter note. I had wanted to remain civil – we needed to, for the children's sake. But from that day on Hans-Peter never ceased to scream. He felt humiliated and had fallen into his own trap: the woman he thought he loved was leaving him for good. He had lived off his parents, off me in London, was supported again by his mother during all our married life and had been incapable of establishing his own base. Although I had not mentioned any of this to him, his inability to stop me from going was a clearer expression than any words would have been.

I tried to soothe the situation and calm his fury by abandoning my lawyer and accepting all his terms. Even surviving with the minimum legal child support was better than venturing into bitter litigation – for the sake of our sons, I wanted a truce. My lawyer told me I was mad. Joachim tried to talk to me:

'Catherine, Hans-Peter is avoiding his responsibilities. If he joined the army rather than accept that offer of a partnership, his reasons are obvious. You have put a lot into this marriage and you will be coming back to London with nothing and two boys to feed. Think of the future. You're thirty-nine. Don't leave before you settle every-thing. Be careful . . .'

'Oh, Hans-Peter won't be able to settle this problem. It's just the way he is. But I can't take it any more. I've waited too long and I can't fight against him. I'll be OK with the boys and hopefully Hans-Peter's anger will calm down in time.'

'You're making a mistake and I'm afraid you may regret it later.'

But my judgement had been right: no lawyer, no more screaming. Hans-Peter practically never called. The storm was over. I later came to believe, Hans-Peter, surrounded by his family and the Monkmanns (all lawyers and a judge), was already embarking on the ultimate plan, set-ting legal traps and examining loopholes. Only later would I realise how right Joachim had been.

Two weeks before the children and I were due to leave, Hans-Peter came to pick up the boys and take them to

Verden while I organised the two sets of moves, looked for a new tenant for the flat, paid off all the bills, packed his things and mine . . . I had no time to think. Amélie arranged a farewell dinner and when all was ready, I drove to Verden to pick up the boys. But first, Hans-Peter wanted to meet me at a notary's to sign our contract. My lawyer had seen the initial draft.

'Don't sign it. It's a very bad deal for you and I can smell a rat,' he had told me.

The children were at Gundel and Hans-Werner's and I knew Hans-Peter would not allow me to take them before we had signed. At 10 a.m. I met him in the waiting room. He looked tense and did not look at me when I said hello.

A young man, who said he used to be at school with Hans-Peter, admitted us to his office. We sat down and he proceeded to read through a long document in German. He spoke slowly so that I could understand. However, German legal language is very complicated and there were many words which were unknown to me. But the crucial paragraph was there and I felt I could relax:

The custody of the mutual children . . . shall be transferred to Ms Volkmann. Dr Volkmann expressly declares his consent to Ms Volkmann moving with the mutual children to London, England, to take up residence there . . . Until a court ruling on custody of the mutual children, Dr Volkmann provides Ms Volkmann with authorisation to represent the children in legal relations, in legal transactions of daily life and in other transactions . . . The parties agree that the children shall live with their father for at least two months (per annum).

The later part dealt with the maintenance Hans-Peter and I had agreed on. The young man asked us to sign and date the last page. We shook hands and left.

Hans-Peter and I drove to his parents' house. He sat in silence, staring straight ahead of him. His bitterness was so intense that I could feel the vibrations emanating from his body.

The children were ready to go.

'I'll see you in two and a half months,' Gundel said, kissing Alexander, and the three of us drove off waving goodbye.

'That's it. I'll never have to set foot in Verden again.' I was so happy, I felt overjoyed. However, I had a strange feeling. Hans-Peter's tense attitude at the notary's office and his mother's ironic expression when we parted were rather disturbing. Oh well, in time, Hans-Peter will quieten down, I thought. He was bitter now and in shock and this was in keeping with his personality. But he loved his boys and for their sake would soon re-establish a civil relationship with me.

Next morning, we were *en route* to our new lives – and freedom. I had finally freed myself from the Volkmanns' domination.

Freedom tasted so sweet ...

Chapter 8
The Conspiracy

For two and a half years you lived with your Mummy in London. We were happy there and I am sure you still have some memories left – because if they were extracted from you, the emotion of them must remain.

The contract I had signed before leaving was notarised five days later in Verden and when I received my copy a few weeks after my arrival in London, I simply put it in a drawer. It was only two years later when I took it out and carefully deciphered it with the help of a dictionary that I got a surprise. The contract stated that our 'first place of habitual residence was in the Federal Republic of Germany' – not only did we first live in London but Alexander was born here! I had not noticed this when the contract was read aloud in the notary's office in April 1992. It had never occurred to me that there might have been some legal catches, but at the time I also had other things on my mind.

Alexander, now seven, was falling behind at school. The academic level in the London Lycée was much higher than at the Hamburg one and he needed to catch up to be admitted into the next grade. Constantin, on the other hand, had adapted well at the kindergarten. Language was not a barrier for him. This was the way I too had learned French. My mother had only spoken Russian to me in my childhood, but within a few months at a French school I was fluent. Most children have this amazing ability. Hans-Peter used to say that in order to speak a language without an accent it should be learned before the age of seven, when the vocal muscles are formed to produce only specific tones. I was so glad both boys would have the opportunity to be fluent in three important European languages.

What was amazing was to watch how Alexander immediately started talking in English whilst Constantin refused to say a word for several months – at least in front of me! Constantin did not like to fail. He needed to feel he had mastered the language before he would speak in it. It became our little joke and I would tease him about it, until one day he forgot, and I overheard him playing with his English friend:

'Don't touch this. It belongs to my brother.'

I peeped through the door of this bedroom and smiled. Constantin looked back at me with a mischievous expression in his eyes. He was very sweet – but I knew proud Constantin wouldn't appreciate me kissing him then. He and I had a special code – we understood each other completely. A look was enough. We accepted and respected each other and were particularly close. Constantin and I belonged to each other and we had a harmonious relationship. For him, living in London meant having Mummy more to himself and he never questioned the separation.

Alexander, however, seemed more concerned, and whilst he did not mention it at first, on his return from the first summer holiday with his father he asked me: 'Mummy, tell me. Why doesn't Daddy live with us in London?'

I explained as simply as I could that grown-ups sometimes decided that they want to live separately but it certainly never changes their love for their children.

'Mummy and Daddy will always love you.' He trotted off and didn't ask much more for a while.

From time to time, Hans-Peter would phone to talk to the boys. He always addressed me in German. This had been a new development which had happened about a year before, when Hans-Peter started to speak to me systematically in German and demanded that I answer in it. This deeply frustrated me since I was unable to express myself properly and often made grammatical mistakes (I never had time to study the language except for introductory self-teaching) and Hans-Peter would constantly correct me. But, as if he had put a barrier between us, he would only speak English when the conversation concerned us personally – which had been more and more rarely.

But my new existence in London had brought me different challenges which were of more concern to me now. During my six years of absence the City had changed dramatically: Big Bang, the Crash, takeovers, mergers, faxes, computers, 'global' markets . . . I felt as if I had landed in a totally different world to which I had to readapt quickly and at my age it was tough. But what was tougher still was the new character of the financial world. Traders were rude, and often aggressive – survival was the name of the game and money its only aim.

My boss was not much more than half my age and in this environment no one was anxious to help me out. I was no longer the little queen with a private assistant. Generalists were out and private clients' business practically extinguished. The new era consisted of specialists and computers, and I had no idea how to use one.

I had to learn fast. For me, too, it was a question of survival. Not in order to make big money as fast as possible, but to survive within my new existence: see to the children's needs, give them a happy home, assure their good results at school and satisfy the au pairs. Otherwise, I knew I would be in danger.

Brigit, our German au pair girl, would take the boys to school in the mornings, pick them up in the afternoons and play with them until I returned home. Tini was always the first one to greet me. He would run up the stairs of our basement flat with squeaks of joy; Alexander would follow and the two of them would start talking at once, each telling me enthusiastically about their day. The arrangements worked well, although it was quite exhausting!

The bond markets opened very early in the mornings, which meant waking up before dawn. Trading was draining and I had to learn the discipline of working again. Sunday mornings were often dedicated to supermarket shopping and the rest of the weekends to the children, who were still young and needed to be constantly entertained.

But, in the circumstances, we managed well. The children liked Brigit and I got on well with her too. But, as any working mother knows, dealings with au pairs are often difficult, as they are neither guests nor staff. I was sad when Brigit eventually left. The children, however, were overjoyed that Isabella would come and live with us after their first summer holiday in Verden.

Isabella arrived in London in September 1992 for the start of the new term. Our arrangement was different. She was not employed as an au pair. In fact this made matters much more difficult for me since she was, like Hans-Peter, extremely disorderly and I would spend most of my time tidying after her and the children to keep our cramped flat in a liveable condition. With the children, however, Isabella was wonderful and the three of them would play joyfully and laugh as I was tidying up. They loved being together and it was a pleasure to see the children so happy.

Isabella walked them to the Lycée (which they both attended now) which was ten minutes away and picked them up at 3.45. She would then supervise Alexander's homework and I checked it on my return from the office. She spoke French fluently and so was able to help him. My philosophy was that he should learn to manage as much as he could on his own. But (unlike Constantin) Alexander was not very studious and, like most boys of his age, he preferred to play. His early results showed that he needed to work harder and unfortunately Isabella was a little too young and slack to discipline him.

Isabella seemed to suffer from the same symptoms as

Hans-Peter. She was constantly tired and unprepared to help with the housework, and that first year was very trying for me. My financial situation was also difficult. The rent was very high in relation to my income but the flat was close to the school and had a wonderful communal garden where the children could play with their friends.

After six months, Isabella became bored. She was now eighteen and had decided that London offered many better distractions than Alexander and Constantin. She started complaining about her monotonous day, and wanted to find a job to occupy her while the boys were at school. I approached a friend and eventually convinced him to employ her part-time in the City.

Soon, Isabella's life became very busy as she started going out in the evening with the young men she had met in the office. I had to organise my outings according to her schedule. She was very attractive, so at her age this was probably inevitable. However, my mother was not of the same opinion. She had recently come to stay with friends in London and warned me: 'Katia, I don't like your Isabella. She only plays with the children, goes out, never helps you and expects you to care for her. She's too young, too self-centred, and I find her rather false. I wouldn't trust her if I were you.'

My mother was always intuitive and I should have acted on her advice on the day when I came home earlier than expected and found Isabella on the phone to Hans-Peter. She was happily talking to him in German as if she was mistress of the house. She continued her conversation oblivious to my presence, then hung up.

'Was that Hans-Peter?' I asked, surprised.

'*Ja*. I was just telling him about the boys. He says hello.'

I later found they used to talk to each other – Isabella was Hans-Peter's London agent. There was nothing specific for me to hide, but Hans-Peter was enquiring about the school, his sons' well-being, my work and my social life. Isabella had always been in awe of Hans-Peter and I now believe that he took advantage of this to collect any useful information that might later help him devise his supreme plan in case I did not return to Germany. Hans-Peter was still holding on to a vague hope that I might fail in London and come back to him.

However, none of these details raised my suspicions then. I simply found it irritating that Isabella should be talking about my private life behind my back. But when she began to invite her friends round in the evening I became annoyed. Then one day her best friend appeared from Germany – Isabella having told her that, since the children were away on their holiday, she could stay here. I finally reacted:

'Isabella, don't you think you could ask me first? After all, this is my flat and I think it is just normal courtesy to ask.'

Unknown to me, this eighteen-year-old would provide Hans-Peter with the testimony he had longed for. 'Catherine was only interested in her work and keeping the flat tidy . . . she was never there for Alexander's homework and I had to do it with him . . . she regularly went out in the evenings.'

In the meantime, Hans-Peter had come to London for a weekend in May 1993 with his friend, Judge Monkmann. When I returned home from work, the two of them were in my sitting room drinking tea with Isabella, and I had a most awkward feeling – as if they had come for an official examination and I was the visitor in my own flat. Hans-Peter made a few phone calls, Isabella poured more tea and they left.

'Katia, I don't like the smell of this. Why is Hans-Peter coming with a judge? You have to get divorced and protect yourself.'

Mother was always too suspicious. Hans-Peter still seemed antagonistic towards me and I didn't feel this was the right moment to anger him further. In a few months he might find a new girlfriend and become better disposed to the final legal break.

*

Alexander was eight years old and Constantin six when the new nanny started with us. Isabella remained in London and was still employed at my friend's office but she contacted me on only a few occasions.

Masha, was Russian, from a small town east of Moscow. She was the antithesis of Isabella: forty-seven years old, unmarried, austere. After my experience of the previous year, I had decided I wanted someone to help me with the organisation of house rather than with the children. Masha would only take them to school and pick them up but I would supervise their homework. The boys were now more responsible and no longer required full attention, only the presence of an adult. They usually played in their bedrooms or in the garden with our new neighbour.

I had recently been offered a good job at an excellent German bank, and bought a three-bedroom flat with direct access to a large communal garden. Masha had her own room and shower. Most of the rooms were spacious and the boys could run in the corridor to their hearts' content.

The 1993 school year had started on a very happy note. The boys had their friends and Constantin was particularly pleased because his best friend lived in the house opposite ours. Alexander's school reports had improved amazingly and he had a new friend in the boy who lived in the flat above ours.

I was still under pressure with my busy days, but since Masha took care of the washing, cooking and cleaning, I was entirely free for my boys from the moment I came home. We usually sat in our large kitchen to do the homework. Constantin was a terribly keen student and as soon as I opened the entrance door, he would come with his satchel:

'Mummy, let's do the homework.'

Sometimes he even did it on his own before my return, to surprise me. Alexander, on the other hand, was irregular and it all depended on his mood of the day. Our weekends were usually full of activity: movies, roller-blading, swimming, entertaining their friends, visiting them . . . If the first year was a little unsettled, adapting to a new environment and living in a flat which was too small for four people, the boys had now established themselves in their new London life – as twenty-four witnesses would later testify!

Constantin would return from his holidays in Germany (about every six weeks) excited to find his room, return to school and see his friends. Alexander, however, found the transition more difficult. He preferred being on holiday and was less enthusiastic to return to school and I noticed that when he was with his father for a longer period of time, he needed a few days to readjust.

Masha adapted amazingly quickly to life in the West. Within five months, she started asking for a rise. Her change of attitude was quick and drastic. When she first arrived, she was grateful for my invitation to London. She cleaned the house and attended to her duties so well, that I suggested: 'Masha, you really do not need to clean the kitchen on your hands and knees. Why don't you use the mop?'

I did not want a slave, and her subservience was embarrassing. I suggested she called me Katia rather than Madam.

Masha, like many who come from the communist bloc, had discovered the magic of capitalism and decided that she should have an affluent life. I tried to explain that unfortunately money had to be earned and that in the West no one had a guaranteed job. But this did not convince her, lost as she was in her fantasies of the glamour of capitalism and its buying power.

Her visa was due to expire in May. On 1 April, I had to announce to her that it was impossible to renew it from England.

'No, I won't return to Russia. I want to stay another year in London.'

'But that's impossible. I talked to the Immigration

Department yesterday.'

'Well, then I'll find another job. But I will not return to Russia.'

Without a visa, her attempts to find another position were totally unproductive. Masha's harsh and inflexible ways did not impress even those who had been prepared to employ someone without a permit. I had no intention of keeping her, and my boys did not like her much anyway. She 'got on their nerves', they said. I started to look for someone else and tried to break the news as gently as possible.

'Masha, you really will have to go by the end of the month. I can't keep you without a visa, so I must employ someone else.'

A few weeks after this conversation, Hans-Peter unexpectedly came to London for the weekend and I could not fail to notice his bitterness at the obvious signs of our comfortable life without him. The flat was attractive, the boys were very happy, had excellent results at school, and my career had been re-established. The signs of our successful reintegration into London were clear. In his usual way, Hans-Peter had failed to face the truth, clinging to the belief that our life here was temporary. But on this visit, he could no longer escape the fact that we had managed well. With hindsight, I feel that this was the turning point for Hans-Peter. He had sown the seeds earlier on but now, unknown to me, he would finally reap the ultimate revenge.

In the past, Hans-Peter had complained to me about Masha over the telephone.

'Catherine, why have you got a Russian woman? She sounds terrible and is always moody with me when I call.'

Suddenly though, after this visit and the discovery that I had dismissed Masha, Hans-Peter would phone before 5.30 p.m. to talk exclusively to her. I learned this through Alexander, who had been surprised that his daddy did not bother to talk to him. I found this extremely odd but consoled Alexander:

99

'Oh, don't worry, you'll see Daddy next week. It's almost Easter.'

The first real warning sign became apparent on the children's return from their Easter holiday in Verden on 24 April 1994. I was in Heathrow's Terminal One waiting for their plane to land. The stewardess came out first and Constantin rushed towards me and jumped into my arms:

'Mummy!'

Alexander stood still as if refusing to move. I was shocked. I walked towards him and kneeled down.

'Alexander?'

He didn't answer and looked terribly grim. Then really quickly he said: 'I am German and I want to go to a German school!'

'What are you talking about, Alexander?'

'I am German.'

'Don't you even say hello to your mummy?'

He kissed me but remained silent. As we walked towards the car, Constantin was jumping with excitement and telling me about his holiday. Alexander on the other hand was staring into space and his movements seemed strangely rigid.

Constantin as usual sat behind me in the car. He locked his arms around my neck, put his cheek against mine and started talking exuberantly. Was his friend back from holiday? Could he see him later? Tini was excited and he was impatient to reach home. Alexander remained motionless and silent. He looked peevish. Constantin went on:

'Do we have school tomorrow?'

'No, tomorrow's free. School starts the day after.'

Tini was just about to suggest an exciting outing, when, in a hardly audible voice, I caught Alexander saying:

'I want to go to the German school.'

The tone of his voice was flat – lifeless. I was amazed.

'Alexander? What's the matter, my angel? Aren't you happy to be back home?'

'I want to go to the German school.'

100

Tini had stopped talking and stared at him for a second. Then, as children do when they have a thought in their mind, he went on unperturbed: 'Mummy, can we go to Battersea Park tomorrow?'

I looked in the mirror. Alexander sat still, with a tense expression on his face. He did not listen to Constantin: he didn't even look out of the window, it was as if he was paralysed. I became impatient with the traffic. I wanted to be home and take Alexander in my arms. What was happening? I had never experienced him like this and was worried.

When we finally got home, Alexander stepped out of the car and stood still while Constantin hurriedly jumped out, took his bag and ran to the front door.

'Mummy, come on.'

I took their suitcase and Alexander walked beside me. As I opened the door, Tini rushed to the bedroom and I knelt down to comfort Alexander.

'What's the matter?' He did not answer.

'What's this talk about your wanting to go to the German school?'

'I just do! I am German!'

'But Alexander, the Lycée is very nice.'

'The German school is better.'

'But you've never been to a German school before.'

'I just know it's better!'

'How?'

'Because . . . Because it finishes at midday.'

'But you often have sports or outings in the afternoons.'

'That's not true!'

Alexander had answered me as if I were a liar. He had never talked to me in this tone before and I was profoundly shocked. What had Hans-Peter done to him? For the past half-hour Alexander had been pulling a face, saying the same sentence endlessly.

Constantin who had come out into the hall interrupted my thoughts:

'Oh stop it! You're boring with your "I'm German, I

101

want to go to a German school!" all the time.' He had imitated his brother's voice with a twinge of irony that made Alexander smile. Tini went on: 'Look, Alexander, this is your present,' and he handed him the parcel I had prepared for him. They trotted off into their bedroom. I brought in their suitcases and started unpacking while my two little boys were happily playing beside me.

Tini was in a particularly chirpy mood. As I ran their bath and called them, he rushed in with more Ninja Turtles than he could carry, threw them in the water and got into the bath.

'Alexander, are you coming?'

I called several times. Finally Alexander appeared, empty-handed. Tini was splashing, talking, laughing, while his brother remained impassive. I had never seen Alexander this way.

'What is it, my angel?'

'Don't call me that, it's stupid.'

I was taken aback, hardly knowing how to react.

'Alexander, why are you pulling a face like this? What's the matter?'

'I am German!'

'Well, of course you are. But you are also French and English. You know you are lucky – you belong to several countries, not just one.'

'I want to go to a German school. In any case, when I'm nine, I can decide.'

'Decide what? What are you talking about?'

'I can tell a court that I am German and want to go to a German school.'

I was dumbfounded – courts, Alexander deciding, being German . . . what had my son been told?

'Who told you all this?'

'I'm not saying!'

Constantin interrupted his brother:

'Will you stop this "I am German". It's boring, isn't it, Mummy? Besides, we are here now. Have you called Karim, Mummy? Can I see him tomorrow?'

102

Tini was getting out of the bath and I helped Alexander, dried him and held him in my arms. He was still my baby and I could feel how comforted he was. He did not move, his body wrapped in the towel, close to mine. I felt so sorry for him, realising what had been done to him. Tini came running back with another question and Alexander followed him into the bedroom, a child again.

The next day, as I was sitting at my office desk, the department manager called me to meet him upstairs in a conference room.

'We've decided that we won't extend your probation period which falls due at the end of the month,' he said.

As if the sky had fallen on my head, I was unable to speak.

'Well, I'm terribly sorry. This wasn't my decision, but I can't help you.'

'But . . . why? There must be a reason.'

There was none, but I was to leave the premises within the hour. The personnel assistant manager whom I went to see later on did not know either. There was nothing negative in my file, no problems of performance . . . she was sorry. I called home to tell Masha I would be late and Alexander answered. As soon as he heard it was me, he coldly stated: 'I'm German!'

I had lost my job, on no grounds, my son didn't even say hello to me and was repeating the same sentence like an old record . . . I collapsed in tears.

I returned home but, thank god, Alexander had forgotten his repetitive sentence. Next day school started and he was soon back to his usual life, with his changeable moods – but they only related, as they always had, to his friends, football and homework. Germany was forgotten.

On 27 April, Isabella, who had not called in months, decided she wanted to come and see the children. Alexander, though, was at a friend's house that evening and I thought it odd that she had surfaced and affected a sudden and pressing interest in the boys.

Since my dismissal, Masha had become ill-tempered and sulky. She had been used to having the flat to herself and my presence irritated her, she told me. The boys found her infuriating: she nagged them all the time and I hoped she would leave quickly. Her visa had expired by now but she was determined to stay in the West and urged me to give her a few weeks' grace to find another job.

Meanwhile, Hans-Peter never seemed to call to talk to the boys any more until one morning Masha announced he was in London for a few days and that she had met him for tea. I was startled and felt terribly uneasy, wondering why Masha (who had never like Hans-Peter) should meet and talk to him behind my back. The explanation she gave me was that she needed some spare plugs from Germany for a friend in Russia. I suspected she was not telling the truth and had an ill-defined suspicion that they were conspiring. She had become insolent; but I was more absorbed with the immediate problem of how I would support the boys without a job. I confided in her later that I ought to talk to Hans-Peter.

Masha must have conveyed my message to Hans-Peter as she told me he would come to see me the next day. It was May, ten days before Alexander's ninth birthday. Hans-Peter arrived, looking tense and nervous. He shook my hand without glancing at me and blasted into the kitchen, a hateful expression on his face. He knew I was under pressure and I could detect scorn in his voice:

'So I hear you lost your job?'

'Yes, I did and I'm really worried. This is why I thought we ought to talk. The bills are mounting and I don't know how I'm going to be able to carry on if I don't find something quickly.'

'Well, don't count on me. I've no money!'

Remembering the scene in Hamburg when he had turned his pockets inside out screaming, I immediately abandoned the subject. I imagined all his travel expenses and visits to London shops had been financed by his mother.

'I could take the boys to Germany if you can't manage.'

'Well . . . I don't know. This would be a rather difficult solution. The point is that we must think of them first. I don't know . . . Yet, if I don't get a job quickly, how am I going to care for them? I have to think.'

Nearly a month had gone by since I had been dismissed and I didn't have a single lead. The recession in England was still hard and jobs were scarce. My situation was alarming and I had believed Hans-Peter would cast aside his resentment and consider the boys' stability. I wished that, as a father, he would say, 'Catherine, I'll help you out for a couple of months, give you time to sort things out.'

But this was another man I was dreaming of. Instead of sharing the responsibility for our sons, Hans-Peter had put a different plan into action.

The phone rang. A headhunter had arranged an interview for me with a bank. Hans-Peter became agitated and in a hurry. He stood up.

'So it's settled! I'll take the boys,' he said.

'Wait, wait . . .' I quickly scribbled the address for my interview and hung up.

'No, Hans-Peter, we have to think.'

It was always the same with Hans-Peter – he would settle matters the way he intended, disregarding my views. The man-child who needed his mummy was a bully who would not allow you to talk, would pull you by the arm: 'I want, I want . . .'

Peter-Pan Hans-Peter who had seemed wonderfully attentive and caring at first was motivated only by his feeling of dependency. I had been attracted by this clever, good-hearted and funny man and it had escaped me that he had no idea how to build a real, adult life. He made unwise decisions about his career, acted irresponsibly and behind all this youthful charm he had been quite lost. He had clung to me, depended on my organisation, drawing on my feelings of guilt and compassion until he had suffocated me; jealous of my friends and my outside interests, he had wanted to possess me until I had finally

105

freed myself by walking out on him.

Today, he saw me weak and stressed and this was his chosen moment to take his revenge and secure his ambition. We parted, both tense.

The next day, I made an appointment to see the new director of the Lycée:

'Both your sons are doing well at school and it would be disruptive for them to go to Germany, even for one term. If your husband continues to pay the school fees, you'll be able to survive with unemployment benefit and if he refuses to pay, you could request a grant. I'll help you.'

In fact, it was still Hans-Peter's mother who settled the school fees and his Bundeswehr salary was presumably his pocket money while he lived with his parents. Hans-Peter still intended to open a practice and Alexander had told me he had found one in Bremen. Ute was redecorating it for him. He had also just moved on to Wilfred and Ute's property, renting their old house while Ute and her family moved to the larger one, fifty yards away, after her mother-in-law had died.

May 1993 was the month Hans-Peter had been waiting for. Unknown to me, the field was now ready for his last move.

Feeling ill at ease, disquieted by Hans-Peter's animosity and Masha's suspicious behaviour, I made an appointment with a new lawyer specialising in family law. That morning I woke up feeling terrible and in excruciating pain but I still managed to make my way to the law firm. I was pale and felt dizzy. The solicitor started to take a few preliminary details but I could not go on and rushed to the loo, where I was so sick that a taxi was called to take me back home. Masha had cooked a Russian dish especially for me the previous evening and I wondered what had gone into it. I was ill for a couple of days and never tried to see the solicitor again.

A week after the meeting with Hans-Peter, I was offered a job as a senior account executive in an Italian bank.

That same evening, I telephoned Hans-Peter:

'I've got a job. We don't need to worry any more. All's well. I start on 28 June and the hours will be much more flexible. I'm so relieved. Besides, I've been to see the schoolmaster and he said it would not have been good for the boys to miss a term.'

Hans-Peter was silent. Then: 'I've already talked to the school here.'

'What do you mean? You only went back to Verden a few days ago and we didn't agree on anything!'

'Well, I'll get my lawyer to write to yours.'

In the meantime, Masha still had not found a job and refused to go. The boys kept complaining about her bickering and I was tired of her complaints. I wanted to be alone with my sons and enjoy my free days with them. Finally I had to send her off, ticket in hand. She was bitter and turned on the doorstep to snap: 'In any case, I wrote to your husband!'

Little did I imagine then that in September I would find her in Verden! Hans-Peter had obviously helped her obtain a visa for Germany for the extended stay in the West she had yearned for. She would later testify against me.

'A mother who works . . . Alexander was unhappy. He wanted to go to the German school and she wouldn't listen to him . . .'

Now, though, she was gone and this was a relief to both the children and me. I felt I had ridden the storm and would finally be able to relax. The boys' holiday would give me time to settle into my new job and reconcile myself with these strenuous years. By the time my angels returned after the summer, all would be at its best, ready for them.

I had also taken the precaution of asking my regular lawyer to obtain legal confirmation of the children's return on 28 August, 1994. However, the additional sentence Hans-Peter's lawyer had added should have made me more wary:

'Dr Volkmann regrets your client's change of mind in relation to the children going to live with him in Germany for at least a year . . . and he hopes that, notwithstanding her new job, she will be able to give them all the time and attention they need.'

My lawyer answered: 'I must inform you that there is no question that my client has not been able to give the children all the time and attention they need, she has always done so and will continue to do so.'

We had never mentioned a year; just a term. I had naively thought these words were unimportant, only reflecting Hans-Peter's acrimony, and that I was legally protected.

I had of course heard about child abduction but this concerned faraway lands with different customs and religions from our own. I had custody, the children's place of residence was London. Hans-Peter was not living in a country where women had no rights. We were in Europe.

Chapter 9
The Nightmare Begins

Alexander, Constantin, my darlings, you are the essence of my life and without you I do not live. Together we managed to succeed – alone I can no longer achieve. My birds of freedom, it was your sight that led me to subsist. It was your sunshine that was my drive. Since you have been scurried away, the house is silent, the night is deep – the birds' nests shrouded in ghostly sleep.

The very day I had been dismissed from the German bank at the end of April, Hans-Peter had called to talk to me. His voice was tense.

'What have you done to Alexander?' I demanded. 'He came back repeating like a robot that he wants to be a German.'

'This has nothing to do with me,' Hans-Peter answered drily.

'Well, *someone* obviously told Alexander to say this! No child could come out with such a ridiculous statement on his own! Alexander is not even nine. How could he understand what a nationality means?'

'It's not me. It's him! He wants to go to a German school.'

'Alexander has never been to a German school. How could he know?'

'Maybe he talked to Ute's children . . . It has nothing to do with me.'

'Come on. It's Ute's children who told him that at the age of nine he can decide? Since when do children know about the law?'

'I don't know. It's not me!' Hans-Peter's voice was trembling and he was now shouting down the telephone. I was furious but composed.

· 'Look. You have no right to use Alexander like this. He is a child. This cannot go on. I am wondering if I should even send the boys to you this summer.'

'No. No. You have to send them.' His tone was that of panic. 'I must see them. They're my sons too.'

'I know they are and this is why I never turned them against you. But you must do the same and not play with Alexander's emotions.'

Hans-Peter continued for a good ten minutes, defending himself as a child would. It wasn't him – he had done and said nothing, he insisted.

This telephone conversation and our meeting a few weeks later when Hans-Peter announced he could take the children to Verden unsettled me. Alarm bells were ringing loudly, but I had not realised that Hans-Peter's feeling of revenge against a woman who had left him for good had become obsessive and that breaking our agreement, defying the law and punishing his own children would not stop Hans-Peter from achieving what I later came to believe he had been carefully planning for two and a half years.

He only needed to be sure that I would send the boys to Verden. From then on – as I was to learn, too late – he would be protected. A lawyer's letter confirming the boys' return to London on 28 August (legally binding) would become irrelevant in his home territory.

I know nothing about German family law, the non-harmonisation of European laws, the Hague Convention . . . and how unprotected one is. I honoured the agreement that the boys should go to Germany on holiday (otherwise I would be breaking our separation agreement) and assumed his lawyer's letter would protect me legally, should Hans-Peter continue to act irrationally.

Furthermore, Alexander had long forgotten about his declaration. Within days of his return from the Easter holidays, he was happily reintegrated in his London life. His school, his friends, his orderly room, all were here. He loved our evenings and weekends together: being valuable and needed in his role of man in the house, protective of Constantin and his mummy. Sometimes, Alexander would surprise me on Sunday mornings by laying the breakfast table. When we needed to go shopping, he often rushed to the kitchen, pencil and paper in hand, to start making a list:

'Constantin, which yoghurts do you want? Mummy, can you check if we have enough Corn Flakes?'

'Mummy, what else do we need?'

By nature, Alexander was easily influenced and his father played on this:

'Poor Daddy, he feels lonely,' he had once reported after his holiday in Verden.

I resented Hans-Peter for playing on his son's emotions, but I knew this was also part of Alexander's character. Consequently, his 'German' statements had not alarmed me as much as they should have. Alexander was sensitive and mercurial. For example, one day Sean was his best friend, the next he didn't like him any more and the third he wanted to invite him to stay for the weekend. Constantin and I were accustomed to Alexander's changes of moods and opinions and we treated them light-heartedly, knowing them to be temporary. Constantin, with his steady character, was a pacifying influence on Alexander. Constantin had found his best friend two and a half years ago and had never changed his mind since. We now lived opposite and they saw each other practically every day; Alexander welcomed their peaceful relationship and would join in.

My boys were so different and it was exactly from these differences that each drew his strength. To Constantin, life was uncomplicated. To Alexander, it was confusing and every day would bring new challenges. Alexander's desk and toys had their specific order, but he would pull out his favourite T-shirt, discoloured by numerous

111

washes, and mess up the neat pile; come home dishevelled, his shirt sticking out of his trousers, bruises on his
knees, happy one day, grumpy the next. Constantin
would carefully pick out the right-coloured T-shirt to go
with his trousers and neatly pull it out of the wardrobe
without disturbing the others, come home well combed,
impeccably tidy. He would do his homework immediately
and perfectly while Alexander always found excuses to do
it later. Constantin loved well-prepared dishes and salty
things; Alexander preferred junk food, chocolate and
sweets.

Constantin was afraid of nothing and knew how to
gain respect. All the girls at the primary school knew him
and I would be amused to hear them call 'Constantin'
when school was out, and see how my self-assured little
son would wave his hand with a smile but continue
towards our car. Constantin was in control and he knew
it but instinctively realised that showing off was not
'cool'. When I read his last school report with an 'A' in all
subjects and 'excellent', I turned and said: 'Tini, that's
amazing! You didn't tell me you were first in your class.'
Quietly he answered: 'But, Mummy, I didn't know I was
good at school.' I could not refrain from smiling proudly
– Constantin was definitely 'cool'!

Alexander suffered a little from Constantin's excellence
at school, his popularity and his self-assurance, yet he was
extremely proud and protective of his younger brother. I
was conscious of how difficult it must be for him to have
a sibling who had so many talents and I compensated by
over-congratulating him – which was possibly a little
unfair for Constantin. But I felt Alexander needed support and approval to build up his self-confidence. He was
wary of everything and let himself be dominated by
others. He was the one who was solidly built, whilst Tini
was thin and fragile – but it was Constantin who would
roller-blade, swim and ski fearlessly. Alexander was careful and anxious.

Odd and even – these were my two sons. One dark and

one blond. One resembling his father, the other his mother.

From mid-May until the end of June 1994, I was with my boys all the time. It was heaven. We did everything together and no one else was there demanding my attention. Grumpy Masha who interfered with our dinner conversations and evening games, jealously interrupting to talk about herself, had left.

Isabella had restricted me to clearing up. Masha had expected me to share my presence. Finally, we had our privacy and our time belonged to us. I never enjoyed my sons' company so much and the three of us had a fun time, laughing and cuddling as if we needed to have extra rations before the summer break. These six weeks were the last memory they would have of their mummy. Apprehensive as I was, following the strange conversation with Hans-Peter, now I was relaxed and confident about the future. My new job would give me more flexible hours; past experience had made me more careful in choosing the next au pair and setting her specific duties; the flat was comfortable and my boys were turning out to be great little guys. I had weathered the storm and there was nothing to be worried about any more . . .

Until that last free conversation I had with the boys. It was in August 1994 and it will remain engraved in my memory as long as I live. Alexander came to the telephone first. He sounded happy and was enjoying his holidays, but with his usual concern he went on:

'Mummy, have you bought the school books I need for the beginning of the term? You haven't forgotten our Lego?'

Then Constantin came on and his conversation worried me:

'Mummy, where are you?'

'In our flat, Tini.'

'Yes, but tell me where, in which room?'

'I'm in the drawing room, sitting on the green sofa and

113

looking out on to the garden as I'm talking to you.'

'Ah. And is your hair long? You didn't cut it again, did you?'

'No, Tini. You'll see by the time you come back it will be just the length you like.'

There was a pause, as if Constantin was trying to visualise the room and me.

'Why, Tini, are you bored?'

'Yes, Verden is boring. When are we coming back home, Mummy?'

'In three weeks. You're going to the seaside first.'

'But where are we going on our holiday with you?'

'I won't tell you, it's a surprise, remember?'

We blew kisses over the telephone. I told him how much I loved him and these were our last words. I hung up and remained seated. Something indefinable worried me. Constantin's voice had been different to his chirpy self. He had sounded sad and worried. It was unlike him.

I usually called once a week, sometimes less often, as I did not want to disturb their holidays there, believing it would be unsettling for them. Constantin was the one who would speak less: his motto was he was either in Germany or in London. Never before had he sounded so uninterested in his holiday, never before had he needed to build himself a picture of London. That night I could not sleep, hearing his voice over and over again.

The next day, I telephoned but Hans-Werner told me they were at the beach. The time after that, he told me they were asleep and the next they had gone out with Gundel and Hans-Peter. But he assured me they were well and happy.

I began to panic. Hans-Werner never used to answer the telephone, yet now it was only he who picked up the receiver. Why did they not allow me to speak to my sons? Where were they? Two weeks were left before their return to London but they were due back in Verden for a few days first. Hans-Peter's home number did not answer and when I tried his parents' house Hans-Werner answered,

114

giving me another excuse. Fourteen days . . . fourteen interminable days before I would be able to kiss my sons again. I thought of nothing else.

Would Alexander come back as he had after Easter? He sounded so happy to return home, but then what was being said to him since we had last spoken? Alexander was like blotting paper, absorbing everything. From the time he was a baby he was anxious and needed comforting. I would calm him by telling him how much I loved him and would hold him tightly in my arms. I often felt inadequate to Alexander's anxious nature, wishing I could climb into his body and extract what made him unsure. In so many ways Alexander was like his father, whilst Constantin was more an extension of me. I never needed to make an effort to understand him – it was simply as if I was looking at myself in the mirror, except that he was much more self-confident, intelligent and gifted than I was! I never worried about my Tini. I always worried about Alexander and wondered what Hans-Peter was imposing on him now. My poor, poor boy was being made guilty about his father's emotional inadequacies.

Hans-Peter kept me for six years through pity and guilt. Now he was trying to possess his nine-year-old son:

'I am so sad . . . Daddy needs you. He needs to be loved. Alexander, do you love Daddy? Are you happy here? You shouldn't leave me on my own.'

I had overheard him in the past, I had seen some of his postcards, and was realising that during these three weeks of silence Hans-Peter was begging for a child's love instead of offering him unconditional love. During the Easter holiday, Hans-Peter had added a new idea: 'I am German.'

I tossed and turned at night, was unsettled during the day and still could not get through to my sons on the telephone.

On 24 August, four days before my children were due back, I opened the door of my flat at six o'clock in the evening and found a large DHL envelope on the floor. I picked it up and as I started to tear it open, the phone rang. It was John, a friend of mine. We started talking as I took out a twenty-one-page letter, starting 'Dear Catherine' in Hans-Peter's handwriting. I was surprised and felt uneasy. I hung up quickly and started reading: 'I find it very difficult to write this letter to you today . . . however, as a father . . .'

I started to shake as I began scanning the paragraphs, trying to understand what Hans-Peter was leading up to. Twenty-one pages, in English – this meant Hans-Peter wanted to make sure I understood; this meant it concerned a personal matter between him and me.

. . . I know it is my duty to speak and let you know the following . . . since you left me two years ago and since you took the boys with you to England . . . the boys have repeatedly, and especially Alexander, expressed that they would rather live and go to school in Germany . . . that Germany was their home and that it was German that they wanted to speak rather than English. You know as well as me that especially Alexander has over the last months become increasingly depressed and you have yourself told me . . . that you had to accept the fact that he felt at home in Germany rather than in England . . .

Since they returned in July Alexander's (and Constantin's!) views about where they want to be have not changed . . . They both vehemently express their strong wish to live and go to school in Germany . . . I have now said to them . . . if you want to live and go to school here you can . . .

As a father who loves his boys I knew and know that I had and have to be honest with them . . . Knowing that something can be done about it I feel (and know) that something had to be said . . . and it is my duty as their father . . . In order to make sure that something will be arranged which I clearly see is in the best interest of the children I have last week

116

contacted the youth authority here who will now interview the boys about what they want and where they want to be. In order for you not to think that I act illegally in any way I have . . . applied for the right to keep the children here . . . Please know and please understand that this is by no means an act of aggression *vis-à-vis* you but something which I feel *must* be done for the boys' sake.

I have always expected you . . . not to let me see them any more. And I can assure you that I would never think of anything like this myself. I know that the boys love you as much as they love me and I also know that you love them as much as I love them . . . I feel rather depressed as I am not sure whether or not you understand why I act now. But I desperately hope that you understand that all I do is for the boys, and that you understand that as their father . . . I have no choice but to speak up in a way which I feel is my duty *vis-à-vis* them.

Please understand, I do not want to act against you and I do not want to sabotage your relationship with the boys . . . I have also told them that should they, after all, change their mind and prefer to live in London there would be no problem . . . and . . . that in that case I certainly would not be upset.

This is a very long letter but I do hope you see I try to act in the best interest of the boys . . . I am giving you such short notice . . . simply because until now I still hoped that their or especially Alexander's sadness would stop . . . I sincerely hope and pray that you understand why I am doing this . . . and you should see them now: they both are very, very happy that we have spoken about the situation . . . and I hope you understand why and for whom I have done this . . .

I was shaking like a leaf, in a cold sweat, in total panic. Automatically I called John, the last person I had spoken to. Then I picked up the phone again and called Leonard at his office. My voice was trembling and I only remember repeating: 'Hans-Peter isn't sending the children back. I've just received a twenty-one-page letter telling me he isn't sending the children back.'

Leonard and John were both on their way from the City. I did not move. I reread the letter, this time carefully, stopping at every word, going over each sentence. I felt as if I were suffocating and all the blood had left my body.

Hans-Peter had nothing to do with this, he wrote, and hoped I would understand! Just as in April when he had never told Alexander to say he was German? He was blaming the children for his actions, quoting Alexander, and Constantin only in brackets, mentioning 'they' when he meant 'him', underlining Constantin's name to convince me that even he had expressed his 'will' to remain in Germany.

I know my children: they were inside me before anyone else had seen them. I knew that Alexander could easily be influenced, but I also knew Tini could not. Hans-Peter was playing with words, trying to tell me Alexander thought we had come to London on holidays, that he had felt homesick and wanted to go to a German school. Was Alexander mentally retarded? Would it take him two and a half years of schooling in London to realise this was not a holiday? How could he feel homesick for Verden when he did not remember living there and it represented holidays for him? How could he and Constantin feel so unhappy about returning to London when their mummy, their friends and all their toys were there; when a few weeks ago they had told me the exact opposite? And when had I ever said that they felt at home in Germany rather than England?

I was scared. My sons were in danger. In a sudden flash, I saw that Hans-Peter had been planning this for months and all the ideas he had been planting suddenly resounded in my mind: Alexander's 'I am German and I want to go to a German school'; Masha's 'I've written to your husband'; Hans-Peter's 'I can take them to Germany if you can't manage'. But it was not until later that I saw the significance of Hans-Peter's wording 'in the interests of the children' and 'the wishes of the children' – the basis of his legal case.

As I picked up the telephone in anger, Hans-Peter was already calling me:

'Did you get my letter?'

'Yes, I've just finished reading it,' I said, and before I had time to say more, Hans-Peter continued in a trembling voice: 'It's not me. It's Alexander. And Constantin too. They want to stay here.'

He was shouting as I had never heard anyone shout before. My voice became calmer than ever, as if I was faced with a mental patient:

'Then, can I talk to Alexander, please?'

'No, you can't. He's sleeping and I'm not going to wake him up.'

'It's 7.30 in Germany! Hans-Peter, please let me talk to him . . .'

'Well, he's not coming back. There's no point in you talking to him. They both want to go to school here.'

'Hans-Peter, you know perfectly well this does not make sense. They've always attended French schools. How can they know about German schools? It would be unsettling for Alexander to change systems . . .'

'It's not my fault. It's him.'

'How can you ask a nine-year-old which school he wants to go to? Verden represents holiday times for Alexander: of course he would choose to stay there. Most children would say the same. Shouldn't you be more interested about continuity, instead of cornering him in a situation he can't understand?'

'Well, it's not me. It's him. He wants to go to school here. I've already told you – I am not sending them back.' His voice suddenly changed to a commanding one. 'In any case, Alexander wants to be German.'

'What are you talking about? No child has any idea

119

what a nationality means. It's not an innate feeling. Besides, our children have always been raised in multicultural environments . . .'

There was a bleep; silence. Hans-Peter had hung up on me while I was talking. I was still holding the receiver, hearing the echo of Hans-Peter's hysterical voice. People say women are hysterical, yet I had never heard a woman talk this way. I sat staring into emptiness until the doorbell rang. It was Leonard.

I handed him the letter. Leonard read through it slowly and I could see the expression on his face become bleaker and bleaker. Finally, he finished and stared at me in silence for a moment. His face was pale:

'Catherine, this is terrible. I can't believe it.'

He was still trying to absorb the content of the letter.

'Hans-Peter sounds completely hysterical,' he went on: 'He repeats himself all the time and he's hiding behind Alexander as if he had nothing to do with this decision – asking you to forgive his actions!'

Leonard was picking out sentences:

'"I had no other choice . . . Please know and please understand . . . this is something which I feel must be done for the boys' sake . . ." *He* feels depressed as he is not sure you will understand. *He* will not feel sad if the boys one day decide to return to you!' Catherine, this is ghastly! Hans-Peter is refusing to return the children and he wants you to understand and forgive his actions! He doesn't want to "sabotage your relationship with the boys" and yet he presents you with a *fait accompli*!'

We were still debating the letter when John arrived. John was an old friend of mine with whom I had got back in contact when I returned to London. He had never met Hans-Peter but knew my boys a little. John was fifty-four, and an extremely successful bantjer in the City, on the board of several companies. He was bright, matter-of-fact and had read law at Cambridge.

He read the letter carefully as if it were a business contract.

120

'This letter is incredibly manipulative and frightening. Catherine, this is very serious. You must get yourself a lawyer tomorrow. One who specialises in child abduction.'

'Child abduction?' I murmured.

'Yes, this is what it amounts to. You have legal custody, your children are resident in London and his refusal to return them is therefore a criminal action. Your lawyer will have to make an injunction and place your children under English court protection.'

I was speechless. My babies were supposed to be back in four days and John was talking about legal action and courts. I had read Hans-Peter's letter over and over. It was explicit, yet I still had not grasped what it implied: my sons were not coming back.

As if in a trance, I could no longer think straight. Leonard, dear Leonard, took over.

'John, do you know a good lawyer for Catherine?'

'Yes, there is an excellent firm I know. I'll call them tomorrow and introduce Catherine. They specialise in cases like this.'

Leonard and John continued talking, but I only caught the drift of their conversation. I was in a state of shock.

'Do you know Hans-Peter well?'

'Yes, I know him well. He is totally immature and irresponsible. But that he would actually do a thing like this . . .' I heard Leonard explain. 'I know Catherine's boys very well. I'm Alexander's godfather and they often came to the country with us. They are balanced, full of life and well behaved. Both Alexander and Constantin had adapted well and were happy. In fact I saw them the day before they left on their holidays. Constantin wasn't even looking forward to going and Alexander was asking me when he could come to the country again . . . I cannot believe that Hans-Peter would do this.'

'Did you notice this sentence in his letter: "and maybe Catherine could come to Verden and stay in Ute's house for the weekend?" It sounds to me as if her husband is try-

121

ing to use the children to manipulate her back to him.'

'Well, Hans-Peter was always very possessive of Catherine and, knowing him as I do, he could never accept her leaving him . . .'

They talked further, then John stood up:

'Catherine, I'll call the lawyer first thing tomorrow morning. You'll have to act immediately. This is very serious.'

He took my arm and squeezed it in a comforting gesture, bid goodbye to Leonard and left. Thank God I had such friends, I thought.

Leonard stayed and as soon as he left I rushed into my bedroom, crushed, sobbing until my eyes had no more tears to shed. Some time during the night I called my mother. Somehow, the next morning I managed to get myself to the office.

As soon as I walked out of the lift into the trading room, my colleague Nicholas rushed up to me:

'Catherine, what's the matter?'

My face must have given me away.

'My boys . . . My boys . . . They're not coming back!'

Nicholas immediately called Nicolette, my friend who worked at the same bank. She came almost at once, took me by the arm into a conference room and closed the door. My whole body was trembling and I could only utter the same words over and over:

'My angels, my angels . . .' Nicolette held me tightly in her arms and I could not stop crying.

Nicolette was a senior manager at the bank. She had some legal dealings in the past that might prove relevant. Once I calmed down a little, she took me to her office and we started to assess the situation. John had left a message with the name of the lawyer and an appointment time. I had brought all the papers John had said I would need and two hours later I was sitting in the office of my lawyer at Kingsley Napley. An assistant was also present to take notes.

Jane looked at the documentation and read Hans-Peter's letter:

'This is a very manipulative letter. Tell me about your husband.'

I explained as much as I could, between sobs.

'This is illegal retention. We'll have to go to the High Court of Justice and make an application for a resident order and a wardship order. We'll also make an injunction under the Hague Convention for the immediate return of the children to this jurisdiction.'

I had no idea what she was talking about. Wardship, Hague Convention . . . I could only think of my boys. Where were they now? What was being said to them? Was Tini asking how many more days were left before he would be coming home to Mummy? It wasn't really happening. This was only a bad dream. Soon, I'd wake up and my boys would be here . . .

'Can we send Hans-Peter a fax first? Maybe he'll return the boys as per our agreement.'

'I very much doubt it. His letter is pretty explicit. He's already taken legal steps and I must tell you that he knew what he was doing well in advance. He's also trying to trick you into going to Germany. You must not go as it will imply that you accept the situation. He also mentions the local youth authority. Do you realise that this means he's trying to get their support? I believe that in Germany they play a major role in child custody battles. Your husband knows what he's doing full well and from the connections you tell me he has, he's in an excellent position . . . But if you wish I'll send him a fax nonetheless.'

Everyone around me kept repeating how serious it was. They were talking about abduction, legal actions, English and international law . . . but I was incapable of grasping the reality of the situation. Hans-Peter was only acting irrationally. He wasn't serious. The boys would be back in three days.

I couldn't remember how I got to the office, how I came home – I was moving like an automaton. I needed to talk to Hans-Peter and make him return to his senses.

123

There was an answering machine at his practice, no answer at his house. I called uninterruptedly. A girlfriend came to see me and brought a take-away dinner. I had no appetite: all I could think of was frantically fast-dialling Hans-Peter's home number. Finally at 11 p.m. Hans-Peter answered:

'Hans-Peter . . .' As soon as he heard my voice he hung up, then took the telephone off the hook. I could no longer get through to him. I did not sleep.

The next day, 26 August, a fax was sent to Hans-Peter's practice in Bremen, with a copy to his London lawyer:

We have been shown a letter written by you on the 22 August which categorically states that you do not intend to return the boys as agreed. We consider this to be child abduction. Our client has instructed us to commence proceedings through the English and German Courts . . . but she very much hopes that the matter will not go to a full-blown hearing and that you will agree to return the children on the agreed flight of Sunday 28 August.

My parents and my friends rallied about me, calling me, offering their help and support. I do not think I could have survived those early days had they not surrounded me with their love and care. Hans-Peter was still unreachable and I did not know where my boys were. My world had collapsed and I was in a constant panic.

The whole bank knew. The director called me in. He was Italian and wonderful:

'Catherine, what's happening to you is absolutely ghastly. The bank is behind you and don't worry, we'll support you in any way we can.'

Thank God I had friends and was working in an Italian bank. How awkward it would have been if I had still been employed at the German one! I had only been at my new job two months and was still on probation. Luckily, I had started with such energy and determination that my results were excellent – at least the bank knew I could be productive.

Finally, I managed to get through to Hans-Peter's parents' house.

'Gundel where are my sons? I would like to talk to them.'

'I don't know!'

'Please. I haven't talked to them for nearly three weeks . . .'

'I don't know where they are. I won't tell you!'

'But I'm their mother! You can't hide them from me. I need to talk to them . . .'

'OK, OK, I'll tell Hans-Peter to have them call you.'

'So you know where they are. Please tell me.'

'No. I promised Hans-Peter I wouldn't say.'

'But Gundel . . . What sort of people are you? You're a mother too. How can you . . .'

'You're the one who left my son!'

And she hung up.

So there it was. My children had been kept to punish me, as it was I who had left Hans-Peter.

The next morning, Hans-Peter called me at the office:

'I'll fetch the boys and in half an hour you can call me at the practice and you'll be able to talk to them.'

'But why can't I talk to them now? Where are they?'

'They are in Bremen. At my aunt's house.'

'Well, can you give me her number? I'll call them there.'

'No, I want to be present when you talk to them. Call back at the practice.'

Half an hour of hell. I was glued to my watch, shaking and scared. My little boys were prisoners – they were not even allowed to talk to their mother.

'Hello, Alexander? How are you my darling?'

'Hello.' His voice was cold, toneless. I was frightened.

'I'm German and I want to go to a German school!'

'But Alexander . . . What about our holidays together? Remember, this was a surprise. All your toys are here, your friends, your mummy . . .'

There was silence. Then Hans-Peter's voice shouting down the telephone:

'Stop it! Don't talk to Alexander this way. Now you've upset him, he's crying!'

And then Constantin. A tiny peevish voice which I could hardly recognise:

'Mummy?'

'Yes, Tini.' I was nearly crying too, but I went on: 'How are you?'

He was silent. I went on: 'Mummy loves you . . .'

'I know. But I have to go to a German school, I have to . . .'

He didn't finish his sentence. His voice was small and sounded scared.

'Tini, I . . .'

'I have to go now and . . .'

He never finished. My little Tini . . . his voice had sounded so sad, so lost . . . I could see his little face: he was probably biting his lower lip to control his tears, probably looking down to escape his father's directives. I saw Alexander's expression, his eyebrows knitted, tensed up in repressed pain.

Hans-Peter was acting like a madman. He was acting like a kidnapper – controlling the conversation, making the children repeat sentences. They sounded rehearsed, forced. I ran down to Nicolette's office, barely able to control my tears. I was petrified. My poor little vulnerable boys, held hostage . . . 9 August 1994 would be the last time I had had a free conversation with my own two children. They were now kept behind a wall, forbidden all contact with their mummy in the hope that they would grow to hate and resent her.

That evening, I received an envelope from the Verden court. A decision dated 22 August, 1994 rejected Hans-Peter's ex-parte demand of custody. In Germany (probably the only country in Europe with this legal arrangement), one can make court applications for child custody without even informing the other party. Hans-Peter had presum-

126

ably asked for custody to be transferred to him some time in July and had waited for the decision, hoping it would be in his favour. On 22 August he had been informed that Judge Moritz rejected his application as he considered that the children should remain with their mother and in England where they had already been living for two and a half years. Irrespective of this, Hans-Peter decided to keep the children and wrote me his letter the same day.

By retaining the children, Hans-Peter had now defied both English and German law.

Chapter 10
Helplessness

My angels, how could I ever describe how I felt when you disappeared? No words can depict how much agony, despair and tortured worry I endured. No words can reach into this dimension of emotions.

The next day, I awoke to the realisation that my solicitor had been right: Hans-Peter knew what he was doing and he *was* serious.

Now I had the proof: Hans-Peter had already applied to the Verden court for custody transfer when I had last talked to the children at the beginning of August, when Alexander had asked me whether I had bought his school books and when Tini had told me he was bored in Verden. This was why the Volkmanns wouldn't let me talk to the boys any more: Hans-Peter was setting up his legal argument based on the 'will of the children' (which as I would later discover is very effective under German law) in case his demand was rejected – he could hardly jeopardise his defence by allowing the children to express an opposite 'will' on the telephone.

Why had I let the boys go to Germany? I thought of them all alone, unprotected, with a father who was betraying them, betraying their mother and pushing her out of their lives. What he had done was horrifying and it terrified me. How was it possible? How could German law admit ex-parte demands for such crucial issues as custody? Had Hans-Peter obtained a decision in his favour I would have been removed from my sons' life there and then and would have had little legal recourse.

I tried to calm myself. The judge *had* rejected Hans-

Peter's conspiring manoeuvre. The law was on my side in both countries and justice would protect the children. Yet I could not suppress my alarm. Hans-Peter was surrounded by lawyers and a judge and his father was very powerful in the small town of Verden. The boys were under their control and I could not even reach them by telephone.

My nights were sleepless and my days full of panic. On the morning of Sunday 28 August, I rose at dawn. Maybe Hans-Peter would change his mind, maybe he would send the boys back today. After all, why would anyone want to embark on bitter legal battles? I had never obstructed his contacts with the children, never complained about him to them, never been unreasonable . . . Why should he want to provoke arguments and drag his sons into it?

By ten o'clock I was frantic. Instinctively, I knew Hans-Peter would not call but I tried to hold on to the only notion that gave me a glimpse of hope: logic. I sat on my green sofa, the phone in front of me, praying it would ring. We were due to drive to Alton Towers the next day, then up north to see my friend Valerie and her boys. Alexander and Tini had asked so often whether we could visit them again. Their presents were lying on their bunk beds, ready to open, their school books and new pencil cases beside them . . .

Everything was ready for their return – but they never would return. An hour later, I dialled Hans-Peter's home number. No answer. Finally at noon: 'I've told you. The boys are not coming back!'

'But Hans-Peter, I'd planned a holiday with them, school's starting in three weeks . . .'

'Well, too bad. The boys are staying here,' and he hung up.

I called back. An answering machine was on. Hans-Peter had obviously just installed it to screen the calls. I tried Ute's number. Wilfred, the judge, answered and he allowed me to speak to my sons, who were in his house.

Both said little, answering only 'yes' or 'no', Alexander

sounded stressed and Tini's frightened little voice startled me again. My self-confident Constantin sounded intimidated and perplexed. What were they being told? I was devastated.

My sons' lives were being dismantled, never to be serene again. They were being held prisoner, spirited away from their mother and prevented from talking to her. I was not allowed to speak to them again until October, except for one evening on 8 September.

Between tears, I managed to talk to my mother, then, once I had regained control, to my solicitor who had given me her home number. Monday was a Bank Holiday, but first thing on Tuesday morning we would apply for the emergency orders at the High Court of Justice. We were to meet at her office at 10 a.m.

The hours passed interminably, alternating sickeningly between moments of rational reflection and gushes of emotion. I imagined my boys lost in the dense woods, walking hand in hand, their rucksacks on their backs, crying for me . . .

On Tuesday, 30 September, my solicitor, her assistant and I went to the High Court of Justice where we met our barrister. He had received preliminary reports from Jane, but there were details he needed from me. He took a few notes, Jane presented him with the papers she had prepared and we sat waiting for the judge to call us in. I had never been inside a courtroom in my life and felt nervous. My sons, my flesh and blood, were reduced to names in a file, to another routine case to be argued. A man whom I had never met would speak on my behalf and a judge would decide our destiny.

Hans-Peter had cast me out of my sons' lives and now barristers and solicitors controlled our future. I didn't even hear the voice calling us through the loudspeaker.

'Let's go in,' the solicitor said.

We walked into the impressive wood-panelled room. Our barrister sat in the front row. Jane, her assistant and I in the one behind. The judge walked in wearing a wig and a black robe and we all stood up. We sat again and the hearing began. Our barrister spoke, but with all the legal language and the various articles I understood very little. I was numb.

Jane woke me from my stupor with a nudge:

'Great,' she whispered, 'we've got an injunction under Article 3 of the Hague Convention.'

I had no idea what she was talking about, but could see that the verdict was good and that we had surmounted the first hurdle.

Jane was pleased and so was the barrister. Justice Ward's decision would soon restore my children to me in London. It was not as though they were in Iran or Yemen. Germany was a signatory to the Hague Convention on child abduction.

I was relieved but not convinced. My boys were far away and in Verden. In Verden, the rules were different: the Volkmanns and the Monkmanns were in control.

'Hans-Peter lives in a judge's property, his father knows everyone in town, his sister is a lawyer, so is his brother-in-law. His uncle is a politician in Bremen . . .'

'Don't worry, the German central authorities will look after things. I'll inform the child abduction unit of our Lord Chancellor's office immediately of the court decision.'

Perhaps Jane thought I was over-dramatising and under emotional stress. She tried politely to take leave and hailed a taxi.

'And you'll need to get yourself a German lawyer as soon as possible,' she advised.

'I don't know any German lawyers.'

'I'll try and find one for you. I'll call you later,' and she was off.

I went back to the office and tried to concentrate on the business – there was nothing else I could do now. Like a robot I talked to my clients, and bought, sold, wrote confirmations. Only one thought was in my mind: my children.

131

Jane called me with the name of a lawyer from Munich who specialised in child abduction cases. I called him immediately and left my office and home number on his answering machine. Nicolette accompanied me home and I spent all evening on the telephone, between my parents and my friends, still unable to reach the children: Gundel's number was not answering and Hans-Peter's new device recorded my eternal unanswered messages.

Two days later, I finally reached his aunt in Bremen who held me on the telephone for ages, playing innocent, until she admitted everyone was away but she couldn't tell me where. I was beginning seriously to panic. Where on earth did they disappear to? School holidays were ending in a week's time in England. In Germany school had started two weeks ago – soon, the children would be missing class here.

The Munich lawyer, Dr Kram, finally called.

'Mrs Laylle? I received a fax from Jane yesterday. So your children have been abducted? Well, I'm familiar with the procedure – I've dealt with many such cases. I'll put the necessary papers through to Berlin first thing tomorrow. Then I'll be away for a few days. In the meantime, would you send me 1,000 marks.'

Dr Kram had spoken in English to me. His voice was strict. He had run through my case. I hung up and felt uncomfortable. He sounded as if he knew what to do and that he would act fast, but he had not seemed interested in listening to my concerns about the boys. However, what choice did I have? Jane had told me he was a reputable lawyer, and though my world had fallen apart, it was just a routine job for him. So many things separated me from my sons now.

Soon, my days became a maze of legal terms, phone calls, faxes, photocopies and my regular office job. My evenings were consumed by further phone calls between helpful friends who had just heard the news, my parents, my sister Véronique, Leonard, Nicolette – and Hans-Peter's answering machine. At night, I could not sleep until finally, too exhausted to think further, I would doze off and be transported into a maelstrom of nightmares. Some were so harrowing that I became afraid of going to sleep.

My boys were calling me, I could hear their cries of help, see the frightened expressions on their little faces – but I could never reach them. Either Hans-Peter came running up, grabbing each child under the arm and vanishing into the darkness, or I would find myself suddenly lost in the dense forest unable to find them again . . . but still hearing their cries.

I tried Dr Kram on Wednesday, but he was not yet back. By Friday, I began to panic again. I called Jane. She couldn't help me further. No one had his home number. I arrived at my empty flat that evening and found another letter from the Verden court. My heart started beating fast: what now?

A short note on recycled paper said something about a hearing time of 2 p.m. on Tuesday, 20th September, 1994. I called Véronique, whose German was fluent, and faxed her the note. A few minutes later she was on the telephone:

'Catherine, this is a hearing for custody. Hans-Peter has lodged an appeal against the decision of 22 August refusing him custody.'

'But that's impossible. There's been an injunction from the English court ordering the return of the children to England under the Hague Convention. This has priority. The Verden court can't decide on custody. It will be determined here in this jurisdiction.'

'Well, call your German lawyer immediately on Monday. Monday is already the 12th!'

'I can't get hold of him.'

Everyone got on the telephone. No one knew of a German lawyer who specialised in abductions and Hague Convention cases. Only Joachim had a friend who was a commercial lawyer, a partner in a large law firm in Munich. Maybe he would be able to help.

'Yes, yes, I've heard about the Hague Convention. I've never dealt with these cases before, but Joachim tells me you urgently need help.'

'Thank you.' His voice sounded soft and considerate. He spoke almost no English and dealing with legal terminology in German would be impossible for me but at least Véronique would be able to help.

I had managed to reach Ute a few days before. Her voice was chilling:

'Catherine, you don't want to understand, do you? Your sons want to live in Germany and you had better get used to the idea. Behave as a mother, respect their will and stop trying to call them.'

'But I *am* the mother. They are my sons. Please tell me where they are. What Hans-Peter is doing is illegal.'

'Don't talk to me about the law. Just leave your children alone.'

'I need to know where they are.'

'I've promised Hans-Peter I won't tell you. But don't worry, they'll be back in two weeks' time. I'll ask Hans-Peter to call you then.'

'Back in two weeks!? From where?'

'That's all I'm going to say. Be satisfied with that. I can't say more.'

Ute, with her forbidding hostility, would not even tell me where my children were and in her self-righteous tone had told me I should content myself with talking to them in two weeks' time. Were these people human?

The next day, I called the Child Abduction Unit. They faxed Berlin and found that the police had instigated a search.

The director of the French Lycée was on the telephone.

'Madame Laylle, I have just received a fax from your husband stating that the children will no longer be attending the Lycée since they "have moved back to Germany after the last school term". Had you not told me about your story, their places would have been given away. You know how long the waiting list is. But of course, I'm keep-

134

ing them open.' I was horrified. Hans-Peter's planning went so far! Had Mr Cock been less attentive, there would have been no places at the boys' London school; another positive legal argument for Hans-Peter.

Nicola and Franz, two of my office colleagues, were helping me with a flood of calls. Nicolette lunched with me to talk things over. Véronique deciphered my German lawyer's court applications, my friends rallied around me in the evening, and my parents were devastated . . . but the German police were still unable to locate the children.

I was beside myself. Finally, I called the local police in Verden. A constable answered:

'Oh, *ja*. We received a fax from Berlin two days ago. *Ja, ja*, I'll check their house tomorrow.'

'But that's the point. They're not there! I'm worried . . .'

'We'll look into it. Tell me, are you married to Hans-Peter or Hans-Jorg?'

The police knew them by their first names. They had not even started their search!

On Thursday, 8 September, Gundel finally picked up the telephone.

'*Nein*, I don't know where your children are.'

'But, Gundel . . .' She was nervous. Her voice was insecure and mistakenly she let slip that they were in southern Germany, in Freiburg.

'Can I have Antje's number?'

Annoyed with herself that she had given out this information, she resentfully gave me the number of Hans-Peter's sister. I dialled at once. It was engaged – Gundel had obviously got through first, not needing the international prefix, to warn her daughter that I would be calling.

When the line was finally free, a disconcerted au-pair answered:

'*Nein*, I don't know where your children are.' But during the conversation she revealed that Hans-Peter would be back later. At that moment, Antje grabbed the phone. Her voice was spiteful:

135

'Catherine, they're not here. The children don't want to talk to you.'

'Antje, please . . . This isn't credible. Why should my children suddenly not want to talk to their own mother?'

'Your children want to live in Germany.'

'Well, this is what you're telling me. But even if so, why should they be barred from talking to me then? I would like to speak to my sons. I haven't spoken to them since the 28th of August. You have no right to forbid my children to talk to me.'

Antje was becoming extremely aggressive. She was shouting down the phone, interrupting me and throwing legal terminology into the conversation. I got scared. She was a lawyer and I had better get off the phone.

But Antje went on:

'You should have come to Verden as Hans-Peter suggested in his letter!'

'But I couldn't. My lawyer told me not to go. It was a legal trick.'

'What trick? It's you who left Hans-Peter, isn't it? You aren't interested in your children. You didn't take care of them. You worked.'

'But Antje, you work too and left your first husband when your son was still a toddler.'

'That's entirely different!'

'That evening, I phoned about ten times. Finally I managed to talk to my boys who 'had just come in with Hans-Peter from an outing in the woods'. It was ten o'clock at night!

Hans-Peter came on the phone first:

'And you accuse me of being a kidnapper! You're mad, mad.' He was hysterical and I was terrified. 'Alexander, tell your mother –' and he passed the phone over to his son, who sounded petrified.

'Mummy?'

'How are you, my love? I've been trying to call you every day . . .' I heard Hans-Peter's voice in the background: 'Tell her, tell her!' Alexander was hesitant. I

136

could sense his disorientation and nervousness:

'I am German and I want to go to a German school,' he said in French.

'Are you going to school?'

'No.'

'But school started a month ago.'

'Constantin and I are going to the kindergarten with Antje's son.'

My nine-year-old son was going to kindergarten, in southern Germany, when Hans-Peter had a medical practice in Bremen, some four hundred miles away?

'Doesn't Daddy go to work?'

'Yes, he goes to the practice.'

'But when he's not with you, who's taking care of you?'

'The babysitter.'

Again Hans-Peter barked in the background. His voice was shaking: 'That's not true. Tell her it's not true.'

Alexander's voice was unsteady. I could feel he was about to cry. In a faint tone he asked me whether I wanted to speak to Tini, and a little desperate thread of a voice came on:

'Hello.'

'Tini? Mummy loves you. I've been trying to call you. I didn't know where you were.'

I was shaken. I tried to choose my words carefully so as not to upset the children, yet I suspected this might be the last opportunity I would have to talk to them and find out what was going on.

'And are you with Alexander all day?'

'Yes, but Mummy . . .' and in a tearful voice, he added quickly, 'I've got to go now.'

Hans-Peter's voice came on:

'Now they're upset. What you're doing is horrible. I don't want you to speak to them any more!' he yelled and put down the phone. My boys had been standing there throughout Hans-Peter's threats and shouting.

I fell to pieces, unable to manage my emotions any more. The pain was so acute that it had become physical.

137

I was crying, shaking, everything inside me was aching. My sons . . . My mind was in total turmoil and I was frightened as I have never been in my life: Hans-Peter was acting like a madman and there was nothing, nothing I could do to rescue my children.

How was all this possible? How could nothing be done to protect two innocent children? Didn't the lawyers, the bureaucrats at the Lord Chancellor's department and in Berlin, realise that this was urgent?

The following day, Jane sent me a fax she had received from Hans-Peter's English lawyer, dated 8 September 1994, the same day I talked to the boys in Freiburg:

'The children are with my client at his home address in Verden. The children are well and happy and there is no reason why your client should not telephone them on his home number.'

A fax from Berlin dated that same day, stated: 'The police investigations have not been successful yet' and on 9 September: 'The police investigations have revealed that the respondent and the children are in Freiburg until the end of this weekend. Then they will come back to Verden.' But they were not, and on 12 September Berlin advised us that they had 'again requested the police in Verden to look for Dr Volkmann and the children'.

I never managed to speak to the children again. Antje's number was switched on to an answering machine, as was Hans-Peter's number in Verden. Gundel did not answer. Hans-Peter's English lawyer and the police were misinformed. The children were not in Verden and they did not return on 12 September. I would find out later that, on that weekend, my sons had been taken on a 600-mile drive to a small North Sea island to spend ten days at a psychologist's private home.

My new lawyer, recommended by Joachim, called me on 16 September:

'Everything's fine. The judge in Verden has been informed about the Hague injunction. He will only deal with the custody after he has heard the Hague Convention case.'

Just after we met and before Hans-Peter moved in with me, taken in front of my London flat in 1982.

Our wedding, June 1984, in the Russian Orthodox Church in London. Léonard, my best friend, is behind us.

In Wiesbaden in 1987. Alexander in the playground. His face behind bars seems to me a premonition of what was to come.

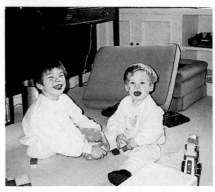

Right: Happy moments in Paris when visiting 'Babouŝia' and 'Grandfather'

Hamburg, 1990. My two angels in my arms in the garden where we used to take them daily.

1990. A happy
family moment.

Below: 1990. A
family still united.
Summer holidays
in Austria.

Christmas holidays in Paris, 1992. Joyful moment shared between Alexander and his grandfather.

Above: Alexander and his grandmother as King and Queen.

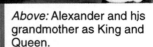

Constantin loved to dress up.

London, 1993. Tea after school… before homework.

Above: Constantin in disguise yet again, wearing Mummy's necklaces.

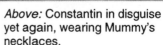

Left: Alexander always proud and protective of his younger brother.

Isn't it fun to have a bath together?

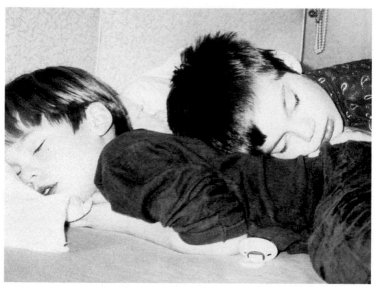

It's much warmer in Mummy's bed.

Constantin and his great friend in May 1994, a few weeks before they set off on the holiday from which they never came back.

Left: The troubled faces of the children just before yet another court decision separates us.

Below: The long muddy track that leads to the isolated house where Alexander and Constantin are retained.

The love of a mother who fights – the love reduced to documents.

'What do you mean?' – my voice was trembling – 'deal with the custody? My sons were illegally retained and under Article 3 of the Hague Convention they have to be returned to England immediately. This is what the Hague Convention is about – to protect children against abduction and illegal retention.'

'Yes, but your husband might argue that their return to England would cause them psychological damage.'

'What?' Alexander's 'I'm German, I want to go to a German school' was resounding in my mind.

'There is an exception under which children need not be ordered back. I can imagine your husband will use it to defend his case.'

'But how could a return to England cause psychological damage to my sons? England is a civilised country. We have no famine nor are we in a state of war!'

'I know, but I am just preparing you for the eventuality.'

'But the Verden court cannot discuss custody in any case. My sons are wards of court; they are under the protection of the High Court of England and Wales.'

'Well, we'll just see what happens.'

I hung up and ran downstairs to see Nicolette, in a panic. Why was my lawyer being negative and dispassionate?

'Most lawyers are the same. But your case is black and white, I shouldn't worry.'

But I did. With the support that Hans-Peter had in Verden, anything was possible.

On Monday, 19 September I took the plane to Hamburg. Véronique's flight from Paris arrived twenty minutes later. Joachim met us at the airport and the three of us drove to his flat where the lawyer was to join us later. This was our first meeting. His colleague who specialised in family law would arrive the next day.

Véronique and I were very nervous. Joachim's friend was a gentle man who seemed detached and unaware of the seriousness of the case. At 6p.m. Joachim's fax

139

machine rang. The Munich office was sending us a copy of Hans-Peter's court deposition which they had just received. My sister and I were perplexed: in Germany, was evidence brought in at the last minute admissible?

Reels of paper were coming out. Joachim gave Véronique some pages and both started reading. There was silence and I saw my sister's face fill with consternation:

'What's the matter?'

'I think it's better if you don't look at it. I can't believe what I'm reading. I'll just tell you in brief. There are testimonies from two of these au-pair girls you had. One from Isabella and one from Masha. What they basically say is that you're a bad mother. You worked all day and did not take care of the children. They claim they had to attend to the boys.'

'But that's ridiculous. And Masha never took care of the boys. They didn't even like her . . .'

'Yes, but the fact is that they have made their statements and with a hearing tomorrow you'll not have time to provide evidence against them.'

'And Véronique, look at this!' Joachim interrupted in a grim voice.

Véronique started reading and her face became even more sombre.

'What is it?'

'It's a report from a child psychologist.'

'What child psychologist?' I asked in a panic.

'Someone who lives in Norderney, an island in the North Sea.'

'What? My children were taken to a psychologist? But that's horrible . . .'

'Well, you had better not see that report.'

Joachim and Véronique were shielding me from the information.

'Catherine, you have to be strong. You'll need to sleep tonight.'

'Let me see that report,' said Dr Schirker, the lawyer.

'Ah, yes, as I thought – your husband is arguing that it would be psychologically harmful for the children to be returned to England.'

'But how could the judge accept a report made by a psychologist whom Hans-Peter appointed? The mother was not even present when the children were examined and the psychologist doesn't mention this rather crucial point,' Joachim interjected.

'Well, we'll see,' the lawyer concluded.

Véronique and I looked at each other in horror.

Chapter 11
Verden Closes Ranks

The book of life is the supreme work that one cannot close or open according to one's will. An interesting passage may not be re-read. But the last page inevitably comes. One would like to return to the page where one loves, and already in our fingers is the page where one dies. *(Lamartine) How much I would give to go back to that page – before you slipped away from my life.*

Joachim had booked us into a small hotel nearby. Before going to sleep, Véronique tried to reassure me as best she could. Véronique, the intellectual, was a professor at 'Le Grand Palais' University in Paris and a lateral thinker. She gave me gentle advice, but I could not fail to notice how worried and nervous she was herself. She had been to Verden once, in the summer of 1987, and had observed the prejudiced and insular atmosphere of Hans-Peter's entourage; she knew that tomorrow would be trying.

The next morning Joachim and the lawyer, Dr Schirker, came to fetch us. We picked up the second lawyer at the airport and all five of us set off for Verden. The second lawyer seemed very young and I was surprised how little English he spoke, considering they were both working for an international law firm.

Finally we reached Verden. Everyone was silent.

'Gosh, it's even smaller than I imagined,' exclaimed Joachim's friend, Dr Schirker.

I directed Joachim to the court: 'Amtsgericht – Verden', Hans-Peter's pride.

Everything was deserted and grey. I was filled with angst.

The small building seemed empty. There was one court-room. In front of it was a large hall with several chairs and to the left another small waiting area; to the right, a corridor with several doors. A small notice on the side of the courtroom read:

12 A.M. VOLKMANN VS VOLKMANN

I gulped. We sat and waited. The loudspeaker called; 'Volkmanns, please come forward.'

The five of us walked into a white-walled modern room. A blonde woman sat on a bench to the left, the judge on a platform on the right. On either side of the room were four wooden chairs and a table:

'*Nein, nein.* Only the client and her lawyers, please. The other two will have to wait outside,' the judge announced.

Véronique and Joachim looked at me and left. My lawyers, with me between them, sat to the left of the judge. I wondered who this blonde woman was but from the way she had looked at me I felt she was there to tes-tify against me. The minutes passed.

The judge leaned down towards the speaker on his desk and called: 'Herr Volkmann, *bitte*.'

Still nothing. My mind was racing. It was 12.07 already. Was he not going to show up?

Suddenly, the door flew open. Hans-Peter's brother-in-law Klaus, who is six foot three, a short blond man, and Hans-Peter frantically rushed in and took their seats opposite us. Hans-Peter looked flustered: his eyes were glazed, staring into the distance, and his cheeks were red. I shivered.

The judge began in German. He spoke slowly and clearly. I managed to understand most of what he said.

Dr Schirker stood up and from what I could make of it, explained how Hans-Peter had failed to return the chil-dren, breaching our agreement . . . how settled and happy the children were in London . . . Hans-Peter's expression did not change. His eyes stared at the white wall behind me. He didn't look at me once.

Klaus interrupted my lawyer in an arrogant tone and

143

began a long speech. he was slouched in his chair and spoke so fast that I did not understand a word. But what was being said was obviously against me.

The judge agreed to whatever demand Klaus had just made and the blonde woman started talking, spitefully glancing at me from time to time:

'I have talked to Alexander and Constantin. They both expressed their strong will to remain in Germany. They do love their mother but felt unhappy in England. They did not like their school. They endured Nazi taunts. They said their mother works and is not around for them. There is a very nice school next to where they live now . . .'

I could not believe my ears. What was this woman saying? My sons, teased at school for being Nazis? This was insane. And what had this to do with a court case about abduction? I stared at her, stared in front of me, stared at the judge. I was horrified.

'What's this talk of Nazis? This is 1994!' I asked my lawyer.

'Don't worry. Keep calm. This woman is a social worker, from the Verden Youth Authority. Let the judge make up his own mind.'

The judge then asked me to present my case which I managed to do with deadly calm. This was very serious. It concerned my sons and I knew I had to be composed.

Hans-Peter then spoke: the children felt German, wanted to go to a German school . . . He still stared at the wall, his lip trembling and his voice too.

I felt as if I was part of a war movie, brought before the court on a nationality trial.

A discussion followed as to whether the children should be brought in. The judge spoke into the loudspeaker: 'Volkmann children, please come forward.'

Suddenly, the little blond man, the local lawyer, stood up and shot out of the room. Dr Schirker exclaimed: 'But this is totally irregular. You cannot just leave the courtroom in the middle of a hearing . . .' The man had already disappeared.

Five minutes later, he was back. The judge asked for an explanation: the children were not in the building but in Café Jens downtown.

The judge called for a recess. Hans-Peter and his two lawyers loudly stormed out of the room followed by the blonde woman.

As my two lawyers and I walked out into the hallway, we saw a crowd of people belonging to Hans-Peter's party standing opposite. We dashed to join Véronique and Joachim who had waited in the small area on the right. They both looked pale and worried:

'Katia, do you know who's here? Masha!'

'Masha!'

'Yes! And I wonder how Hans-Peter got her a visa.'

We quickly recounted the hearing.

'But the children should have been in the building. This is completely irregular,' Joachim interjected.

Joachim was deliberating on strategies when we heard the judge's voice calling us back in. Both Véronique and Joachim squeezed my arm:

'Courage, Catherine!'

We went in first and sat down. I looked at Hans-Peter walking in; his movements were uncoordinated, his expression bitter. This was the man I had married, with whom I had had two sons and now he had declared war.

The judge said something and started reading his decision. My mind was too paralysed to focus on any discernible words I might recognise. Then: 'The respondent, Dr Volkmann, is ordered to surrender to the petitioner the two children of the marriage to enable their immediate return to the United Kingdom. The court orders the immediate execution of the ruling. The obligation to surrender the children may be enforced with the aid of a court bailiff. The court bailiff is empowered to enlist police support where necessary. The order for surrender may where necessary be enforced by the application of physical force.'

145

My sons were coming back! We would be reunited at last! The nightmare would end, yet I could not rejoice: something inside me could not believe it. Hans-Peter's face had disintegrated into the most hateful expression. His lip was shaking. His eyes were glazed. Klaus and the other lawyer said something to each other, then:

'Dr Volkmann would like half an hour to bring the children,' and before I had time to react to the meaning of the request, Dr Schirker answered: 'Of course, I am sure I can trust my colleagues. Police enforcement will not be necessary. Half an hour to bring the children to the court building . . .'

I stared at him with horror but Hans-Peter, his two lawyers and the social worker had already charged out of the courtroom.

We packed our papers, thantjed the judge and walked out; the corridor was deserted. Only Véronique and Joachim stood by the door. We kissed and sighed with relief.

'But why did they all gallop downstairs? We saw Hans-Peter run out of the courtroom, his party behind him, and in a flash they'd disappeared. 'There's something fishy about this,' Joachim interrupted. 'Catherine, where's this Café Jens? I think we should go there immediately. You stay here with the lawyer, in case the children are brought back. Véronique, Dr Schirker and I will go and see what's going on.'

The three of them left. It was 1.30 p.m. the building was deserted. The atmosphere felt ominous. I knew something was desperately wrong. Why had my lawyer allowed this half-hour. Dr Schirker was an honourable man and probably couldn't imagine that a forty-year-old doctor would behave irresponsibly. Had Joachim been in court, this would never have happened. He knew Hans-Peter's capricious and obstinate character. He knew how his family would bend to all his demands and how Hans-Peter saw the boys as his possessions.

We waited. I sat down, weak and unnerved. The

minutes dragged on and the tension became insufferable. I lit a cigarette.

We heard hurried footsteps. Véronique, Joachim and Dr Schirker came rushing towards us breathless. Joachim reported:

'We walked into the coffee shop and Véronique heard children's voices coming up the basement stairs. She turned round and saw Alexander and Hans-Peter. Constantin and Antje were behind them. Véronique hardly had time to say "Bonjour Alexandre" when Hans-Peter grabbed him by the hand. Antje grabbed Constantin and they ran out of the café. For a second we stood there stupefied, then we started running after them along the pedestrian walkway. I shouted: "stop" but they didn't. Passers-by were staring. Antje turned and yelled at Dr Schirker: "You criminal. We'll never return the children." Then Hans-Peter and Antje threw the children into the back seat of a car, slammed the doors and accelerated away. Antje was at the wheel. As she drove past us, she opened her window and yelled, "In any case, we're off to Celle" and their car vanished round the corner. It was incredible. She and Hans-Peter looked as if they were mad, nearly possessed.'

'And Antje is a lawyer!' Dr Schirker exclaimed in disbelief.

I was speechless. For some unknown reason, Dr Schirker had taken his heavy briefcase with him. I could just imagine the scene: my polite and subdued lawyer carrying a load of files, my sister overwhelmed – only Joachim would have had the quickness of mind to grasp the situation but he was unable to run due to his physical disability.

Dr Schirker muttered: 'We need to get the court order and present it to Hans-Peter's local lawyer,' and he set off down the corridor. Fifteen minutes later he was back.

'I can't believe it. There's no one around. The judge has gone home. We seem to be the only people in this desolate building. But I finally managed to find a secretary. She'll type the order.'

147

We waited. My sister and I lit more cigarettes.

The secretary was ready and Dr Schirker went off to deliver the order. He came back, beside himself:

'Do you know what's happened? Hans-Peter's Verden lawyer has closed his office. There's no one there. They've all walked out and simply shut down for the day! I couldn't serve the court order.'

Joachim was the only one who still had his wits about him.

'We'll have to find a bailiff. Is there a phone anywhere?' he asked.

We found a small room with a telephone equipped for local calls only. Court order in hand, Dr Schirker began dialling the numbers on the list the secretary had given him. But Verden was closing its ranks and its doors to outsiders. No bailiffs were available. One was out to lunch, another was off duty, a third otherwise engaged . . .

'Phone Hans-Peter's father, maybe he'll see sense,' Joachim suggested.

'Dr Volkmann? This is Dr Schirker, I am your daughter-in-law's lawyer. Your son is acting irresponsibly . . .'

'My son isn't here. I don't know where he is.'

'Dr Volkmann, this isn't a game. This is extremely serious. Please tell us where your son is. He has abducted the children and defied a court order. Are you aware that he's risking a jail sentence? You must be sensible and realise that this behaviour is not in your son's nor your grandsons' interest. I urge you to co-operate – for everyone's sake.'

'It's none of my business. Nor is the court's decision!'

The conversation was hopeless. Dr Schirker hung up, furious, and disappeared out of the room. There was still no one to be found.

'Where are we? I've never seen a place like this!'

It was four o'clock. The children should have been returned by two.

The door of our room opened and a smiling man walked in.

'I hear you're in a spot of trouble. Tell me,' he said.

Dr Schirker explained the situation and said that we could not locate one bailiff.

'Ah *ja*. I know Hans-Peter Volkmann. A very prominent family in Verden. Dr Hans-Werner Volkmann is a member of the Rotary Club . . . I was never admitted as a member.'

Joachim immediately caught on and joined in the conversation, understanding that we might have discovered an ally. Indeed, within half an hour, two court bailiffs were waiting downstairs for us.

They were both very young and looked hesitant.

'Hm . . . Judge Monkmann? We have to go to Judge Monkmann's property?'

They got into their car with the young lawyer and led the way out of Verden and down a country lane. It was about five o'clock when we turned off on to the forest track leading to Wilfred's and Hans-Peter's houses.

We proceeded along the muddy track, across the abandoned railway line and into private property. All was uncannily quiet and eerie. We stopped the cars between the two houses. The court bailiffs and Dr Schirker got out. Ute's daughters came out of their house on the left and walked towards them. The eldest said hello whilst her twelve-year-old younger sister stood behind her with such an expression of hatred that I shivered. One of the bailiffs asked the fourteen-year-old where the children were.

'No one's here,' she answered, 'and I don't know where they are. Goodbye,' and both girls retreated into the house. My sister, Joachim and I had stayed in the car, frozen by the chilly atmosphere of this desolated place. Even Joachim's zeal had evaporated.

I looked at Hans-Peter's house. Could my sons be hidden there? I got out of the car and asked my lawyer whether we could look inside.

'There's no one here, I'm certain!'

We drove away and tried Hans-Jorg's house back in Verden. The bailiff timidly rang the doorbell. He was extremely ill at ease. He knew the Volkmanns and dreaded his present duty. Hans-Jorg opened the door. His expression was worse than I had anticipated. Arrogant, spiteful, his lip curled as he dismissed us as if we were beggars seeking a handout:

'Neither my brother, nor the children are here. I don't know where they are. Goodbye, gentlemen,' and he closed the door without having said hello or looked at my sister or me.

Dr Schirker was horrified. He turned to his friend, Joachim:

'My God, he was just incredible! I thought the sister was ghastly, arrogant and rude, but this one!'

Our next stop was Hans-Werner and Gundel. My sister and I got out of the car as if we were living through a bad dream.

No answer. The bailiff rang again.

Finally Gundel opened the door. Hans-Werner, standing behind her, looked old and tired. As usual Gundel took over.

'*Nein*, the children aren't here and I don't know where they are.'

I moved forward.

'Gundel, please,' I said. 'Tell me were my sons are. I'm their mother . . .' I had tears in my eyes and although I knew the appeal would prove useless, I still hoped.

'You think I'm hiding them? Please search the house!'

The bailiff was getting very embarrassed.

'Catherine I do not know where your children are and I don't want to know. This has nothing to do with us. I've always been a good grandmother to them,' and she shut the door on us.

We returned to our cars. The bailiffs quickly took their leave, relieved their job was over. I had no tears left. My mind was empty and my body drained.

'I'm leaving,' the young lawyer announced. 'Tomorrow I have an early meeting at the office. Could you drop me at the train station in Bremen.'

I had lost my *sons*. Two small boys had been spirited away from their mother in a most horrific conspiratorial way. Justice was on my side, Hans-Peter was acting like a criminal – but my lawyer had another meeting to attend.

Only Joachim seemed to care.

'But what about Celle? Isn't that where the higher court is? It's only forty minutes away. I think we ought to drive there first.'

'Well, I don't know. Let's wait till tomorrow,' suggested Dr Schirker. My sister and I were too overwhelmed by our day to add anything.

However, knowing the end of the story, I do not believe it would have changed anything had we driven to Celle – the Volkmanns and the Monkmanns were far too well established.

After we dropped the lawyer off, we found a hotel in Verden for a sleepless night. The next morning, the four of us met the bailiff in front of the court building as arranged.

Dr Schirker dropped the court order into Hans-Peter's lawyer's office just opposite. Then we set off on our vain search. Our last stop was Gundel's house. She still claimed not to know the whereabouts of the children. As we were about to drive off to the police station to report Hans-Peter, we saw Klaus walking towards the house, carrying a bag from the bakery. It must have contained more than a dozen buns. Dr Schirker jumped out of the car. The two of them stood in the street, talking for what seemed to be a very long time.

'But the children must be in the house!' I exclaimed.

'Klaus has certainly brought enough buns for an army,' mused Joachim.

'Well, why can't we go in and have the order executed?'

'Calm down. Dr Schirker must be dealing with this,' my sister answered.

We waited. Dr Schirker finally came to the car.

'Well, we may be getting somewhere. Klaus wants to

151

meet me at eleven at a coffee house to discuss handing over the children, but let's go to the police station and report Hans-Peter first.'

I was worried. Dr Schirker seemed to be overcome by what had happened. He had never come across such difficult people in his customary commercial litigation. I feared he was being naive.

I could not blame Joachim's friend. Joachim was a very loyal person. Criticising his friend would be unkind, especially when he had been so helpful and supportive.

And at that time I did not know about German law or its application and felt insecure, yet instinctively I realised we were being too 'civilised', especially when my sons' future was at stake.

I conferred with my sister in Russian. She felt Dr Schirker was a lawyer and no doubt knew how to deal with the situation.

I fell silent. We reached the police station. A constable calmly led us into his office and began taking long notes about our case which he then dictated to a secretary. He wanted us to stay until she finished typing it to check if all was correct. Why did he need a full report? I wondered. We had the court decision in hand, ordering the immediate return of the children to England – with the help of the police force, if necessary. I had expected him to launch a police search. I remembered how, the year before, a Frenchman who had abducted his son, had been chased by the French police and sent to jail for seven years. But here in Verden the police saw Hans-Peter as their next-door neighbour and a pal, court order or not.

Time was speeding by. It was five minutes to eleven. Dr Schirker was getting impatient. Finally, the policeman was satisfied with his well-written report and let us go. We rushed back to the car.

'Joachim, you'd better go to the court building with Véronique and Catherine and get an Interpol alert while I go and meet Klaus. We have to make sure Hans-Peter doesn't leave the country.'

'Leave the country?' I thought. Hans-Peter wouldn't leave the country – where else could he be better protected than in Verden!

Véronique, Joachim and I walked into the red brick modern block. Today there seemed to be people around, but none were ready to help:

'*Nein*, it's the other office, down the corridor.'

'Oh, they must have made a mistake, I don't deal with these matters, try the second office on your left.'

'Sorry, he's out on his coffee break.'

Joachim was furious. I could see the veins on his forehead dilating. A woman approached us.

'What can I do for you?' she asked in a severe, unsympathetic voice. Joachim explained.

'Let me see the court decision.' Véronique handed it to her.

'Well, I see . . .' and she went on without my being able to understand. Then she pointed towards another office door and turned to leave.

'Véronique, the papers?'

The woman was holding them tightly to her chest as if she wanted to keep them.

'Oh, yes of course,' and she handed them back.

We knocked on the door and a voice called: 'Come in.'

Joachim walked in first. I followed him and turned towards my sister in horror: 'It's Wilfred Monkmann's sister!' I exclaimed in Russian. We looked at each other as if we had just seen a ghost.

'Hello, Catherine.'

'Hello, Sophie.'

Joachim started to explain what he needed, completely unaware of the situation.

'Well, I'm sorry. I can't do anything for you.'

'And why not?' Joachim's voice was trembling with anger, but he remained courteous.

'Because your lawyer is not here.'

'This is completely irrelevant. Here is the court order – '

She looked at it.

153

'No, I'm sorry. I can't help you.' She stood up and led us back to the door. Then she turned towards me:

'Yes, and how are you, Catherine?'

I do not know what came over me, but I smiled and answered her politely. I had been so affected by the daunting events of the past two days that I was too frightened to reply otherwise.

We walked towards the Café Jens on Verden's main street. My thoughts were in a blur, I felt strange, the blood was streaming away from my head and suddenly everything went blank . . . When I opened my eyes Joachim and Véronique were leaning over me, trying to help me up from the footpath.

'Catherine, we'd better go and eat something. Are you all right? How's your head? You fell backwards, straight on to the ground. Are you sure your head is OK?' Véronique held me by one arm, Joachim by the other, until we reached the coffee house.

My head did not hurt – but everything else did. We ordered some food and waited. It was three o'clock when Dr Schirker finally appeared.

'I had a long conversation with Klaus. In principle they agreed to return the children by five o'clock . . .' Then he hesitated, as if realising for the first time the meaning of what he was about to say, 'but Klaus mentioned something about the Celle court. I'd better be there.'

The children back? At five o'clock? I so desperately wanted it to be true – but I couldn't believe it. Dr Schirker came back:

'I've just talked to the judge in Celle. He said Dr Volkmann has lodged an appeal against yesterday's decision. The judge accepted it and ruled that until the case is heard Hans-Peter should keep the children, because you might try to hide them in England if they are given back to you.'

'What? What do you mean, accepted the appeal?'

'Well, Celle is the higher court and appeals can be lodged there.'

'But that's impossible! How could the judge accept an appeal when Hans-Peter was in contempt of court, when he was reported to the police? How could he accept an appeal without even informing us and letting us defend ourselves? How can the children not be returned to England when the judge in Verden ordered their return?' I was beside myself. I guess Judge Monkmann accompanied Hans-Peter to Celle. We were tricked and Celle is supporting Hans-Peter's illegal actions!'

Véronique took me in her arms:

'Calm down. All is not lost. Hans-Peter can't get away with this!'

'But the boys! Where are my boys? I want to see my boys. They've been tricked, too, by their own father. Imagine what they must have been told when they were running out of the café! What lies are they being fed? And what were my boys doing at a psychologist's house for ten days? My poor, poor boys.' I was sobbing, my head in my hands. Joachim and Véronique were silent, absorbing the full tragedy of the situation.

Dr Schirker spoke first. 'Well, there's nothing more I can do for the moment. I'd better return to Munich. I think I can catch a plane from Bremen in a hour. As for you, there's little point in staying here now, you had all better go home, too.'

The three of us drove back to Hamburg. I sat in the back of the car, resigned and depressed, looking blankly at the fields streaming past. My children were hidden away somewhere and held prisoners, their little minds tortured . . . Joachim saw my blank expression in the car mirror.

'Catherine. Don't worry so much. We'll win in Celle! I know how you feel, but try to look at it just as a snag, not the final outcome. Hans-Peter won't be able to defy the law for ever. Our only problem will be that here family law is different from England and France. In Germany, the "will" of a child is taken into account – even at Alexander's age. This is what Hans-Peter is basing his

155

case on and he'll continue to influence the boys into saying they want to remain in Germany. However, the judges in Celle will be aware of this and will have to consider Hans-Peter's illegal behaviour. They'll also have to examine the evidence. Your boys were excellent at school and everyone knows how indicative this is of a child's mental stability and home environment. What you must do is get your friends who know Alexander and Constantin to give their testimony. Catherine, I know how much Alexander and Constantin love you. Hans-Peter won't be able to destroy that – at least not in the long term.'

The three of us parted, sad and exhausted. I felt lost, betrayed and frightened and could not stop worrying for my boys. There was something so threatening about the Monkmann property lost in the woods, the abandoned railroad track, the mist hanging over the long muddy road and the two lone houses, cut off from the world. It reminded me of the scary fairy tale 'Hansel and Gretel'. My sons were out there, lost in the forest without my arms to protect them. Verden, the social worker, the drawn curtains and closed doors belonged more to a horror movie than to reality. I was overwhelmed by an awful sense of fear.

But this was only the beginning of the most terrifying nightmare my sons and I now live.

Chapter 12
The Abyss

*The evil of modern society isn't that it creates racism
but that it creates conditions in which people who
don't suffer from injustice seem incapable of caring
about people who do.*

— Louis Manand

I returned to my empty London home. The presents were
still lying on the beds with the school books. The Lego
knights and pirate boats were still neatly arranged in the
wardrobe, the cars lined up on the windowsill, the big
American flag hung on the yellow wall of my babies'
room. All was still.

I closed their bedroom door. The entrance hall grew
dark, no longer lit by the sun shining through their window. I opened the door again and tried to find solace in
Joachim's words:

'Think of it just as a snag. Your children will be back!'

But everything was worrying: 'In Germany, a child's
wishes are taken into account.' I felt sure their wishes
were being manipulated. This would be the only way of
conditioning children to reject their own mother and I
knew now that Hans-Peter was capable of even that.

On Friday, 23 September, surprisingly I reached Hans-
Peter at home:

'Hello, Hans-Peter? It's me.'

'What do you want?'

'Well . . . I'd like to talk to the children.' I heard Hans-
Peter's voice: 'Alexander. Tell her!' Alexander came to the
telephone.

'Hello.'

157

'Hello, Alexander. It's Mummy.'

Silence.

'Alexander, I was in Verden two days ago. I wanted to see you, but I didn't know where you were.'

'I won't tell you!' His voice was aggressive, shut off and distant. He had obviously been told that he was being hidden from me – the enemy! Alexander was repeating coldly a series of ready-made sentences conveyed to him by adults.

'Alexander, aren't you going to school? School started six weeks ago.'

'That's not true! You're lying!'

'Of course I'm not lying. Why should I lie? I've never lied to you.'

'Yes, you lie. And the judge lied too. He's an idiot!'

Alexander had never spoken in this way. Even his voice was different: cold and bitter, similar to his father's. I was horrified at what my son was saying and of how alien he was to the boy who had left London three months ago. I tried to change the subject but there were few avenues open. I found out that Masha was still there, and how nice she was!

'But you never liked Masha. She was too strict and grumpy. Don't you remember how you and Constantin used to imitate her nagging? And we were so pleased when she finally left.'

'That's not true. She was strict because you forced her to be strict.'

'Do you want to speak with Constantin?' And Alexander passed the phone over without saying good-bye. Tini was different. There was no bitterness or aggression in his voice. He did not retire into self-defensive coldness. On the contrary, a thin little whine of a voice came on:

'Mummy?'

'Yes, darling. How are you?'

'OK,' he said in a weak and unconvincing tone. I felt so sorry for him.

158

'Tini?'

'Yes . . .'

I felt he wanted to say something, but was scared to.

'Tell me, Tini?'

'No . . . I have to go now, Mummy. Bye.'

I pictured them – Constantin abandoned and distressed, Alexander overburdened and angry. I imagined how Hans-Peter and Antje had panicked after seeing Véronique, Joachim and the lawyer in the café. How hysterically they had executed their next move, insulting Dr Schirker and the judge, screaming at the children and defaming their mother. Maybe Tini had asked, 'But why are we running away from my mummy?' and had been scolded.

Alexander was probably terrorised by his father's aggression and single-mindedness. Cornered, under his control, he had no choice but to conform. Yet the upheaval in his mind was such that it had made him angry and aggressive.

I agonised about my sons' well-being, grieved at their loss, and was tortured by the thought of what was being done to them. As their mother I could sense how deeply unsettled Alexander was and I could hear Constantin calling for me in his dreams. How did Hans-Peter respond to their fears? What was he doing to harness them? Thinking about what they were undergoing made me shudder.

I was also increasingly alarmed by the legal development of the case – justice was on my side, yet the courts' decisions had not been carried out. My sons were still unreachable and the way Hans-Peter had obtained a stay of execution on Celle boded ill.

On 20 September 1994, a further summons had been issued by the High Court of Justice under Article 8 of the Child Abduction and Custody Act of 1985 and Article 15 of the Hague Convention with an order for it to be disclosed in the proceedings in Celle. The Verden decision had also been explicit: 'The retention of the children is unlawful . . . The children are only 7 and 9 years old and

159

in the view of the court there can thus be no question of considerable intent on the part of the children . . . The expert opinion obtained by the father is to be viewed with reservations. It has been obtained for the sole purpose of supporting his view . . .'

A consultant physician at a prominent London teaching hospital with professional experience of children and senior lecturer in medicine at London University read the report and wrote:

It is not clear to me why the children had to travel to this island to see this particular doctor. My information is that Dr Schoen is not a leading expert in child psychology and that other experts could have been more easily contacted (closer to Verden). It would be important to determine why Dr Schoen was specifically requested to issue this report . . . It is extremely important to note that the report was prepared following interviews with Hans-Peter Volkmann and the children but in the absence of the mother . . . This failure to interview independently all the parties involved, indeed even to comment on this failure, seriously prejudices the professional integrity of the report. Dr Schoen identifies a number of disturbing factors: discontinuity of care, that the mother is not around, the nervous symptoms of the boys, the angst displayed by Constantin, the aggression of Alexander towards his mother, the sense that the children are being verbally manipulated . . . Whilst these symptoms are presented as evidence that there is a poor relationship between the mother and the children, alternative interpretations of these symptoms should have been considered. At the time of the interview the children had not seen their mother for three months. It is quite extraordinary that an expert in child behaviour would not take account of this important issue . . . An alternative interpretation is that the children's behaviour at the time of the interview reflected the problems encountered since their abduction . . . [and] the effects on children in a disrupted environment who have been under the care of one parent who is aggressive towards the other parent . . . These symptoms could be the result of discontinuity of care, the fact that the mother is not around, the nervous symptoms of the boys, the angst displayed by Constantin, the strong aggression of Alexander towards his mother, the sense that the children are being verbally manipulated . . . Dr Schoen's professional independence is in conflict with his interpretation of much of the data presented. He has concluded that the children's return to London would cause severe psychological damage. This is a most serious allegation, yet his professional judgement must be questioned. In summary, I found this report fundamentally flawed. It has a biased interpretation of the observations.

In the meantime, Dr Schirker was still unable to obtain a date for the Celle hearing – he would be advised in due course. By the end of the first week of October I was frantic, realising that the longer the children were under Hans-Peter's influence, the more rehearsed they would become. I implored Dr Schirker to enquire further. The judge could only be reached in two days' time. Two days later he was celebrating his birthday with the staff and could not be disturbed. We had to wait – but how can a mother wait patiently when she believes her children are in danger?

Finally, a date for the hearing was set: 20 October – just within the one'month limit. The director of the Lycée, teachers and friends provided me with detailed statements. The teachers praised the boys' academic results; the director testified how well integrated and popular with their classmates they were; parents confirmed how polite, gentle and happy they were; my friends (most of whom have known me for over twenty years) testified how devoted a mother I was, and my past and present

161

employers, that I was a responsible individual. Everyone told me not to worry, that justice would prevail, the law was on my side, all the evidence was in the court and Leonard, Alexander's godfather, would accompany me as a witness and for moral support.

I hesitated about which lawyer to use. Dr Kram, the Munich lawyer, had reappeared and was willing to take the case back. He was a specialist in Hague Convention cases. Dr Schirker was not. I conferred with my parents, my sister and my close friends until we reached a unanimous consensus: stay with Dr Schirker. He would surely be less trusting now that he knew what we were dealing with.

On 19 October 1994, Leonard and I flew to Hanover where we met Joachim, my sister and the two lawyers and we drove to Celle that evening. I felt nervous and unsettled. How would my sons react to me? They had not seen me for four and a half months, had hardly been allowed to speak on the telephone and I assumed Hans-Peter had indoctrinated them further, perhaps taking them to his psychologist again.

The atmosphere in Celle was very different to that of Verden with its quaint streets and picturesque houses. The High Court of Lower Saxony, situated in this town of 50,000 inhabitants, was in an old building in the town centre. Winter had arrived.

The court building was deserted and we waited apprehensively in the cold corridor.

At five minutes to two, the two lawyers and I went to sit in the empty courtroom, leaving Véronique, Joachim and Leonard outside. We waited in silence. At ten minutes past two a crowd of people arrived. Hans-Peter, Klaus, two other lawyers, Judge Monkmann, Frau Kranitz (the social worker) and my two little boys walked straight into the courtroom while the rest of their party remained outside in the small ante-room. They had an aura of hysteria about them. I could see Ute, Antje and two men I did not know standing outside. Hans-Peter and his lawyers went to sit in their allocated places opposite the judges' tribune, to our right. The rest sat on a bench behind us, my sons next to Wilfred Monkmann. At that moment the three judges, in black robes, walked through the door opposite us. It seemed they had arrived with the others.

My boys . . . I left my seat and hurriedly approached them. I knelt on the floor to kiss them. Alexander's face was hardly recognisable – angry and tense. I bent forward.

'Hello, Alexander,' I said in French.

He did not look at me and started to hit me with his arms and legs. I was flabbergasted, shocked, staggered. Wilfred stared at him fixedly. What had they done to my children? I turned to Constantin, tears in my eyes:

'Tini?'

He turned his head to the side to avoid looking at me. My God, what have they done to the poor boys! I ran out of the courtroom, sobbing. My friends surrounded me, but I felt alone in my agony. Anyone could hate me but being rejected by one's own children is beyond human endurance. Dr Schirker came over quickly:

'Don't worry, the judges must have realised how manipulated your sons are. No child would react so to his mother. Just stay calm.' I wiped away my tears and went back into the courtroom in a complete daze. Nothing could have hit harder, no emotion could have been deeper.

I looked at Hans-Peter, surrounded by his lawyers. He was staring at the top of the wall opposite, his hands joined together as though in prayer. I shivered.

The judge started talking and the boys were led out by Wilfred, who then returned to his seat behind me. My second lawyer stood up to speak his only sentence during the whole hearing:

'We would like to ask the court whether court bailiffs could be provided as we would not like to see a repetition of last month's events.'

He sat down and the main judge proceeded. He talked

163

at length while his two colleagues looked straight ahead.

I did not understand a word the judge said, nor any of the long statements made by Hans-Peter's lawyers. Finally, the three judges stood up and took off their black robes. My lawyer whispered to me: 'They're going to interview the children now.'

'But they've been brainwashed for months. You saw how Alexander reacted! This is awful . . . and awful for them.' I was saying the words but was incapable of thinking straight, overpowered by events, unable to understand the procedures, dependent on my lawyers.

Hans-Peter's party rushed out of the courtroom into the small ante-room immediately outside and Hans-Peter led Alexander into another room for his private interview with the judges. We joined my party; they had been waiting in the larger waiting area leading off the ante-room. All three had a quiet doom-laden expression. Leonard and I decided to go back to the ante-room. Little Constantin was sitting on Hans-Peter's lap shielded by a group of tall adults. As we walked in, Hans-Peter turned Constantin round on his lap so that his back was to us. His party was sitting all around the room: however, one chair in the far corner was free, so Leonard and I sat down, sharing it. Leonard said hello to both Hans-Peter and Constantin but was completely ignored. He persevered with Constantin, asking him how he was, but he would neither answer nor look at Leonard; his head was still turned away. I tried as well, softly calling his name. He moved his head but he would not answer. Hans-Peter kept distracting him with little toys and some sweets that were lying on the table. As both Leonard and I periodically tried to talk to Constantin, Hans-Peter readjusted him on his lap to face the opposite way from us while Ute, Antje, the social worker and Klaus were actively talking to each other in excessively loud voices – as if to muffle mine.

Constantin's unease was obvious and I detected an expression of irony on his face – as if this was part of a game he had to perform. He sat still and let himself be handled. This was so unlike the little boy he used to be, independent, full of energy and endless talk. Leonard and I were so struck by it that we sat silent for a while.

A man came up and barked at us: 'Get up, I want to sit here!' Leonard's basic German was enough for him to understand what the man had said. We looked at each other, shocked by his rudeness, and ignored his request.

This was Dr Schoen, the psychologist. I felt frightened. Constantin turned his head towards me as I tried to say a few words. I sensed he wanted to tell me something but Hans-Peter immediately turned him and took out a book to show Constantin. I turned around and noticed that Dr Shoen had remained standing behind me, his eyes fixed on Constantin. Automatically I jumped up to stand between them to block Dr Schoen's field of vision and shield my son.

At this point, the door on the side of the room opened and Alexander walked out. His face was pale, his hair dishevelled; he looked tormented. Hans-Peter hurried towards him,

'So what did you say?' he asked. Taking him by the hand he rushed out of the ante-room through the waiting area and into the corridor. Constantin was led by Ute through the door for his private interview. The psychologist, Ute, Antje, Klaus, Wilfred, the social worker and the other man (another social worker, apparently) hurriedly left to join Hans-Peter and surround Alexander.

Véronique, Joachim and the two lawyers stood at the other end of the waiting area. Véronique and Joachim were still distraught and shocked by the hysterical behaviour and belligerence of Hans-Peter's party. While I was in the courtroom, Véronique and Joachim had tried to say hello to Ute and Antje but had been ignored. Ute's fiercely hostile expression had paralysed them. My lawyers had an unmistakable air of defeat about them. Only Leonard had any strength left and could think coherently.

'Let's try and talk to Alexander,' he suggested.

We walked down the corridor, Leonard leading the way. As soon as Hans-Peter saw us, he grabbed Alexander by the hand and directed him towards the men's room.

'Leave him alone!' Hans-Peter screamed at me. Leonard and I stood still. Finally, they came out. Leonard walked forward:

'Hello, Alexander. How nice it is to see you.'

'You can keep your money and your chocolates and go away,' Alexander shouted aggressively as he was whisked away towards Ute and the psychologist.

Leonard was speechless. Alexander used to love his godfather, whom he saw often. They had a running joke about their mutual love of chocolates and when Leonard telephoned, Alexander would rush to talk to him first – about chocolates! For Christmas and for his birthday, Alexander would receive some money. This was his favourite treat, and he would proudly put it in his own bank account.

When Constantin emerged from his fifteen-minute talk with the judges, there was a slight ebb in the hysterical behaviour of Hans-Peter's party. The judges called us back into the courtroom. Hans-Peter, his three lawyers, the social worker, Judge Monkmann, my two lawyers and I went in; the rest stayed outside.

The senior judge spoke, but the only moment I was able to follow was when Frau Kranitz spoke. The Verden Social Services had themselves appealed against the decision of 20 September. I never understood how this was possible. Neither Frau Kranitz, nor anyone in her department, had ever talked to me nor to the boys' schoolteachers and no enquiry about the children's lives in London, their school results or our social conditions was ever made. I wondered how their testimony, which represented one side, could be acceptable.

Frau Kranitz used exactly the same words as she had done the month before in Verden, and again mentioned the word 'Nazi'. I turned to Dr Schirker and muttered that he should intervene. He held my hand still:

'No. Let the judges decide. They have the information we've sent them and they know. Stay calm, don't worry.' But I worried like mad and felt uncomfortable and helpless. The court recessed for a second time – the judges were to make their decision.

Before the first recess, Leonard had managed to approach the children as we were in court. As he recounted in his later report:

Following the children's interview, I sensed a slight lifting in the constant shielding and escorting of the two boys by members of Hans-Peter's party . . . I entered the ante-room and found the children sitting with Hans-Peter's sister, Ute and Dr Schoen. I said hello and sat down with them and was, as before, completely ignored. They continued to talk amongst themselves in German as if I was not there . . . After ten minutes, Dr Schoen was called out . . . There followed a silence so I turned to Antje and asked her how she was. She seemed startled, but she did reply. I was so encouraged by the first civil interchange that I had had with any member of Volkmann party that I continued to talk about my children and asked her about hers . . . The door leading to the waiting area opened behind me and the boys looked over and ran out. I did not see who beckoned them out . . . I then suggested to Antje we go out to the waiting area to find something to drink. The two boys were sitting at a table fiddling with some playing cards. I walked over and sat with them. Antje followed me and sat opposite me. I suggested playing cards. To my surprise, Alexander (who had still not spoken to me except for the one hostile remark) began to deal the cards . . . Constantin began to laugh and joke with me – for those few minutes he was the jolly little boy I know. Alexander was more guarded, asking Antje where his father and Ute were. However, he also began to loosen up . . . Catherine appeared from the

167

courtroom and I called her to come over. She pulled up a chair and joined us while we played the game. This continued for a few minutes, till I saw Hans-Peter appear in the distance. He saw us and immediately gesticulated to Alexander to come. Alexander put his cards down on the table at once and ran to him. Constantin followed behind him. We never finished the game.

I had no further chance of direct contact with the children again as they spent the remainder of the time sitting in the small ante-room surrounded by members of Hans-Peter's party.

Leonard and I tried to approach the children, but again it was impossible. Ute held Constantin in her arms facing the window, the psychologist standing next to her and other members of Hans-Peter's party surrounding them. Alexander had disappeared with Hans-Peter. We had no choice but to wait and worry in silence while Joachim and Véronique were talking about the members of Hans-Peter's group, trying to work out what could link them together.

We were called back. This time, Véronique also sat at the back as we decided that since Judge Monkmann had been present during the whole proceedings, there should be no reason why members of my party could not listen in. The tension was high but I felt resigned. The same judge, sitting in the middle, spoke and started reading out the decision. He glanced at me above his glasses while reading. I knew then what the outcome would be but I hung on to the rational notion that the law was on my side:

'. . . We declare that the children, and particularly Alexander, have expressed a strong desire to remain in Germany . . . The appeals of the father and the Youth Welfare Officer are upheld . . . The [return of the children] is rejected pursuant to Article 13 of The Hague Convention, since the children have decisively opposed such return . . .'

I burst out: 'But I'm their mother! You haven't even heard me.' Silence.

I collapsed in tears. Hans-Peter, Klaus, Wilfred and the social worker hurried out to the ante-room to join Ute, Antje, Dr Schoen and the other man, who were all standing at the door. There was uproar followed by delirious whoops of joy. I heard voices shouting several times: '*Wir haben gewonnen! Wir haben gewonnen!*' – We won! They laughed and kissed each other noisily, jumping and punching the air as if they had just won a football match. Alexander participated in this unbridled joy. Constantin looked puzzled and uneasy.

I was still crying and completely ignored by them all, when I saw Alexander marching into the courtroom, as if he were a little soldier in Red Square, up the steps of the tribune to shake the judge's hand. I was wide eyed, horrified and destroyed.

Still shrieking with joy, they began to lead the children away. I stood up and rushed behind them trying to say goodbye to my children as they left. My attempt was quickly rebuffed by Hans-Peter who shouted at me in German: 'Go away!' As my boys were led quickly away, surrounded by the large group, including the social worker and the psychologist, Constantin turned round to look at me, a deeply sad expression in his beautiful blue eyes as if to say: 'Mummy, help!' But Antje pulled him away and I only saw my little Tini being dragged by the hand, his head still turned towards me.

The crowd disappeared and silence fell on us. I slumped on a chair, my head between my knees. My lawyers were discussing the proceedings with Joachim who was desperately trying to find a way in which we could save the situation. For a moment I felt antagonistic towards these professionals who had been so passive and intimidated. They would be returning to their families now, having simply lost one case amongst many others and their lives would go on undisturbed. I had lost my sons.

We left and once the lawyers had gone, Véronique,

Joachim, Leonard and I went over the details of the day and the attitude of Hans-Peter's group. What had been the most shocking and traumatic was their hysterical behaviour and the jubilant cheering which followed the decision. They had vociferously celebrated their triumph – the separation of children from their mother, before the very victims whose lives they had destroyed.

As Leonard wrote:

The continual shadowing and shielding of the children not only by their father, his sister and his neighbours, but also by the professional experts brought into the case by Hans-Peter – the social worker and psychologist. The latter, Dr Schoen was particularly pervasive, constantly talking to the children, following them about or staring at them . . . The aggression and hostility of Alexander towards his mother and me was particularly shocking. This is a boy whom I have always known to be a well-balanced, well-behaved and gentle child. Catherine could not go near him (or Hans-Peter) without being shouted at with great hostility. Constantin's docile, blank and puzzled expression, his passive avoidance of both his mother and myself was so sad to see in a little boy who I again know to be so full of life, as well as of spontaneous affection towards his mother. These were simply not the happy, well-balanced children who had left for their summer holiday to Germany four months ago. Only for those few minutes, during our card game did they begin to resemble the children I know.

I had asked Leonard to write a report on what he had witnessed: 'But can you do it soon, while all the details are fresh in your memory?'

'Catherine, I could write as detailed a report in ten years' time! I will never forget what I saw today. It was a ghastly, unspeakable nightmare that will stay with me for ever. Those poor children – what has been done to them?'

My parents were – thank goodness – in London for my return, sharing the tragedy and trying to comfort me. I sobbed through the night unable to rest or calm myself. Nothing and no one could console me any more and my agony was uncontrollable. I was in a horrendous nightmare. Justice had betrayed my sons and deprived them of their birthright: their own mother.

My friends and my parents were outraged and heart-broken. They rallied around me with warmth and determination. Some wrote letters to the central authorities, others gathered legal information and two girlfriends secretly set off to raise money to help me with the legal bills. Charlotte, a Greek woman whom I had only met a few times, contributed £2,000 to my cause, as did a Danish friend; even a man whom I had never met chipped in as well; all in all, over £20,000 was raised. The unstinting support of my friends and their profound generosity has touched me deeply. Without their loving care, I would probably sunk then. They kept my belief going and with it my life.

A few weeks after the Celle hearing, I received the court decision. It was faxed to me in the office. I sat in the conference room and read through the twelve pages:

Following the hearing of the children, the court is also persuaded that they have attained an age and maturity in view of which it appears appropriate to take their opinion into account . . . [since] a 7 year old child faced with the decision to join either the judo or football club generally knows which decision to make . . . Alexander buried his head in his arms on the table and remained sobbing . . . Alexander justifies his decision . . . not on grounds of the personal characteristics of one or the other parent, but primarily with the statement that he is German. In response to the simple enquiry as to whether the English are 'different' he was unable to

171

explain . . . He confirmed that he has no friends at school, apart from his brother, as he is the only German there and is teased and called a.'Nazi' . . . In Hamburg he did not apparently feel restricted in terms of the available facilities for play since the French Lycée in Hamburg is attended by many German children . . . The mother always bought only the most expensive clothes for herself, while buying clothes from cheap shops for the children . . . the mother was never there . . . weekends (were) spent in polite walks through Hyde Park . . . Alexander's entire environment is based on a foreign language, since German is not spoken either at school or at home . . . the court is persuaded that the boy is undergoing considerable suffering and is convinced that his mother 'simply took' his brother and him away with her. He thus feels even more abandoned in what he regards as an alien environment . . . In view of the other social and cultural differences, in particular the apparently demanding school tuition . . . Alexander's refusal to return to his mother is perfectly understandable . . . The members of the court are also not lacking in appropriate personal experience, in that they are all fathers and grandfathers . . . [and in less than a page] Constantin also conveys his own opinion, rather than one externally imposed on him . . . he felt out of place at the school and had no friends and the older children were always teasing him . . . His opinion is also not based on a childish whim but on careful consideration . . . the severe psychological strain is revealed by a manifest physical restlessness which is no longer appropriate for his age . . . His brother was the most important person . . . as he was the only person with whom he could speak German . . .

Hans-Peter had flagrantly violated the law. I had abided by it – yet the court was penalising me and rewarding him, using nationalistic references as the ground for their decisions.

None of my witnesses had been called and I, the mother, had not been heard by the judges. Yet, after interviewing my sons for thirty and fifteen minutes respectively, children who had been under the influence of their father and a psychologist, the judges concluded that it was the boys' 'own' will to remain in Germany. And whilst the Verden judge had estimated that the children were too young for their view to be taken into account, now Constantin was deemed mature enough at seven to decide on his whole future! Yet Alexander, at nine, constantly changed his mind about whether he preferred rugby or football!

I was shaking like a leaf. The Celle court overruled two previous decisions, ordering the 'immediate' return of the children to England under an international convention because they had decided that my sons were 'suffering' in an alien environment and because 'German was not spoken at home or at school'. Although my sons were trinational and trilingual, to the Celle judges they were not French, not English, not European; they were solely German – and this overrode everything else.

The judges felt it was better for children to be raised as Germans and considered that my boys should only play with German children. Pupils at the French Lycée represent sixty different nationalities and in both Alexander and Constantin's classes there were half-German boys like them. The judges considered that the English were 'different' and referred to Alexander having stated that he 'communicates in English to his school friends' when French, his maternal language, was spoken at the French Lycée. 'Alexander obviously thinks in German and is obliged to translate in order to communicate' when no child has a capacity of 'translating'. I, their mother, a foreigner, was of no consequence. Not speaking German amounted to the affliction of psychological harm. Being denied a mother did not!

A German lawyer I met read the decision:

'This is a historical piece!' he exclaimed. 'It could have been dated fifty-five years ago! It only has one aim – the glorification of one nationality. As far as the boys are concerned, it is inconceivable that in the space of such a short interview their psychological state could be established - especially when judges are not qualified child psychologists.'

I took the decision to show it to my friends; I faxed it to the central authorities, to the Foreign Office, convinced that someone would take action. No one did. The Lord Chancellor's department wrote me letters, saying that under the provision of Article 13 children could not be returned . . . My Member of Parliament said there was nothing he could do, the German Central Authority in Berlin stated that the Celle order 'is not appealable – unless the decision violates Constitutional law. However, I would like to point out that the acceptance of a complaint through the Federal Constitutional Court in Karlsruhe really is an exception.' In fact over 95 per cent of applications are rejected. 'However, Ms. Laylle can apply for custody of her children at the Family Court in Verden at any time.'

Under the international Hague Convention, the children should have been returned to England and final decisions on custody taken by the authorities of the children's habitual residence – England. By not returning the children, the Celle court therefore extended the meaning of the Convention by giving an artificial jurisdiction on custody decisions to its own courts.

Not only had Hans-Peter managed to have all his illegalities sanctioned, but he now held an additional advantage, since it was he who had chosen the forum in which custody was to be decided – a forum favourable to him: the Lower Saxony courts.

I had trusted the judicial system yet my boys and I were betrayed by the very institution that should have protected us. Ever since Hans-Peter had realised that our life

in London was a success and that I would not be returning to him, he had embarked on his premeditated and
unscrupulous plan. I had not noticed because I had been
too busy with survival. Now the law was his accomplice
in the ultimate revenge: to strip me of my sons for ever,
regardless of their suffering.

Every night I dreamed the same dream: Alexander in a
dark cloud, tense and tormented, Constantin scared and
distraught, calling out: 'Mummy, help, help . . .' and I
would wake up with a start, sweat pouring from my face.
When I had no more tears left, I would fall back to sleep,
but the dream never left me. In the office, I would try to
switch my mind off – if only for an hour, if only for
minutes. But the nightmare of my days was no better,
divided between panic and despair.

Hans-Peter had proudly married a foreigner, consciously raised his children to be international but since he
was incapable of coping with an attack on his ego, he had
sought refuge in the insularity of his narrow minded community.

Chapter 13
Behind the Wall

My darling angels, finally we were allowed to see each other . . . Alexander, your eyes were sad, and they brought sadness to my heart. You were not free to speak, not even to softly whisper what was in your heart . . . but through your hesitating smiles and faltering eyes, I knew of the shame and pain you were shouldering . . . Constantin, you did not speak in the silence of the house. My ears could not hear you. My heart did. Your gentle smile revealed the secret longings of your heart.

Dr Kram contacted me immediately after the Celle hearing and my parents, my sister, my friends and I decided I should switch to him. After all he was an expert in the field. Dr Kram decided he should meet me, and flew to London the next morning.

Although I was £1,000 poorer, I felt Dr Kram could redress the situation. He presented himself as determined and committed. The Celle decision, which was legally watertight, was particularly 'unusual'; so was the role of Verden Youth Authority. However, as its scope was restricted only to the 'non-return' of the children under the Hague Convention, it had not changed their legal residence, which was still in England, nor the custody provision: under the English law, my sons were wards of court and under German law I still had care and control. Dr Kram stressed we should move fast as time was working against me. Not only were the children under Hans-Peter's control and influence, but Klaus, Hans-Peter's lawyer, would soon benefit from another argument, namely that the children would now be settled in their new environment. 'In custody cases, possession is everything,' he added.

Since Hans-Peter refused me any access, Dr Kram proposed that we apply to the Verden court for an order for access rights immediately. However, our request was rejected. Following the October Celle decision, the Verden judge was on a three-week holiday. The replacement judge stated he could not make a decision since he had not yet received the file from Celle. Furthermore, he could not see the 'urgency of the matter'.

'But I haven't seen my sons for many months. And I don't understand why the judge should not allow a mother to see her children, files or no files, when Celle was able to stay the execution of a court order on 21 September without any files.'

We made further applications – all were rejected. The judge now required a report from the Verden Youth Authority before deciding whether a mother could visit her children. I was incensed:

'But this is crazy! We know in advance what report Frau Kranitz will write. She's testified in court against me twice without having ever met me and was celebrating their "victory" in Celle!'

'Well, let's first wait for the report, then we'll attack it. Frau Kranitz will no doubt contact you soon,' said Dr Kram.

But I did not hear from Frau Kranitz, and therefore no report could be prepared for the court. On 29 November Dr Kram decided to telephone the director of the Youth Authority. An hour later, he rang me:

'I have just had the most outrageous conversation with Mr Lecker, the director of the Youth Authority. He told me that Frau Kranitz has no free time available for you. The earliest she could talk to you would be in two weeks – but only if you personally come to Verden. Telephone or written contacts are out of the question . . . He also advised you to accept the Celle decision and leave your children alone. The quicker you withdraw your demand for custody in the Verden court, the better.'

Dr Kram was fuming. He would send Mr Lecker a fax to record this conversation and stress how inconceivable it was for Mr Lecker to take such a blatant position when he had never met the children, never spoken to the mother, nor enquired about our lives in England, concluding that in his twenty years' experience in family legal matters he had never come across 'such biased attitudes from the Social Services'.

I was up against an insurmountable wall. Even telephone contact was impossible. The few conversations I managed to have with my sons were monitored – Alexander would repeat his same repetitive sentences; Constantin would answer with a tense yes or no. I recorded two of these desperate conversations. The sound of Alexander's blank and robotic words was too depressing and frightening to listen to again.

The boys' friends were upset, particularly Sean. Alexander had given him his phone number in Verden before he left on holiday and had wanted to ask Hans-Peter if he could invite him to stay for a week during the summer. Sean – also aged nine – had tried to call Alexander, but Hans-Peter wouldn't let him speak to his friend. Sean called me, tearful. For six months he kept the desk next to his free for when Alexander came back to school. The boy upstairs reacted in the same way. He would come to see me and ask whether I had heard anything. Then he would walk into the boys' bedroom, sad and petulant:

'I miss them so much. When will Alexander and Constantin be back?'

I would look at this nine-year-old grieving for his friends. Hans-Peter was breaking the hearts of so many people. I wondered if my eighty-two-year-old father would see his grandchildren before he died.

At the beginning of November, I sent a fax to Hans-Peter urging a meeting, whenever he wanted, wherever he wanted, with the help of a mediator. Two weeks later I received a letter from his lawyer, written in German, explaining that no such meetings could take place and accusing me of being a bad mother – I should leave the children alone, stop trying to phone, and comply with their wish to remain in Germany.

Two weeks after that I telephoned again and had my second and last conversation ever with Hans-Peter. He literally yelled. He was illogical and interrupted all my sentences. Throughout our conversation, he was shouting 'I forbid you'. He made no sense.

It started with:

'What do you want?'

'I would like to talk to my sons.'

'Well, they don't want to talk to you. They are afraid that you want to take them away.'

'Over the telephone?'

'The children are scared.' His voice was trembling.

'Why should my children be scared of their own mother? It is -'

'You accused me of being a kidnapper! You are lying. You lied before the court in England. You made your friends lie.'

'I made my friends lie?'

'Well, I don't want to talk to you on those terms.'

'Which terms?'

'I want you to stop making the children's friends phone them, especially when I'm not here. You force their friends to phone them. I forbid you to make their friends phone them. Why don't you forbid their friends from calling? I want them to stop.'

'How could I force their friends? I thought you said in court they have no friends . . .'

He hung up. I dialled again.

'Why did you hang up?'

'I didn't hang up. What do you want? I haven't time to talk to you. I'm busy.'

179

'I would like to talk to the boys. You can't throw me away. I'm their mother. You must realise what harm you're doing the children.'

'I know you're their mother! But what's the point? What do you mean by that?' His voice was quavering even more.

'I think that a mother should be able to speak to her sons when -'

'Well, you can. I'll tell them to call you on Friday.'

'Why should I make appointments to talk to my -'

'On this basis I don't want to talk to you. If you insist on making their friends call I will leave the answering machine on. Especially when I'm not here.'

'But . . .'

'Look I have no time, I don't want to talk to you. You can send me a fax. I don't want to discuss anything with you on the telephone.'

'Well, I'm their mother . . .'

'What do you mean by that?'

'I think that maybe a mother and a father could -'

'Send me a fax in the office. I don't want to talk to you like this. I don't have time.'

'Do you think your children will be proud of the way you speak to their mother?'

He hung up.

Five court demands had now been rejected. I had not spent any time with my sons for six months and the central authorities were avoiding the issue. I knew I had to seek other avenues. Desperation gave me strength. In consultation with friends and after hours of discussion, we decided there was only one alternative left: the media.

I telephoned Dominic Lawson, at that time editor of the *Spectator*, for an appointment. My friends had agreed with my suggestion. The magazine, with a circulation of around 60,000, is a high-calibre and serious weekly and read by people in the government. Approaching the *Spectator* was a cry for help; to publish my story in a

180

tabloid might have been interpreted as a call for scandal which I wanted to avoid.

On 2 December 1994, that week's edition came out. I rushed to the newsagent's. My heart was beating fast as I picked up a copy and saw that my story had hit the front page. The article written by Alisdair Palmer 'Is this what we mean by European Union?' was the main feature on three pages. It was powerful and extremely well-written. Surely something would happen now to help my sons and restore them legally to me.

That very day, the *Daily Mail*, the *Mail on Sunday* and two other major newspapers phoned the *Spectator* wanting the story. I felt unsure and decided to go on hiding, but the *Mail* published our story next day, based on the *Spectator* article: 'Germany defies High Court in tug of war case'.

For months I had fought with my lawyers, written innumerable letters, gathered evidence – all without results. I got thinner, poorer, my sons were still unreachable, yet no one could help! Suddenly, doors opened following the article. My Member of Parliament agreed to meet me, and the authorities in England reacted. I had heard criticism of the press often but I certainly cannot share this view: without its help and support, my sons and I would have remained in oblivion and the issue of child abductions would never have been brought to the public's attention.

In the meantime, a friend wrote to Peter Hartmann, at the time German Ambassador, to bring the article in the *Spectator* to his attention. The Ambassador sent a curt note back.

The following week the *Spectator* published a letter the Embassy had sent them in response to the article. It was signed by the Legal Counsellor to the German Embassy and read:

I refer to your article dealing with a German court's decision concerning the place of residence of two minors. Verdicts in family affairs involving children always have high emotional content – especially for the unsuccessful party . . . If one reads the 11-page judgment in full, every unbiased reader will understand that the judges took great care to ensure the well-being of the two minors – as stipulated by the pertinent Hague Convention of 1980. One would learn that the two children requested rather forcefully to stay in Germany because they were tired of frequently being victims of taunts, such as 'Nazi'. This – by the way – is, unfortunately, an experience they share with many children in the German community of this country.

The German Embassy was taking a stand and jumping to the defence of one of its nationals without even having recorded that the court decision did not concern the place of residence (which was London), but illegal abduction! They referred to me, the mother, as the unsuccessful party when it was I who had abided by the law and as if children were an object of reward. The aim of the Convention was said to be the well-being of the children (which is not the primary aim, but their immediate return) and the Embassy ignored the fact that their interest could hardly be served by separation from their mother for half a year and referred to 'Nazi' when the article had not mentioned the word.

I was so incensed that I spent the weekend preparing my reply:

I am the Franco-British mother whose two boys have been illegally retained in Germany. The views of the Legal Counsellor to the German Embassy in London – and therefore presumably the views of his Ambassador and the Government he represents – were contained in a letter published in your 17 December issue.

The writer sanctions the fact that two young boys

182

were taken away from their mother 'because they were tired of frequently being victims of taunts such as "Nazi"' (allegedly at an international school in London) and gratuitously observes that this is – by the way unfortunately an experience shared with many children of the German community in this country – a truly diplomatic observation!

My children do not belong to the German community. They live with me in London and I am not German. Nor for that matter do we belong to any specific national community – we belong to our friends, irrespective of their nationalities. My children have British, French and German nationalities.

If the word 'Nazi' was ever used (which I doubt very much) shouldn't our reaction as citizens of a united Europe be to disregard such stupid comments? Is this not exactly what we are trying to achieve with a United Europe: the end of such narrow-minded, discriminating attitudes . . .? I find it surprising that the Embassy supports the arguments put forward by my husband: a man who has twice abducted children and defied both English and German courts . . . I have deep respect for the German legal system and its integrity, but I strongly feel that somehow a miscarriage of justice has been committed. I am deeply disturbed to note that your correspondent has not expressed the slightest sympathy or humanity towards a mother whose life has become a horrific nightmare; a mother who has been enduring endless, sleepless nights aching for the proximity of her children and worrying to death about their well-being . . . I am not a politician and certainly not a diplomat, but I will fight – fight for justice, fight against narrow-mindedness. But above all, as a mother, I will fight all the way to restore my boys the human rights and freedom of mind of which they have been stripped . . . Whether I remain alone or not, I will keep alive the hope that somewhere there is still justice, decency and kindness in the world. I will continue to hope that someone will finally hear the cry of two helpless boys and put an end to this human tragedy.

The *Spectator* didn't publish my answer, which was very long. Instead, a letter appeared in the 7 January issue, written by the father of Alexander's best friend in London:

I happen to be the father of one of the children's best friends who often came to our house. I checked with my son and there has never been any Nazi taunting at school. If Mr Trautwein wants to defend his country's legal system, which in the circumstances has behaved weirdly to say the least, he should not use blatant falsehoods which play on the cheap emotional issue of Nazi taunting. He might be drawn into dangerous territory, as the way these children have been snatched away from their mother bears a frighteningly close resemblance to what happened in his country not so long ago.

The distance separating my sons from me was increasing day by day. Germany was pushing me aside. Most of my letters were unanswered. To the first English intervention, the German authorities had abruptly answered that on one occasion three children had been abducted by an English mother and had not been returned to Germany!

Since the beginning of this nightmare, I had spent every free minute of my day writing letters, telephoning and trying to gather support. Two innocent boys were paying the price of Hans-Peter's devious moves and now, as far as I was concerned, the German Embassy was backing his illegalities, heedless of the barbaric treatment of the children.

I telephoned the French Embassy and talked to the Ambassador's secretary, Madame St Gilles. She reacted with ready sympathy:

'You haven't been with your sons for six months? But that's absolutely terrible – you are a mother! I'll tell the Ambassador immediately, of course . . . We'll have to do something to help you.' Two days later, the Consulate was on the telephone with an appointment. This is how I met the Consul, Monsieur Perrier. He was a very busy man, but he listened to my story attentively and with solicitude. We were no longer a file to attend to, but Alexander, Constantin and a mother: 'You have not been with your sons for six months! This is outrageous!'

It was M. Perrier who alerted the French government. It was M. Perrier who rounded up the support and attention of the French authorities. He had nothing to gain from helping me, only an increase in his workload. M. Perrier was there simply because he was a kind and caring human being who was concerned about children and human rights.

My father, who is a man of principle with a strong sense of duty, as most officers of that generation were, became our Paris link. Although no longer of an age to endure such stress, he galvanised himself into making appointments and writing letter after letter. He could not accept such flagrant injustice and corruption – but above all, he was a grandfather. He was depleting his finances, helping his daughter, ruining his weak health, but he would not surrender.

In the meantime, Dr Kram was getting nowhere with the Verden court, nor with Herr Lecker. The latest court refusal stated that I might abduct my sons if a visit were granted!

The local youth authority had finally succumbed to the pressure of the press (the *Daily Mail* had gone to Verden) and the supportive intervention of the British Consulate to concede a two-hour meeting with my children. However, the brief meeting was to be held in the youth authority buildings, under the supervision of the social worker.

'But that's outrageous. My sons were snatched away

185

from me. I haven't seen them for over six months and Frau Kranitz must be present!' I exclaimed to Dr Kram over the telephone.

'I know, Catherine, but you have no choice. They will not let you see the children otherwise. Frau Kranitz told me she will meet you first in order to write the report the court needs.'

I was traumatised and knew this was yet another set-up. I telephoned the British Consul in Hamburg.

'Mr Sullivan, I can't go to this meeting on my own. I need an independent witness to be present – otherwise Frau Kranitz will write a report to suit their ends, irrespective of our conversation.'

Mr Sullivan kindly suggested that a consular representative could accompany me. The Consulate then telephoned the director of the social services, Mr Lecker, to confirm the arrangements for the children's visit and politely requested that a consular representative should attend the meeting with Frau Kranitz.

'Why don't you just bring a whole British delegation while you are at it?'

His tone had been aggressive. It was surprising that Mr Lecker should speak in this insolent way to an accredited member of the diplomatic corps.

We had little choice, but realising the strain I was under, Mr Sullivan suggested that his chauffeur Alan should take us to Verden and that the representative of the Consulate would still accompany us and wait outside the building during the meeting. Nicolette, who knew how distressed I was, kindly offered to join our party, which also included Dr Kram. We left Hamburg early on a Monday morning. I was extremely nervous. I had been through so many emotions during the past months and now finally I would be able to see my children. Yet the thought of the antagonism of Verden, Frau Kranitz's biased attitude and the eerie house frightened me.

My meeting with Frau Kranitz lasted an hour. She greeted me politely and I began, in my inadequate

186

German, to explain the children's lives in London and our relationship. Frau Kranitz took no notes. If, as Hans-Peter (and she) insisted, it was the children's 'will' to remain in Germany, why had he taken them to a psychologist? How could a professional psychologist testify blocking all forms of contact between us and how was it that the children looked so happy in London? To illustrate my point, I showed her a picture of the boys before their summer holidays. She looked at the photograph of little Constantin, blond and blue-eyed amidst his dark-haired French schoolmates, and exclaimed: 'Gosh, there are so many foreigners in his class!'

I did not comment.

'Well, Mrs Laylle, you have to understand that your children are scared. Their father thinks you will kidnap them.'

'But it is he who abducted them! When the boys were living in London, Hans-Peter could see his sons whenever he wanted.'

'Well, maybe. But that's the past. The current situation is that he is scared. In fact, the children are not coming to meet you here later. Dr Volkmann has changed his mind and will only agree to our seeing them at his house.'

'But it has been agreed, and also confirmed with the British Consulate. I am scared to go to Hans-Peter's house and I would like to be with my sons on neutral ground.'

'Well, I'm sorry. I was unable to convince Dr Volkmann. If you want to see your children, you have to accept his terms. I'll meet you back here at three.' We parted.

After lunch we dropped the consular representative at the railway station, met Frau Kranitz as agreed and set off in two cars. It was a cold December day. There was snow on the ground. I was shivering. Would Hans-Peter be waiting at the door? How would the children react? So long without their mummy, prisoners in this fortress and subjected to Hans-Peter's manipulations! Six and a half months at their age would have been an eternity – comparable to years at my age.

We drove into the dense forest, along the misty driveway in silence. A mother was simply going to see her own children, yet this was more like an official statesman's visit: a consular car and the protection of Dr Kram and Nicolette. Both cars turned right and parked in front of Hans-Peter's house. Frau Kranitz and I got out and walked towards it. The other three remained outside in the freezing cold. My heart was pounding but I knew that nothing could prevent me now from marching forward to see my boys.

Hans-Peter was standing in the large entrance hall with Judge Monkmann; both were wearing grey Bavarian jackets; both stood straight and impassive. They greeted Frau Kranitz and shook my hand with contempt. Impatient to see my boys, I walked straight through into the drawing room ahead. It was sparsely furnished and cold. Frau Kranitz followed me. A very tall woman was sitting in an armchair in the left-hand corner of the room. My boys were standing still, facing the door. They did not move as I walked in and although I had expected this in these intimidating circumstances, observed by two strangers and under strict control, the sight of my children, usually full of life and mischief, threw me into dismay.

Constantin did not move, let alone jump into my arms as he had always done. His body was frozen. Yet I could see a gleam in his eyes reflecting the excitement. Immediately, I knew that notwithstanding what he had been through, he was happy to see his mummy, maybe hoping that she could change the course of his existence.

Alexander, on the other hand, seemed distant and his gaze was empty. His eyes, which had always sparkled with life, were dead. The Alexander I knew, naughty, dynamic and emotional, had dissolved into a shadow which was not even that of a child. My boy of nine looked old, as if he had been through too much and was resigned to the cruelty of his existence. My heart sank. The great excitement of seeing my boys had changed to utter help-

188

lessness. The two women remained in the room, watching over us.

My sons . . . No child reacts as they did, passive and controlled – unless he is scared. If only I could take them into my arms, cuddle and comfort them . . . I knew that with gentle words and warmth we would be able to find each other again. Instead, two women were monitoring every move, following Hans-Peter's wish for there to be no privacy between mother and sons, hoping to cut the instinctive bond that ties them together.

Aware of their stress, I retired calmly and sat on the sofa. Constantin walked towards me but he did not dare sit. I asked him what he had been building, pointing at the Lego box on the floor. His movements were slow and inhibited. He answered my questions in an even, flat voice. Despondently I remembered how ebullient their voices once were; how, like all children, their enthusiasm would make them unable to sit still . . .

I had the impression I was sharing the world of two tiny prisoners. Both were pale, drawn and obviously too frightened by the circumstances of this visit to relate to their mother.

They quietly led me upstairs to show me their bedrooms. To my amazement, I saw that the walls of what had been Ute's house had been knocked down, leaving one room to the left, one to the right and a large open space in between where Hans-Peter's mattress lay on the floor. It was as if he was guarding them even through the night!

The bedrooms were small, uninviting and cold. There were hardly any toys, only some Lego and a few books – no Ninja Turtles, no modern games and only one old cuddly bear in Tini's room. The contrast with their bright yellow London bedroom, filled with bears, cars, dinosaurs and other modern toys, was startling. Alexander seemed resigned, as if embarrassed by the destitution of their home. Tini however began to relax, as the two women had remained downstairs. For an instant he forgot himself and did a stand up:

'Mummy, look at what I can do,' Constantin called in German. His voice had livened up and he laughed. Alexander stood limp and silent but I knew I could not venture to take him in my arms.

'Shall we play a game?' I asked.

'I'm not in the mood,' Alexander answered. 'We'd better go back downstairs,' he added. He led the way, hesitating at each step. Constantin climbed on my back, then jumped down startled as he saw the two women waiting for us. Alexander marched towards the sitting room and sat down. Constantin and I joined him at the table, followed by the women. The five of us started a card game. Alexander's expression had not changed but as he lost first he watched over my game and helped me to collect my cards, as if he wanted to look after me and protect me. Constantin was cheering up, making cute grimaces and laughing at what I said. If only I could be with them alone. This was like a trip to hell – my flesh and blood and I could not touch them, not give them what they had been starved of for many months: their mother's love.

Suddenly the room was lit up. I looked at my watch. Two hours exactly. Someone, maybe Judge Monkmann, had switched on all the spotlights on the property to announce the end of the visit. Frau Kranitz turned to Alexander:

'This time your mother came to see you here. How would you like to meet her in Hamburg next time?'

Alexander looked panic-stricken and before we had time to speak, he shot out the door into the hallway. A few seconds later, Hans-Peter stormed in, Alexander shadowing him. Constantin, who had been sitting next to me, immediately ran to the other corner of the room and hid his head in the Lego box. Hans-Peter marched across the room and sat on the windowsill opposite, with Alexander on a chair beside him.

Alexander was looking at his feet and Tini was motionless. The atmosphere was icy.

'Dr Volkmann, this visit went very well,' said Frau

Kranitz. Hans-Peter's lip began to tremble. 'And I suggested to Alexander that since his mother came all the way to Verden, maybe next time a visit in Hamburg could be arranged?'

Hans-Peter was raging with anger. He turned to his eldest son and said in a cutting tone: 'Alexander, do you want to go to Hamburg?'

This sounded like an order, not a question. Without lifting his head, Alexander replied: 'No.'

I felt as frightened as my sons. Hans-Peter's voice had been so commanding, so filled with hate.

'But Dr Volkmann, you must understand . . .' continued Frau Kranitz.

Hans-Peter exploded.

'She's accused me of being a kidnapper. She's talked to the press. Did you see what she said to them? She's a liar.' Hans-Peter stood up, pointing his finger at me: 'She must stop talking to the press . . .' Constantin was inert, head deep in the Lego box, as if he wished it would swallow him up. Alexander looked down, head still lower, at his feet. I felt an overpowering desperation to halt Hans-Peter's delirious screaming in front of the boys. I rushed out to get the presents I had brought from London, to alleviate the tension.

I had been so shaken and distraught that I apparently tripped on the way to the car, Nicolette told me later. As I returned to the house, I could see Hans-Peter through the glass door leading to the drawing room kneeling on the floor, pleading with Frau Kranitz:

'*Bitte*, you must understand . . .' I walked in and Frau Kranitz stood up. She motioned to the children to move forward and the three of us went into the kitchen at the side of the hall. I gave them their presents. They both stared at their parcels. I had never seen my children, any children, not unwrapping presents. I helped them and took out their favourite model, Aliens. Both were quiet. As I turned my head towards the entrance hall, I saw Hans-Peter standing still, glaring intensely at Alexander as if conveying an order to behave in a particular way. I wondered how long these toys would remain in their possession.

I was as subdued as my sons. Judge Wilfred was standing at the door. Hans-Peter snapped his fingers and the children went to stand next to him. I tried to kiss them goodbye, but they stood frozen, too terrified even to say goodbye. I went back to the car and collapsed in Nicolette's arms.

Hans-Peter's house had large windows and Nicolette, Alan and Dr Kram had watched all our movements from the car. They saw my boys and me go up the stairs, Constantin jump on my back and Alexander's unnatural walk.

'Two hours alone with your sons and they would be back to normal,' concluded Dr Kram. 'I've dealt with cases like yours before, but I can tell you the bond between your sons and you is particularly strong. Constantin was nearly like a normal child at one stage. This is quite extraordinary, especially since his father remained in the house during your entire visit.'

'What?'

'Well, as you walked into the sitting room right at the beginning, only Judge Monkmann left the house. Hans-Peter locked the door from the inside, went into the cloakroom and never left the house. Alexander knew he was there. We saw him run to get his father there.' Nicolette went on: 'We were sitting in the car looking at what was happening inside, when Alan heard a truck coming from Judge Monkmann's house. We saw it pass by and presumed it was a man working on the land. Dr Kram thought it was rather odd and decided to go and see. It was Judge Monkmann: he parked his truck across the driveway, blocking the property's exit.'

'This is illegal retention,' Dr Kram commented.

No one could have imagined such a remote, oppressive environment. There is something sinister about it.

The coldness of the house, the bareness of their rooms

and the sadness of their faces were haunting. I remembered the days when we used to snuggle together, how little Tini would tiptoe into my bed, Alexander behind him, and how I used to wake up in the mornings with them stretched across it. Today I saw how they had missed the warmth of our cuddles even more than I had.

All of this had only one apparent justification, one refrain rising from the past and echoing on the lips of those who defended this terrible injustice: German nationality. Two children and their mother had been torn asunder and stripped of all their legal and human rights on the sole strength of four words uttered by a nine-year-old boy: '*Ich bin doch Deutscher.*' Was a united Europe only a chimera? Would my children remain prisoners of a resurgence of deep nationalistic feelings operating against internationally agreed human and judicial rights?

Chapter 14
Man's Injustice

It is hard to accept the injustice of God. Yet, with the passage of time, the pain is assuaged simply because of the recognition that death is the very essence of life. One learns to assume the pain as an intricate part of oneself: there is a confusing beauty in death which draws you closer to God. It is impossible to accept the injustice of Man. Time does not soothe the pain. It only intensifies it – because of the realisation that it is the evil in Man that is its cause. Man's injustice was not only imposed on me but imposed on you, my sons. No mother could live in peace henceforth.

The report from Frau Kranitz was more or less as I had expected. I was still in a state of nervous indignation when I read it:

the visit of December 12 went well. Dr Volkmann is prepared to have a discussion with his wife. Both children reacted positively towards their mother and their initial angst was shed. At the end of the visit, Mrs Volkmann suggested a meeting in Hamburg with the children. Dr Volkmann adamantly refused, stating the wife would take the children back to England. Even with the effort of the youth welfare he would not change his position although he finally agreed to a further visit of four hours in his house, in the presence of Frau Schwarz. The youth welfare would therefore suggest a next visit to be carried out according to Dr Volkmann's wish.

'Brilliant! Another well-sealed report! Frau Kranitz is pretending to take a neutral stand and then blatantly sanctions Hans-Peter's demands!' I exclaimed furiously to Dr Kram who had sent a fax to Klaus reaffirming our request for a ten-day skiing holiday at Christmas. The offer I got back was to spend two hours with the children on the 23rd, and four hours on the 26th and 27th, only in Hans-Peter's house and in the presence of Frau Schwarz.

'They must be joking! I am expected to travel to Verden twice – or do they expect me to spend Christmas alone in a hotel there?'

'Don't worry, I'll write to the court.'

Dr Kram sent an angry report stating that these conditions were entirely unacceptable, especially since last time Dr Volkmann remained in the house and locked me in while Wilfred Monkmann blocked the exit from his property with a truck.

The Verden judge answered that since the parties could not agree he would hold a hearing on 23 December to resolve this matter and that I would be able to see my sons for two hours afterwards. This time, my mother would accompany me. Dr Kram intended to return to Munich after the hearing and it was inconceivable to go to Verden without male protection. My mother is an elderly woman and I was too terrified for words, so I asked Keith to accompany us. I had met Keith once, through a policeman I was in contact with. He had a friend he was visiting in Germany and did not mind chaperoning us.

Keith and I flew to Hamburg together where we met my mother. Alan, who later became my friend, decided he would drive us to Verden. He had been shaken by the reception at our last visit and, as a father himself, felt deeply for me. Dear, kind Alan who spoke fluent German would protect me, then and later.

Verden had become a dreaded ordeal and as soon as we drove into it I was filled with anguish. The memories were oppressive. Dr Kram, my mother and I walked into the red brick court building while Alan and Keith stayed in the car. We were ten minutes early. Again all was deserted and I had a sense of foreboding. My mother, who was experiencing the strange atmosphere for the first time, was extremely nervous.

Suddenly, we heard men's voices coming up the stairs. Hans-Peter, Klaus, the blond lawyer, Frau Kranitz, Hans-Jorg, two unknown giants who looked like bodyguards and a man in his fifties in a black leather jacket and a Russian fur hat surrounded my two children. My mother rushed towards the landing, looking for the grandsons she adored, who had stayed many times in Megève and Paris with my father and her.

'Alexander!' she called, bending down and trying to see his face, which was hidden behind the shield of tall men. Alexander did not answer but continued walking in the middle of the crowd.

'Constantin!' my mother murmured. Tini moved his head towards her, but did not answer. The group of men, my little sons still in the middle, continued walking as a pack towards the larger waiting area. I stood behind my mother, unable to talk, unable to think . . . I heard the judge calling us in. I looked back and saw my mother leaning against the wall, sobbing. I had never seen my mother cry before.

We sat in exactly the same place as on 20 September, except this time I was alone with Dr Kram. Opposite were Klaus, the little lawyer and Hans-Peter. To our left sat Frau Kranitz and the man in the black leather jacket, his Russian fur hat still on. I understood he was the director of the local youth authority, the one who had insolently answered our Consulate. His appearance frightened me, I shivered and looked towards Dr Kram, the only ally I could expect to have in this antagonistic atmosphere.

The judge listened to the two sides and then asked the opinion of the social welfare workers. Herr Lecker spoke. The view of the Youth Authority was that the children should only see their mother in Dr Volkmann's house. They felt they were German, etc . . . and they refused to

196

go skiing with their mother as they feared she would use this opportunity to take them back to England! Herr Lecker glanced at me as he was talking. He had never spoken to me, yet the contempt he seemed to feel for me as a foreigner was so violent that I felt overwhelmed by it.

The judge said he could not make up his mind as to whether I could have the children for Christmas and that he would announce his verdict on 27 December.

'But that's after Christmas!' I whispered to Dr Kram.

'Let's go out for a second. We must discuss a way you could see your children outside Hans-Peter's house this afternoon.'

We asked for leave and went into the waiting area where my mother was standing. A few seconds later, Herr Lecker came out of the courtroom and walked towards us:

'Dr Kram, if your client transfers the custody to Dr Volkmann now, I am sure we could come to some arrangements for Christmas.'

'This is blackmail!' I exclaimed.

We went back into the courtroom to suggest my seeing the boys in a Verden public place of their choice.

'My client is prepared to surrender her passport to the court and for police protection to be brought if need be. My client has no intention of taking the children away.'

Hans-Peter's face was red with anger. He started shouting: 'I won't allow it!' The judge declared I should see the children in his house under the supervision of Herr Lecker!

As before, the Volkmann party rushed out of the courtroom with the social workers and disappeared downstairs. I groped my way out to find my mother. She was clearly very upset. While we were in the courtroom, she had tried to find the children. She had searched everywhere, until at last she found Alexander and Constantin in a bare room, guarded by Hans-Jorg and another man. She had tears in her eyes as she described the circumstances:

'Katia, they looked so frightened and tense, sitting still between the two men. They had no toys, no books – just a blank look on their faces. I have never seen children, let alone your children, capable of remaining motionless like this . . . Katia, I am frightened for them!'

We joined the others downstairs and Alan drove us to a restaurant. Dr Kram turned to my mother: 'Oh well, we'll just apply for another hearing,' he said matter of factly and left for Munich.

The four of us met Herr Lecker as agreed. He sat in the passenger seat without saying a word, looking severe and hostile.

Alan stopped the car and Lecker marched stiffly towards the house, my mother and I nervously scurrying behind. Herr Lecker opened the door, let me in and turned to my mother:

'You wait outside. You are not allowed in.'

'But I'm their grandmother and I haven't seen the boys for over eight months!'

My mother returned to sit in the car and Herr Lecker locked the door behind me. My children were standing in the drawing room as they had been last time, motionless and subdued. I kissed both of them and handed them their Christmas presents. They hesitated. I helped them with the wrapping paper. Tini sat down on the small sofa and I followed him over. Alexander stood still with his new magnifying glass in his hand. Tini seemed pleased with his gift – a quiet pleasure I could detect only from the expression in his eyes – and we started assembling the pieces of the model car. Alexander walked slowly towards the window. Herr Lecker, still wearing his black leather jacket and fur hat, sat in an armchair opposite, his arms crossed, staring at me reprovingly. The atmosphere was tense and intimidating. Alexander was expressionless and lifeless.

An hour passed without the slightest movement from Herr Lecker; his eyes were tenaciously anchored on me. The doorbell rang and Alexander walked over to unlock

198

it. It was my mother, who was frozen to the bone and needed to use the bathroom. She then walked into the sitting room and told Herr Lecker she wanted to take some pictures of her grandchildren. She first took one of Constantin and me sitting on the small sofa on her left, then one of Alexander in front of her.

'Alexander, smile. It's for your grandfather.' Alexander smiled sadly.

My mother turned towards Herr Lecker and took his picture. I suppose she was so frustrated and incensed at the demeaning and vicious treatment we were receiving that she simply wanted to make a point. This was surely not very wise but it was a minor demonstration of her outrage that she, as the children's grandmother, had not been allowed into the house and had had to sit in the car in below freezing temperature.

Herr Lecker shot up:

'*Geben Sie mir die Kamera sofort!*' he ordered and blocked the door. My mother did not speak German but could not fail to understand his order.

'*Nein.* It's mine.'

Herr Lecker stretched out his arm to grab the camera from my mother, who was holding it tightly to her breast. I panicked and ran to protect her:

'Don't you dare touch my mother. She is an elderly lady!'

'If you do not give me this camera immediately, I will write a negative report for the court!'

'This is blackmail!' I said in English not knowing the German word for it.

My mother was terrified and managed to escape through the side door to the dining room, through the kitchen and back to the entrance hall. Constantin was hiding under the table and Alexander crouched in front of him as if to protect his little brother.

Herr Lecker continued to threaten me:

'I order you to give me your mother's camera. I do not want my photo in the press.'

'Look, this is my mother's camera. These pictures are for her and my father . . .' I was frightened too, and tried to reason with him. He moved to the side and Alexander, who had been observing each of his movements like a cat watching its prey, slipped through the door and ran into the entrance hall, through the cloakroom and towards the Monkmanns' house. Constantin trailed behind him. I grabbed my bag and ran behind. As I reached the neighbouring house, the children had already vanished. I walked in and stumbled on Ute who was decorating a Christmas tree:

'Get out of my house!'

'But Ute, I want to see my children. At least to say goodbye to them . . .'

'Get out. This is private property and I'm not allowing you in here.'

My heart was thumping, my body trembling and I walked into the adjoining room where I found Hans-Peter sitting engaged in a conversation on his mobile phone. He stood up, his six-foot body blocking the way. I panicked and rushed out through the other door back into the entrance hall. My children were obviously upstairs, probably with the two bodyguards, Hans-Jorg and tall Klaus. I did not dare go up, so I ran back towards Hans-Peter's house. Herr Lecker was standing in the hall. He let me in and locked the door behind me, taking me into the far corner of the sitting room, away from the peering eyes of my party outside.

'Herr Lecker, please. You must understand, I love my sons, this situation can't go on . . .' In my desperation, I was trying to reason with a man who would rather die than move from his position. The doorbell rang. I rushed to unlock the door and quickly slipped the keys into my pocket. There was no way I would be locked in, alone, with these two threatening men. In answer to Herr Lecker's explanation, Klaus put on a show of the conciliatory lawyer:

'Well, Mrs Volkmann, I believe that you should surrender the camera to Herr Lecker.'

'But it's my mother's property!'

'I'm sure you wouldn't want him to file a negative report in court.'

'But you can't blackmail me like this. We are talking about my sons.' I looked back and saw Keith and Alan standing beside the car, waving for me to come. I ran out towards them and we drove off. I sat in the car, still shaking with fright and crying. Several miles down the road, I noticed I still had the bunch of keys in my pocket. We all laughed.

'Hans-Peter will have to change all the locks now!'

This moment of light relief was short-lived. I would be accused of having 'threatened' two men (Herr Lecker and Klaus) and stolen the keys for the purpose of walking into the house and 'stealing' my children away.

On 24 December, I could not reach the boys to wish them a Merry Christmas. Although one concession had been made by the Youth Welfare – that I would be able to talk to my children once a week on Thursdays – the last time I was able to get through to them was on 12 December 1994.

On 27 December the Verden decision was delivered:

'The court rejects Mrs Volkmann's demand for a Christmas holiday with her sons . . . The children, especially Alexander, expressed a "wish" to remain in Verden as he is afraid his mother would take the opportunity of such a holiday to take them back to London . . .' Herr Lecker stated that it would be against 'the interests of the children to visit their mother in Megève. She [the mother] should, as an adult, listen to her children's "wishes" and not the other way round . . .'

I cried all through the night. Those two weeks in Megève were the bleakest days of my parents' and my life. Faced with bias and injustice, devastated by the absence of Alexander and Constantin, neither my parents nor I could weather our pain. My father was beyond outrage:

'You should listen to your children and not the other way around! Are they not even ashamed of what they write? When a nine-year-old wants to play truant, or take drugs, would Herr Lecker expect the parent to conform to his "will"?'

I tried to contact newspapers, Members of Parliament, human rights organisations – all were celebrating Christmas.

Dr Kram had left for a holiday in the Far East. I decided to find a new lawyer. It was suggested to me that because Germany is a federation, it would be advisable for me to appoint a lawyer in Lower Saxony.

'You need to find someone who knows the local proce- dures and is known to the court. Not only will it be cheaper for you as you do not need to pay their travel expenses, but a local lawyer will not be faced with dis- criminatory attitudes which sometimes prevail between the north and south of Germany.'

Four lawyers (one from Bremen) refused to take on my case as they knew the Volkmanns or the Monkmanns and did not want to defend me. The stress, outrage and panic I was under is barely describable. I was losing weight and could not sleep. I was surviving on nervous energy and strength of mind.

By early January, I could not cope any more. All my attempts to reach the boys on the telephone were blocked – even on the allocated Thursdays. More and more people, including politicians and authorities, knew about my case. But the situation remained unchanged. The Child Abduction Unit in London was not getting any results from Berlin. Dr Kram was getting nowhere. Jane was unable to help me since matters were now in the hands of the German courts – and I could no longer live without knowing how my children were. I had written to the Youth Authority, the police and the school they were supposed to attend, to obtain the boys' end-of-term reports. My letters were ignored.

On Thursday 5 January I tried calling. Hans-Peter's

answering machine was on as usual. I asked the Lord Chancellor's department to telephone for testimony. On 12 January the same result. I decided to fly out and see for myself where my sons were. I asked Keith, who was in Germany, if he would accompany me. He came to pick me up at Hanover airport and we drove to Verden in a rented car. I planned to wait outside the school and steal a few minutes alone with my boys – talk to them away from the intimidating environment of Hans-Peter's house, away from Herr Lecker. Then I intended to drive on and spend the weekend with my Hamburg friends.

The school Alexander and Constantin were supposedly attending was in a tiny village, a mile down the country road from their house. The lane which led to it, up a hill, past five or six houses, continued into open fields beyond. From mid-morning, Keith and I waited in the car park opposite. I had no idea what time it finished (in Germany school is a half-day affair) and I heard that some days schools closed as early as 11.30. It was freezing and we had to start the car several times to warm up. At noon, a school bus parked in front of us and we saw children come out and climb into it. There was no sign of Alexander and Tini.

'Maybe they don't go to school here,' I sighed, disappointed.

The bus left. It seemed there was no one else left in the school. We were about to drive off when we saw several cars drive into the small car park, and another school bus appeared. Maybe my sons were still inside! Soon, children started coming out, and there was a knot of people standing around and blocking our view. Keith switched on the engine and drove closer to the school gate. He spotted Constantin first:

'Catherine, look – there's your Tini, wearing the red hood!'

I jumped out of the car in excitement and called his name in front of all the other parents. He was surprised to see me and to my incredible astonishment, after a few seconds' hesitation, he ran off in the opposite direction. I was shocked, and continued to call: 'Tini, Tini.' A Volkswagen, which I recognised as Hans-Peter's and which I used to drive in Hamburg, pulled up near him. Ute Monkmann was at the wheel. She opened the passenger door, pulled Constantin in, slammed the door and continued driving down the hill. I was shattered. I had come all this way to see my sons and this ghastly woman was driving off with them. My immediate reaction was to run to her door and open it even though the car was still in motion. I wanted her to stop! She could not drive fast as there were a lot of children, parents and cars blocking the narrow country lane. I opened her door but Ute continued to drive on, pushing me out of the car with her left arm and leg. Constantin started screaming hysterically. Ute is twice my size and her determination gave her even more physical strength. I was sitting on the running board, hanging on to the door as she was hitting me – but I wouldn't let go.

Keith, still in our car, saw my struggle and rushed to help. Ute's car was close to the trees at the edge of the road. Keith made a run towards the other side and opened the passenger door. I looked at him in desperation. His reaction was to take Constantin, presumably thinking Ute would stop the car then. Tini continued his screaming and Alexander, who was sitting in the back, started pulling Keith's hair. (I had not seen Alexander come out of the school and can only presume he attended another one or had been picked up earlier.) Finally Ute switched the engine off. Keith let go of Constantin but stood by the open door to prevent her from driving off. Constantin continued to yell unabatedly.

'What are you doing here?' Ute spat at me.

'Ute, they're my sons. I only want to speak to them.'

'Leave your children alone!'

'Please . . .' I begged.

She was yelling at me and interrupting every single word I was trying to say to my boys. Suddenly a menacing woman marched towards the car. Ute stopped screaming and smiled at her. This was the headmistress and, as I found later, an acquaintance of Ute who had obviously been 'warned'.

'What are you doing here?' Her tone of voice was so dictatorial that I began to cry: 'I'm their mother. I want to see my sons . . .' I sobbed. There was instant peace. I turned to Tini, who had stopped his uninterrupted scream as abruptly he had started it:

'Why were you screaming like that?'

Alexander answered for him in a cold, flat voice:

'Oma (grandmother) told us that if we ever see you outside school, we should run and scream. She repeated this to us this very morning.'

'But I love you. I'm your mummy and I want to see you – they just don't let me . . .'

'You're lying. Daddy told us you could come whenever you wanted, but you never did.'

'But that's wrong. Look, I'm here . . . and you're being taken away from me.'

'That's not true. You're lying!'

'Alexander, I don't lie. I'm here to see you. I love you.'

'We know, but you don't want to see us!'

In the presence of the headmistress, Ute had been forced to let Alexander speak. The genuine words of a child, who had it endlessly drummed into him that his mother had abandoned him, had naively revealed all.

Three other women and a man marched towards us and surrounded the car. One of them told Ute to drive forward to the school gate. The headmistress opened the passenger door. Constantin and Alexander stepped out and they all headed towards the school, encircling my little boys.

Keith and I followed them at a distance. The group quickly went into the school and the headmistress blocked the door:

'You're not allowed in!'

'But . . .'

She slammed the door and gave instructions to the care-taker not to let me in. I stood leaning against the panel, trembling with cold and upset, tears rolling down my face. Finally the doorman, feeling sorry for me, unlocked the door.

'It's much too cold outside. Why don't you stand here, at least it's warm.'

'Thank you, thank you.' It is extraordinary how grateful I felt for this simple civility. I could not stop my tears and went on: 'I'm the mother. I need to know where my children are. I came all the way from London to see them . . .'

'Come with me, they might be in the teachers' room.'

Keith and I followed him through the empty corridors until he stopped in front of a door:

'This is the room.'

Keith, who did not speak German, was worried. He went back outside to see whether his German friend (who was supposed to meet us to drive Keith back to Hanover) had found his way to the school. Alone, petrified by these people's hostility, my maternal instincts pushed me forward. I opened the door. Eight or nine teachers were sitting around a table, amongst them the four I had seen outside. No one acknowledged my presence. With tears in my eyes, my make-up running, my body shaking, I demanded, 'Where are my children?'

Eight pairs of eyes looked up, stared at me silently and returned to their conversation. However, the man I had seen outside stood up, smiled and led me back into the corridor. Naively, I thought he wanted to help.

'Now, tell me your story,' he said.

I tried to explain who I was and why I was here.

Patiently he listened to my disjointed speech. He asked questions, appeared sympathetic and I did not realise he was detaining me only to gain time.

Finally, a young policeman and a policewoman arrived. Keith's car had blocked the road and the driver of the school bus had called them. I threw myself at them, glad

206

to find someone neutral who could enforce the law.

'I'm the mother. I live in London. I came to see my sons. I haven't seen them for months and I desperately want to talk to them.' I had barely started to explain when Gundel and Hans-Werner appeared in the corridor side by side. They were determined, on home ground and important people in Verden.

'Don't listen to her. She's lying. The children live with their father, on Judge Monkmann's property.'

Keith had found his friend and they were just walking in.

'Ah look!' she pointed at them accusingly, 'she has come to snatch the children. Here are her accomplices.' Keith stood there numb; his friend wondered what on earth was happening.

'That's not true. I have custody. My children are wards of court in England. My husband has abducted them twice!'

Hans-Werner stepped between the policeman and me, looking important:

'I am Dr Volkmann. Don't listen to this woman. She's lying. I want you to phone Herr Lecker, the director of Social Services. He'll tell you the truth.'

I was horrorstruck:

'Keith, do you have a mobile phone? I must call my lawyer.'

He looked at me regretfully: 'No. I don't have a telephone,' he said.

'Why don't you call the judge? Herr Lecker is completely on their side. The judge will tell you.' I beckoned to the policeman.

The two young police officers were utterly bewildered. They had been called for a parking offence and found themselves faced with screaming people and an unmanageable situation. Gundel was waving at me dismissively, blocking every word I tried to say to the policeman, Hans-Werner imposing his power as if he was an army commander. Hans-Jorg marched in arrogantly pointing at me:

'Ah. She's here to snatch the children. Look, two men are with her . . .'

I was unable to talk, my eyes pleading for help from the policeman. He called the court: the judge had gone home for the day.

'Well, call Lecker!' Hans-Werner ordered. The policeman was unsure and decided to take a few notes instead:

'Tell me please, your name and address,' he gently asked me.

Gundel and Hans-Werner interrupted me, still pointing at my 'accomplices' standing dumbfounded behind me. The policeman turned to me:

'Come with me.' He led me into a quiet room to take down my details away from the commotion.

As soon as we returned, Hans-Jorg started attacking me. The policeman interrupted:

'This is a private matter. I can't intervene,' and turning towards me he said, 'You'll have to sort this matter out with the court on Monday. In the meantime, the children will have to return to their father.' The Volkmanns were delighted. Having got their way, they could stop being aggressive.

'Yes, of course, officer,' Hans-Werner quickly agreed with a smile.

'But can I see my sons? Please. At least to say goodbye to them?' I asked the policeman.

'Dr Volkmann, you wouldn't object, would you?'

'Of course not.'

'Will you come with me, please?' I asked the policeman, my fright probably written on my face.

'Of course.'

He led me into the teacher's room and through to a room behind it. This was the headmistress's private office. She was sitting behind her desk telephoning, presumably talking to Hans-Peter in Bremen after she had alerted the rest of his family in Verden. Opposite, Ute was sitting poker-faced between my two boys. No one moved; only Tini looked up at me. The policeman stood at the door as

I walked towards them. Ute sat implacably still. So did the boys. I went round behind her chair and knelt on the floor, seeing my little boys in profile, their necks stiff.

'Alexander, I love you. Tini, I love you. Both so much . . . I brought your Game Boy, you know?'

Tini's eyes brightened and he looked at me. I smiled, barely able to contain my grief:

'I suppose you don't have a Game Boy here.'

'No.'

Alexander was silent, but he, too, turned towards me. He looked sad and stiff at the same time while Constantin looked straight into my eyes lovingly.

'*Wir gehen!*' Ute interjected.

Both boys immediately stood up, like two little soldiers under orders. I rushed towards the policeman beside the door. Ute, with Alexander and Tini trailing behind her, passed in front of me.

'Alexander? Goodbye . . .'

'Bye!' and he marched forward behind his master.

'Tini? Bye, bye . . .' I was bending down trying to steal a kiss from my baby. He leaned forward. 'Bye, bye, Mummy' – he kissed me and he was gone.

'This is so sad. Poor kids,' the policeman mumbled.

We walked out into the corridor in time to see Hans-Werner, Gundel, Hans-Jorg and Ute triumphantly marching away. Only Tini dared to look back at me.

They were gone. The doors were closed. Silence. I was alone, lost in a pain that tore me apart, no shoulder to cry on . . . I was forty one years old and yet I longed for my mother to be there and take me in her arms, like a child.

I returned to London, unable to face anything except the solitude of my sorrow. A week later I received a copy of Hans-Peter's court application for an 'immediate transfer of custody, without a hearing' on the allegation that I had come to 'abduct' the children on Friday 13 January 1995. This was accompanied by a fourteen-page report stating that on my previous visit I had 'stolen' the keys to his house, 'threatened' two men, that I had come to the school with two 'accomplices', one of whom had physically 'attacked' Constantin who had been bleeding and had to be taken to hospital. These claims were witnessed by Ute, who testified that I have 'beaten' her. The bus conductor, the schoolmistress and the four teachers supported these allegations.

The lies, the hate, the injustice were scandalous. How could they make such outrageous allegations? They weren't even credible! How could I physically be capable of beating Ute, threatening two men, one who was over six foot tall when I was not even five foot seven and weighed seven and a half stone! How could Constantin be bleeding when he was wearing an anorak and was seen by the policeman peacefully kissing me goodbye?

I was mad and panic-stricken. Dr Kram had no time to help me prepare the answers to these accusations. Fourteen pages written in German had first to be translated into English before any lawyer could help me. Jane was busy with other clients so another lawyer had to be found urgently, increasing my debilitating expenses. By 23 January, I found one. We spent the whole weekend working but my answers still had to be translated into German, adding to the additional £1,000 I had already spent.

But on 25 January – the day before my birthday – the Verden court transferred the residence of my children from London to Verden (the closest thing to custody, under German law), without even having given me the chance to present my evidence against the unproved allegations. The decision was based on Ute's testimony and a medical report, dated 26 January (the day *after* the decision and thirteen days after the alleged injuries).

Two months later, we discovered that a police report dated the day of the decision stated that 'as far as the police are concerned, Mrs Volkmann had no intention of taking the children back to England . . . no child was physically injured . . . these claims were only put forward by the other party.'

Haunted by the image of my children's faces, the hatred and barbarism of these people, the outrageous injustice and the feelings of despair and helplessness which accompanied it, I saw no end to the dark tunnel my life had become. People speak of medieval tortures; I would have swapped anything for the mental torture which was imposed on me.

I could no longer bear to stay in my flat, looking at the empty rooms filled with memories of happiness and laughter that would never be again . . . Whatever happened, Alexander's mind was slowly being warped for life. I had to save my children but I did not know how. I telephoned the United Nations in Geneva: they were not empowered to intervene in individual cases; the Luxembourg Court of Justice: they had no competence to deal with judicial matters other than those concerning disputes arising from Union laws. The Mediators to the European Parliament were under the same restrictions.

To date, the Union has not succeeded in harmonising European laws. The third 'Pillar' of the Maastricht Treaty (dealing with justice and home affairs) has not been ratified and therefore no common policy has been established. Each of the fifteen member states still has its own independent legal system and only goodwill will enforce its recognition by another state provides only for 'inter-governmental cooperation' in the fields of justice and home affairs. I was discovering the complexities of the European Union and the embryonic state it was in.

Europe was still unable to protect its European children.

Chapter 15
Hopelessness

There can be no light without hope. When hope is only held in the shadow of a dream all is darkness. The image of your souls will remain the only flicker of light on the distant horizon.

My two little boys had been barbarically kept away from me yet there was nothing I could do to spare them the trauma nor restore to them the most basic human right. Hans-Peter and his clan had used an exception within the Hague Convention. Irrespective of the English High Court orders, irrespective of Hans-Peter's abduction in Germany itself, the Celle Higher Court had sanctioned his illegalities, thus leaving the way clear for Verden to endorse it for ever.

Suddenly a change of judge in Verden led Hans-Peter to apply for custody (I had been advised to withdraw my demand) and a hearing was set for 23 February 1995. In Germany, judges have full control of the proceedings. Again, no independent psychologist was appointed to examine the boys: the judge had deemed it unnecessary. Instead, a report from Frau Kranitz was requested. Apparently, English evidence was of no concern to the Verden court, as none of my witnesses who had flown in specially from London were called.

Hans-Peter, who had brought witnesses for the custody hearing he had hoped to have on 20 September 1994 with Judge Moritz, brought none for this hearing with the new judge. I felt this was suspicious.

Herr Lecker and Frau Kranitz testified with great determination, adding that I had threatened Herr Lecker, stolen keys and tried to abduct my children, who were living in terror at the thought that they might stumble on their mother in the streets of Verden. The references to 'Nazis', to a 'foreign environment' and to 'life in England' were made again. I had the impression that I was part of a sacrificial ritual in a mock trial. Herr Lecker's blue eyes were staring at me malevolently as Frau Kranitz concluded that, in the 'interest of the children', custody should be transferred to Hans-Peter and any visit be held in his house only and in the presence of a social worker.

I sat in the court, by turns despondent, resigned, incredulous and outraged. I had no illusions. The verdict had been inevitable. But I still hoped that mercy would be granted to the children. The Volkmann vs. Volkmann case had attracted the attention of the press and the eyes of Europe were watching Verden. A crew from the German television station, Sat 1, had accompanied me to the hearing and were waiting outside the courtroom.

My new lawyer, Herr Struif, the most caring and human lawyer to handle my distressing case, tried to present my defence. Children need a mother; our bond was extremely close; I was a responsible mother who had promoted the boys' regular contact with their father, I came home from work at 5.30, which meant that they would only spend two hours with a sitter . . . On the other hand, Hans-Peter's actions had proved his irresponsibility and his determination to demolish the children's relationship with their mother; Hans-Peter worked in Bremen and the boys were left all afternoon with a third party . . . The children were happy in London, had excellent school results and many friends.

I stood up and presented to the judge a scrapbook Alexander's classmates had done for him: *Reviens vite* (Come back quickly), Sean had coloured on its cover. There were photographs, drawings, words of friends. One wrote, 'I am half German like you and I really miss you. Please come back soon.'

The judge – a woman – did not look at it. Instead, she

213

interrupted me, stating that all this belonged to the past and so did Hans-Peter's illegal behaviour. The past was no longer relevant – we had to look ahead now. The fact was that the children were in Germany and that, when she had interviewed them a week before, they had expressed a wish to remain in Germany.

'But these children are totally manipulated and under pressure to express this "wish"!' Herr Struif interjected. 'Herr Lecker claimed that Ms Laylle had "threatened" him. You said that Alexander told you his mother had "hit" Herr Lecker. This is clear evidence of how confused and pressurised he is!'

The judge interrupted again. She did not want to spend the whole afternoon in court discussing this and would deliver her verdict on 30 March. The Verden court – which last month had needed to make such an urgent decision (on the day of the police report) that it had not allowed me any time to present my defence – now required five weeks to make up its mind!

Hans-Peter's abductions had created a *fait accompli*: the children were now resident in Germany; delaying the decision would strengthen the argument that they were settled there. I was in a no-win situation: little by little they were legalising their actions.

'My client has come all the way from London and she would like to see her children today,' my lawyer went on.

Since their abduction, I had only seen them for three and a half hours under supervision.

'That will be difficult,' the judge said.

'Why?'

'The children are not here,' Klaus answered.

'Where are the children?'

'Somewhere.'

Klaus refused to disclose where the children were being hidden and the judge did not intervene. In Verden, a mother had no right even to know the whereabouts of her own children? I could no longer contain myself and ran out of the courtroom, in anguished tears.

As I rushed out, distraught, the cameraman filmed me. My mother took me in her arms, crying as well. Nicolette, Leonard, Alan and David (who had been Hans-Peter's boss in London) all stood in the waiting area filled with consternation. They had seen Hans-Peter, his lawyers and the two social workers belligerently marching together down the corridor for the hearing; and had seen me approach Hans-Peter, say 'Hello, Hans-Peter' and seen him determinedly ignore me.

I finally composed myself and went back into the courtroom. Herr Struif was still trying to negotiate an immediate access right. Klaus refused all his suggestions. Hans-Peter was silent, staring into emptiness. Finally, Herr Lecker made an offer:

'Next month, under my supervision.'

'But that's impossible. He locked me in the house last time. I couldn't even speak to my sons. I am scared to go to Hans-Peter's secluded house. Do you know where they live?'

'Yes, I do,' answered the judge.

I was dumbfounded.

She looked at her watch and declared the hearing over. Hans-Peter, his two lawyers, Herr Lecker and Frau Kranitz stood up. The woman judge showed them through a back door and the six of them disappeared together down the corridor. The cameraman immediately went after them and filmed Hans-Peter running off, the others speeding behind.

'How can you justify a mother not being able to see her own children?' shouted the journalist to Herr Lecker. Ignoring him, they all vanished down the back stairs.

On 30 March the decision on temporary custody (i.e. until the divorce proceedings) and on access rights was delivered to Herr Struif. Custody was transferred to Hans-Peter 'in the interest of the children'. The arguments were similar to the one used by the Celle judges, with some additions – the 'massive bodily harm' supposedly inflicted on Tini, my claimed 'threats' to Herr Lecker and

215

my 'disruptive press campaign'. '. . . The mother is not the most important person in the children's lives . . . especially since last summer . . . Alexander used to love both his parents now he loves his father more . . . The mother works . . . since both parents work . . . the children feel German . . . they had no friends in London . . . the social environment is right in Germany . . .' The Verden judge had granted Hans-Peter custody, although the children were wards of the High Court of Justice of England and Wales!

The decision on access rights was as follows. The mother's

right of access . . . is suspended until June 30th, 1995. From 1 July 1995 the mother shall be entitled to spend 3 hours on one day each month with her children Alexander and Constantin either at the father's residence or at the District Youth Welfare Office in Verden. Commencing in October 1995 she shall be entitled to spend the period from 10.00 a.m. to 6.00 p.m. on the first Saturday of each month . . . As a result of the incident on January 13th . . . the children feel insecure . . . The court takes the view that the children's negative attitude to their mother is solely due to the fact that the children have no confidence in her and that their current experiences with her are entirely negative. In the view of the court a certain period of peace and stability is a matter of urgency, so that the children do not need to live in constant fear that their mother will appear unannounced and that they will be left to face her without protection . . . in order to enable the children to gradually reestablish trust in their mother, the Court deemed it necessary to ensure that the established periods for contact are not excessively prolonged . . . [since visits can be held at the Youth Welfare Office] no particular day should be specified in order to ensure that they can be consulted as necessary.

I was up against a brick wall. English summons and wardship, European treaties and conventions, the UN Convention on the Rights of Children, freedom of movement (Schengen Agreement) and the evidence brought from England – none of these had evidently been brought to Verden's attention. Verden belonged to another world – unconcerned with Europe, defiant of progress and antagonistic towards 'foreigners'. Verden had its small, close-knit community, its hierarchic order and self-sufficiency. It even had its own court – and under the German law, my case could not be transferred to another federal state. Decisions on custody and access rights could only be made in Verden, and appeals lodged only in Celle, the High Court of Lower Saxony. Beyond that, there was no recourse, except to the Constitutional court which rejected most appeals.

Indeed, on 9 March 1995, the Karlsruhe Constitutional court rejected my appeal against the Celle decision not to return the children under the terms of the International Hague Convention. The verdict was summarised as follows: 'the Celle court had formed their opinion following an interview with the children who express their strong wish . . . no breach of Constitutional law . . . This decision is unappealable.' After yet more legal fees, there were no avenues left.

A few weeks later, Herr Struif learned that Antje, Hans-Peter's sister who had helped him abduct the children, had obtained a position in the Ministry of Justice of Lower Saxony.

In the meantime, back in December 1994, Lord Mackay, the Lord Chancellor 'regretted that he could not assist me . . . it would be improper for him to raise questions about judicial decisions abroad'. The ensuing correspondence with the Lord Chancellor's department was inconsistent and discouraging.

The Lord Chancellor's department had taken an initial view not to question Celle's dismissal of the Hague Convention. Although 'no doubt I was disappointed' by

217

the decision, I was however reminded that 'an order refusing the return of the children under the Hague Convention was not an order granting custody'. I had repeatedly expressed my concern regarding the possibility of 'a fair hearing' in Verden but was still encouraged to make 'an application for custody in the German courts' and to 'continue to consult my legal advisers in Germany'.

However, once my application was filed in the Verden court, I was informed that the Lord Chancellor's department could not intervene while custody proceedings were pending in Germany. And when custody was transferred to Hans-Peter on 30 March 1995, I was told that the Lord Chancellor's department could not intervene in court decisions abroad. What is the purpose of England's wardship if it can be entirely ignored by foreign courts and England has no power to enforce it?

Members of Parliament, however, showed concern and many were outraged by the treatment my sons and I had been subjected to. The few who did not wish to help simply answered that they 'very much regret' but there 'is a firm rule of the House of Commons that Members of Parliament do not intervene in the constituency matters of another MP'. While this is true in constituency matters, it is not the case in matters of national interest.

Others reacted warmheartedly, and particularly thanks to Bill Cash's kind support and energy, seven MPs joined together and on 5 July 1995 in an adjournment debate at the House of Commons, they gave evidence on the way in which European courts flout the Hague Convention to the Parliamentary Secretary, Lord Chancellor's department. John Taylor's answer implacably repeated (now officially) the previous arguments, again omitting to mention Hans-Peter's abduction in Germany

It is not the unit's role [Lord Chancellor's department] to intervene in private custody disputes that are being contested in foreign courts ... the [Verden] court ordered that the children be returned, but the father successfully appealed to the higher regional court. Ms Laylle engaged lawyers in Germany . . . While I sympathise with the difficulties in which Ms Laylle finds herself, I do not consider that there is any more substantive assistance that the British Government can provide . . .

In essence, because I had acted legally – because I had abided by a legal agreement, trusted the law – I had lost. My husband – who had acted illegally, twice abducted children and been in contempt of court – had won! My pain was transforming into anger. As if losing my sons was not traumatic enough, I was now faced with the real-isation that the machinery of the country I so loved and respected was simply not yet ready to support three of its citizens. A new tenacious will awoke in me and took over my entire existence. My life had only one aim and nothing would or could deter me from attaining it. Justice became my obsession and my sons were my *raison d'être*. I could talk of nothing other than my case, think of nothing other than my boys and survive on nothing other than my new sense of consuming purpose.

Although the Lord Chancellor's department remained impassive, the Foreign Office soon showed sympathy. Our Consul-General in Hamburg became involved in my story and gave his support. His kindness, humanity and concern never wavered throughout my ordeal. He has done his utmost to assist me and gather support. Soon, our Ambassador in Bonn was informed and he immedi-ately reacted with compassion and deep concern. Both instigated interventions on my behalf.

Meanwhile, the French government, although not directly involved (since it did not concern its jurisdiction) took a unified position and treated my case with great concern and humanity. France is a country which cares for children. My father and I received extremely sympa-thetic letters from the Ministry of Justice and the Quai d'Orsay, from senators and deputies. They expressed their deepest sympathy for the 'extremely distressing time we were enduring' and on 16 February 1995 Mr Balladur's diplomatic adviser wrote to my father that France would also intercede with the German authorities to try and find an equitable solution for the children.

The co-operation of member states in the European Union was being put to the test. The results were surprising: the unofficial interventions made by our Embassy in Bonn were rebuffed. Germany's federal government, who relied on the independence of their judicial and legislative system to justify it, said that once a decision had been made by one of its courts, the government was unable to interfere.

The answer to the French official intervention made on behalf of my parents (who reside in France and under French law are entitled to visitation rights) was received only on 18 May, after temporary custody had been transferred to my husband. It was biting:

> judicial decisions in custody matters are often perceived as an injustice by the defeated party and attempts are often made to modify the decision through recourse to the media or political interventions . . . under German family law, grandparents are not entitled to visitation rights . . . In Germany it is not possible to go against the wish of the parent who has custody.

I had cried, agonised and grieved, hardly able to endure the pain. The memories were everywhere I went, associated with everything I did . . . How could I go on without my children? How could I go on, knowing that they were kept prisoner, betrayed, lied to and manipulated? There was no solace. I was scared. Day and night I wondered how they would survive through all this. If these people needed them testify in court to protect their illegal acts how far would the manipulation of their minds go?

I had been dragged through complicated legal proce-

dures, one lawyer advising me one way, another the opposite. I had sat through hearings I was unable to follow. I
had watched people I had never met testify against me,
staring at me with hatred. I had been accused of things I
never did, had not been allowed to submit my evidence,
and had my life and that of my sons destroyed by these
people. I had been blamed for everything I did or did not
do. When I tried to telephone my sons, I was described as
a 'bad mother' as I 'disturbed their peace'; when I didn't,
I was accused of 'not caring'. I was blamed for having
lifted the wardship in April 1995 (when custody had
already been transferred to Hans-Peter) and now the
German government was intimidating me into silence!
But how could anyone in my position be silent? How
could a mother not react to the injustice? How can my
sons ever respect me when they grow up if I do not fight
for them?

For months on end, I had fought for our human rights,
summoning all the energy and acumen I did not even
know I possessed, to put an end to this tragedy. I had
exhausted my reserves (selling my jewellery, my flat and
my furniture), I had borrowed from friends, from my
parents' life savings – only to be faced with more injustices, disgraceful behaviour and trauma – and I was still
excluded from my sons' lives.

I had believed that such an injustice would be rectified,
believing that in the 1990s a mother could no longer have
given birth to children to have them snatched from her in
such a barbaric way. Even women in prison are allowed
to see their children – but Germany did not allow me even
that. A mother's cry for help, a mother's cry for love, has
been brutally ignored.

In France, President Chirac was elected in April 1995.
Fresh interventions were made by the President himself,
but Chancellor Kohl withdrew behind the argument that
each *Land* was independent and he could not intervene. A
few months later an acquaintance wrote a personal letter
to the Chancellor, whom he knew well: 'although I am

aware of the independence of the judicial system in Germany . . . I am appealing to your commitment to Europe and your interest in family life, to find a human solution to this tragedy.' Five days later he received an urgent fax:

> The Chancellor has asked me to answer you . . . The fact that Mrs Laylle considers the decision as unfair cannot be used as a basis for polemics nor for media campaigns . . . I believe that it would be in the interest of all – and the media should realise this – that a purely judicial 'case' should not become an incident which spoils Franco-German relations.

There was no way out of this. I had come a long way from my former life. I had learned about family law, politics, the media, public relations, the human rights convention that stipulated that an individual has a right to be treated with respect, the right to freedom of expression, the right to a family life, the right to be heard equitably and without discrimination . . . but all of these rights had been denied me.

There is a level beyond which one can no longer accept degrading treatment: one's esteem goes to pieces or rises like a phoenix with new resolve. There is no middle road. In the name of my sons, in the name of all I have been raised to believe in, I chose the latter. I will go on fighting until justice is brought to bear on my case, and others like it. I've already lost everything but the determination to fight.

Once, I wrote to Chancellor Kohl explaining my case and asking for help. My letter was never acknowledged. No articles were published in the German press, although two prominent weeklies had interviewed me and one had gone to Verden to investigate. At the last minute, the editor suggested that, after all, this story was of no interest and things like this happen all the time.

'Well then, even more reason to talk about it. Isn't it

time someone protects children?'

A mother in distress had become politically unaccept-able.

Even in England I had the impression that my case had been labelled as representing the 'Euro-sceptic' point of view when Bill Cash, Conservative MP for Stafford, had come forward to defend our rights.

In July 1995 I had my first access right. The Verden Youth Authority announced to Herr Struif that no access would be possible as the children were on holiday with their father.

'Where?' asked my lawyer.

'I'm not telling you.'

Then in August: 'Dr Volkmann says the children do not want to see their mother,' stated Frau Kranitz.

In the first week of September, a television production company contacted me. They were working on a docu-mentary for ITV about child abduction and the Hague Convention and had heard about my case.

'We would like to take you to Verden in two days' time,' the journalist told me. I hesitated, aware that this could be used against me even though I was within my rights. (The Verden court had granted me a three-hour right of access, without stipulating day or time.) However, I knew that if I did not try to see my children, this would also be used against me, and if I appeared in Verden alone I would be accused of intent to abduct my sons. Whatever I did or did not do would be presented as incorrect. At least if I went to Verden, I could hold the faint hope that I might glimpse my boys and that a televi-sion programme might provoke a reaction in England. I agreed to go.

The producer and a researcher from London met in Verden with two crew from Berlin, on 4 September 1995. A photographer from *Paris Match*, which had already reported my case in an article in April, also joined us. We decided that I should ring Hans-Peter's house early next morning and try to see the boys before they set off for school. This would be the first time I would have seen them since 13 January 1995. I was apprehensive but determined.

It was 6.50 a.m. when the six of us reached the dividing line of the public path of the Monkmanns' property. Ulricke, the camerawoman, and Niko, the sound man, unpacked their equipment and started filming the panel PRIVATE PROPERTY under which a handwritten board read 'No entry for the press'. A microphone was attached to my anorak and I walked on alone with my bag of toys and teddies on my back. All was quiet. The day had just dawned. I felt uneasy. I rang the doorbell. No answer. I rang again. And again. Odd. If the boys were still asleep, they would surely have woken up by now. I pressed my nose to the window pane and suddenly saw Hans-Peter coming out of the shower-room opposite, a bath towel around him, sliding along the wall, into the drawing room. He had obviously seen me. His ridiculous behaviour gave me courage. Hans-Peter could not even answer the door without the protection of his entourage.

I rang again, with more determination and whispered into the microphone:

'The children are not here. They would have heard the doorbell. Hans-Peter is hiding. I'm going round the back of the house to see what he is up to.'

I started off. My heart was thumping. I passed the kitchen window – no one there; and went past the sitting room – no one. It was silent: no birds were singing, even the leaves were still. I wished one of the journalists were there with me. But I went on and reached the end of the side wall of the house. Then I continued round the back where there were large bay windows. I looked in but could see no one. It wasn't possible. I had seen Hans-Peter walk into this room. I pressed my face against the glass. There he was – crouched behind the sofa, hoping I had not spotted him.

I knocked on the window pane:

'Hans-Peter, will you open the door?' I shouted. He

shot up, panic-stricken, grabbing his towel with his right hand and reaching for his mobile on the table in front of him. I knew he would be calling his friend, the judge. I ran towards the front house.

As I reached the front, Hans-Peter put down the mobile and opened the door: '*Was machst du hier?*' (what are you doing here?) he barked.

'I've come to see the boys. I haven't seen them for many months. I'm their mother.' My voice was as calm as it could be in the circumstances.

'Well, they are not here!' Hans-Peter answered in German.

'What do you mean? Don't the boys live with you?'

'In any case today is a holiday. They're going to Hanover with my parents,' he said angrily and pushed the door shut. My right hand was on the frame and Hans-Peter pushed past me and slammed the door, nearly catching my fingers. I screamed as I tripped backwards.

I started walking back towards the journalists. One thought was uppermost in my mind: the boys don't even live with Hans-Peter. Judge Monkmann had come out of his house, obviously in response to Hans-Peter's call for support, and stood still.

'Wilfred, I've come to see my children,' I said in a half-begging voice, stupidly hoping that someone around here would have compassion.

'This is a matter for Hans-Peter and you,' he answered coldly, without moving towards me.

'What do you mean?' I said. 'He lives on your property and you're the one dictating and protecting every single move he makes.'

I looked back at Hans-Peter's house. Feeling protected by Wilfred's presence, he had come out and was standing, still holding his towel in one hand, talking on his mobile. I went up to him:

'I've got to go now, she's coming!' he said in a panicky voice. I presumed he had just telephoned his mother. I turned and ran back towards the crew.

'And I'll call the police now!' Hans-Peter screamed behind me.

'Great,' I thought. 'The police are being called because a mother wants to see her own children.' At least this time everything would be on film, for the world to see. Were even the Verden police controlled by the clan?

The media crew packed their equipment and we retreated to our cars, which we had left parked on the roadside. Jacques from *Paris Match*, Jonathan, Debbie and I got into one car; the crew in the other. A few minutes later we set off towards Verden. A police car drove past us and turned into the track leading to Monkmanns' property.

'Amazing!' exclaimed Jacques. 'They took ten minutes to arrive and it's not even 7.30 in the morning!'

Jacques knew Verden. He had been here in March with a *Paris Match* journalist and had experienced the atmosphere of the place. It had taken them three hours to find the road leading to the Monkmanns', hidden in dense woodland. They had been followed and late that evening, two policemen had come to their hotel rooms to inspect their papers.

They had rented a car with German plates in Hanover and had talked to no one. Both had been shaken by this experience. Jacques, who had seen a great deal in his life as a photographer, was astounded that the police should be checking people's papers in hotel rooms at 10.30 at night.

We arrived in Rosenstrasse where my in-laws live and parked a few metres away from their house. The small residential street was quiet. No one had set off for work yet. We were tense. The Monkmann and Volkmann power in this town affected the whole group. None of us moved as we examined the house with its drawn curtains. It was still.

'They aren't there. This house looks as though it's been closed for the summer,' Jonathan concluded.

'They *are* here,' I said. Gundel never drew the curtains

226

of the downstairs room as she had nets at the windows. 'They wouldn't have had the time to leave since Hans-Peter's call.'

In a mad burst of courage, I stepped out of the car and walked alone towards the house. Both family cars were there. 'They're here,' I signalled to the others, ready to go to the front door.

Jonathan ran behind me:

'Wait. We need to unload the camera first.'

My children were here, a few yards away from me and still I had to wait! Ulricke and Niko took out their equipment and I could now walk up the steps to find my sons. I rang the doorbell. No one answered. I rang again. Then rang uninterruptedly. No one answered. My sons were behind this wall. What were they doing? I was at my wits' end.

I walked around the house calling: 'Alexander, Tini, Mummy's here to see you.'

The cloakroom window had no curtains. Amongst the coats hanging up were my boys' anoraks. Two pairs of children's shoes lay on the shelf beneath. I called again and turned to Jonathan. The camera was no longer filming but was directed towards the street. I looked up. A police car was speeding along it; it parked beside the group of journalists and two policemen in uniform stepped out. I immediately ran towards them.

'My children, my children are in there. You must help me. I only want to see them, know they're still alive.' This was surely not what the policeman had expected – a mother in distress surrounded by a camera crew. His expression softened. There was a genuine look of concern in his eyes.

Before we could say any more, a second police car and a police van blitzed in and encircled us. A few curious neighbours peered around their net curtains. They had never experienced such a commotion in Rosenstrasse. Ulricke was running her film camera trying to capture the action; Jacques was taking pictures. Niko was rushing behind me with his large microphone; Jonathan and Debbie were wide-eyed, trying to direct.

Two more policemen stepped out of the second car, one in uniform, the other wearing a black leather jacket and khaki trousers. Their expressions contrasted starkly with the policeman who had first approached me. They looked as if they meant business. The uniformed policeman walked determinedly towards me, gesticulating to the first lot to go – he was taking over. The first car drove off. The police van remained. I repeated what I had just said to his colleague. He remained impassive. I guessed that someone had called him to say I had come to abduct two children.

'But I am their mother and I am within my rights. My husband is denying me all access.'

The policeman wouldn't listen to my explanations.

'Debbie, get me the court order, please.'

The court decision explicitly stated that: 'From 1 July 1995 the mother shall be entitled to spend 3 hours on one day each month with her children Alexander and Constantin.' No days were specified. Poker-faced, the policeman started reading it and his expression finally relaxed. Jacques came and stood behind me and whispered, 'This is the policeman who came to check our papers at the hotel room.'

I tried to reach Struif on Jonathan's mobile but at 8 a.m. the office was not open. There was a rattle behind me. A silver BMW whizzed past and parked recklessly: Hans-Jorg leapt out of the car and walked aggressively, his right arm pointed at the camera:

'Stop filming at once,' he ordered in an arrogant tone. Then, turning towards me: 'What do you think you are doing here?' His lip curled in an expression of disgust.

Ulricke continued filming as Hans-Jorg added: 'If you resort to this kind of action, you'll never see your children again!'

'But Hans-Jorg, I'm their mother. Can't you understand?'

He didn't even acknowledge what I'd said. Instead he

walked over to the policeman.

'I am Hans-Jorg Volkmann!' he said, expecting this declaration to cow the policeman into total obedience. 'The children live with my brother. She has no right to be here and only wants to abduct them.' I believe that even the policeman realised how ridiculous this statement was, given that I was obviously and publicly accompanied by the media. The policeman replied in a slightly embarrassed tone: 'She has a right to see her children.'

'Well, the children don't want to see her!' He walked into the house, ordering the police: 'And remove these people', with a dismissive wave towards us.

We were all speechless. Polite Jonathan had never experienced such a demonstration of aggression and arrogance. Even the stern policeman hesitated, his face registering doubt. Only Ulricke, a strong, resilient character, was bearing up. She was appalled by the behaviour of these people and had been determined to capture every expression and demonstration of spite in Hans-Jorg.

'This place is incredible!' she exclaimed. 'If I wasn't here, I would not believe it! In Germany!'

I walked over to the policeman in an attempt to gain his sympathy.

'The Volkmanns and the Monkmanns act as if they own Verden. I have no chance here. They have been blocking me from all contact with my boys.' I was interrupted. Niko had turned around and taken the microphone behind me, where there was some agitation. I turned around. Hans-Peter had appeared.

'Hello,' I said.

He passed by me without looking and walked straight towards the policeman, putting himself between us to exclude me from the conversation.

'Hans-Peter, listen . . .'

His lips were tense.

'She wants to abduct the children,' he said.

'Hans-Peter, they are *our* children . . .'

He simply spoke over my head. I turned to Ulricke and

229

saw her camera turned towards a car stopped in the middle of the street, with a man at the wheel. It was Judge Monkmann. Hans-Peter was pleading with the policeman in his usual fashion. They had walked away from us to speak in private, Monkmann overseeing the situation. It was 8.15. Debbie had finally managed to reach Struif. She passed the mobile over to me. I explained quickly and beckoned the policeman over to have a word with him. He walked towards me, passing Judge Monkmann's car. I saw them exchange a wink and Monkmann drove off.

Left alone, Hans-Peter immediately made a run for his mother's house:

'Why won't you let the mother see her children?' Debbie rushed forward, followed by Niko's microphone.

'The children are scared since she tried to abduct them.'

'Why are the children scared?' Debbie insisted. Hans-Peter ignored her question and escaped in the direction of the house.

'Please, let me see them,' I begged, running behind him. I did not dare walk into the small front garden which separated the house from the street. I was crying. The door was ajar:

'Alexander, Tini, Mummy loves you, Mummy hasn't abandoned you . . .' Hans-Peter had already slammed the door behind him.

That was it. I turned to the policeman:

'Please. I only want to look at them.'

He seemed better disposed towards me now that he had spoken to Herr Struif, a member of the Verden community.

'We don't know what's happening inside the house. Maybe my children did hear me, maybe they're asking why they can't see me.' I was sobbing, my head against the garden wall, the camera long forgotten. My boys were so close to me, only a few yards away, but separated by a wall.

The two policemen had gone back to their cars. Debbie approached them.

'In Germany court orders regarding access rights can't be enforced. It's not like in England or France. I'm sorry, I can't help you.'

'But how do you feel about this?' Debbie asked.

'I feel bad,' one of them said.

They drove off.

I had no tears left. We all stood in silence. Ulricke was angry. This was her country – things like this could not be allowed to happen:

'Who are these people? I have never seen anything like this. And Hans-Jorg's attitude -'

They started packing up their equipment. Ulricke and Niko were still talking. I went to sit in the car, trembling all over. I looked at the white house imprisoning my sons. Where had they been taken – to the attic, or stashed away like hostages in the cellar? I wished we could just stay, sleep in the street and wait until they finally walked out of the house. But filming was over. They had collected all they needed for the programme, scenes that they had never expected. Now it was time to go back to London and edit the material.

It was my pain and mine alone. Except for Ulricke, who was still sharing it. She looked at Niko:

'But . . . today's Tuesday, the 5th of September. There isn't any school holiday!'

We decided to have breakfast and then drive to the school in time for the break. We parked the two cars in the car park opposite. I was too scared to get out. This place carried so many horrific memories for me. Ulricke unpacked her camera and focused it on the school. She was right. A school bus appeared and the conductor got down. He looked at the film crew and then walked back to his bus, reappearing with a pocket camera. It was the same bus conductor who had testified I had come to abduct the boys on 13 January. He walked into the school. As children began coming out, Ulricke filmed them. Hans-Peter had lied again.

Suddenly, the headmistress, followed by the four

teachers I had encountered before, marched towards Ulricke:

'What do you think you are doing here? You have no right to film!'

They looked so menacing that everyone fell silent, except Ulricke, who was outraged:

'This is public property and I can film whatever I want! In any case, with a scandal like this, you'd better get used to the press. This is only the beginning.'

We turned and left – we hardly cared where we went, as long as it was out of this sinister, threatening environment. We were drained and shocked. We stopped in a small town nearby. Ulricke said:

'We're not in Iran! These people can't get away with such behaviour. I really wonder what bonds them all together. Everything has such an eerie feel to it.' She said she would contact the *Panorama* programme on her return to Berlin, then warmly hugged me goodbye and we left for the airport.

Two days later, 7 September 1995, the programme went out on ITV's *The Big Story* at 7 p.m. I had gone to Nicolette's flat, round the corner from me and a few friends gathered to watch the documentary.

Dermot Murnaghan explained: 'The Hague Convention, which is an international convention signed by forty-one countries, is designed to ensure the speedy return of abducted children to the country of habitual residence . . . [It] does not seem to function as well as it should.' He introduced four cases of British mothers who had married foreigners and had subsequently returned to England with their children. Their husbands had cited the Hague Convention and the English courts had immediately ordered the children's return to their country of origin, irrespective of the conditions that awaited them and their mothers. Some were seen practically squatting while their husbands refused to give them financial support.

These cases illustrated how England abides by the letter of the law, systematically returning children. However, 'foreign courts often won't play by the rules,' he went on. Here was a clear-cut case of an abduction whereby the 'father was completely in the wrong and should have been ordered by the German courts to send the children back to England. Instead, the father was awarded custody and Catherine given minimal access rights, amounting to three hours a month. But he refuses her even that. Catherine's children were not snatched away to some faraway land, but to Germany, a fellow member of the European community.'

The film showed me walking along the path through the woods in a bid to see my sons. I looked small and vulnerable against the big trees, a large dog in the distance. A short clip of the conversation between Hans-Peter and me was heard, before I ran back towards the camera: 'Let's go to the other house.' Then the police scene, Hans-Jorg, Hans-Peter and a shot of the pupils coming out of school. The programme took a strong moral stand, conveying the mood of the Volkmanns' aggression towards me.

Then a switch to the presenter, Dermont Murnaghan, standing in front of the German Embassy in London.

'The German Embassy here, in London, refused to give an interview although they said they were fully aware of Catherine Laylle's case. A spokesman for the Embassy said that Germany always abided by the *International* Hague Convention. But when asked why they did not return Catherine's children to England, his answer was, and I quote, "it had been settled correctly under *German* law" and they had no comments to make when they were told Catherine was not even allowed to see her children.'

Nicolette, her husband and my friends sat in silence for several minutes, scandalised. Not only was my case different inasmuch as the children had been snatched away from me, but I was the only mother who had been separated from them. We talked until after midnight. I returned home to find a message from my neighbour upstairs:

'Catherine, call me immediately. Your car has been set

233

alight. The police and the fire brigade have been here to put the fire out.'

A few minutes later, two police constables came to take my details, which were later transmitted to the crime squad. Both had seen the programme three hours earlier. The next day a small article appeared in the *Daily Express*: TV ABDUCTION MOTHER IN VENDETTA CLAIM.

I knew this could not be Hans-Peter. He had been trying to serve me the German divorce papers to ensure that the proceedings would be held in Verden, but did not know my new address. This was much more important to him than setting my car alight. So, then, who did it?

Chapter 16
The Trap

My darling sons, how can I ever express the extent of my pain? How can I ever portray my distress in knowing it is you who are suffering most? How can you ever forgive me for being unable to bring you your freedom back? It is I who have brought you into this world and I have not been able to protect you from it.

This latest incident worried my parents and friends. The police put on a special watch and a CID officer came to see me the next day. A week after my car was set on fire, a note left by another neighbour informed me that someone had tried to break into my flat. It could be a coincidence, but it seemed unlikely. There were too many odd circumstances. My friends advised me to be careful and Nicolette asked me to give her copies of important documents and people to contact, just in case something happened to me.

But strangely enough, I was totally calm. Now, I had lost absolutely everything. There was nothing else to go: my Renault 5 was a total write-off, I was overdrawn at the bank and had even been dismissed from my job. Yet despite my ordeal, I had remained the largest producer on the international desk, and the bank, or at least the director, had assured me of his support. Then in June 1995 he was suddenly transferred back to Italy. Seven days later I was called upstairs and told that I had to leave immediately. On what grounds? No answer was given but the bank was ready to make a settlement which I should not disclose.

Instead of feeling intimidated, I returned to my daily routine with more determination than ever: telephone calls, faxes and letters to England, France, Luxembourg, Belgium . . . the list went on, and I now had seven files thick as phone directories on my case. If my friends could express their alarm, I could not. Any sign of weakness would be used against me: 'she's hysterical, she has a persecution complex'. Besides, if anyone thought I could be frightened away, I would show them how wrong they were!

These were my sons – my own flesh and blood – I was fighting for. Nothing would ever stop me. Furthermore, many people now knew about my case. It had been well publicised. Even in Germany, leading papers had now published full-page articles – they were the best and most poignant ones of all. If the government was not sympathetic, many Germans were. I received letters of support, and in Hamburg shop assistants who had recognised me came up to me and showed their concern. I felt many were embarrassed that such events could take place in their own country.

The French government had reacted warmly and the public had read of my case or seen me on television. In Britain, where my story had been talked about most, people had come up to me to bid me courage and I had received many letters of sympathy; even companies like the AA conveyed their best wishes and condolences. If I was alone in my pain, I had discovered how many people were sensitive and cared. I would like to thank them all, in Britain, in France, in Germany and in Holland, because they have given me the courage and the belief I need to go on.

If I was a political embarrassment to some, others showed their kindness and humanity many times over. Four very special people kept my faith alive: Mr John Sullivan, our Consul-General in Hamburg, Sir John Stanley, MP, Catherine Urban, Conseil Supérieur of the French abroad and Mr Philippe Perrier, the French

Consul in London. I can never adequately describe how much I owe them.

On 11 September, four days after the ITV programme, Klaus submitted a fifteen-page application to the Celle court. Hans-Peter was seeking to cancel my visitation rights altogether (not that I had been able to exercise any!) on the basis that I was a terrible mother since I had 'threatened' Herr Lecker in December 1994, tried to 'abduct' the children in January 1995, and now had appeared in Verden accompanied by the media. The claims, which were also signed by Judge Monkmann, were that there had been ten journalists (in fact, there were five) and that they had trespassed on private property (they had not: filmed evidence of this exists).

I did not receive a copy of this application until 17 September and, four days later, Herr Struif received a notice from the Celle court which stated that we needed to file our defence. The allegations had to be answered point by point. I had a translation made and asked *Paris Match* and the ITV journalists to prepare written evidence to counter these false allegations. The Celle judges, however, did not allow me to file my defence. On 4 October 1995, without informing either my lawyer or me, they simply made a decision based entirely on Hans-Peter's unproven claims. My access rights were halved: from October 1995 I would be able to see my sons four hours per month, instead of one day as per the March decision!

The Celle court stated as fact that I had 'threatened' Herr Lecker, had attempted to snatch my sons (again ignoring the police report and the fact that at the time I had legal custody), had physically attacked Frau Monkmann and injured Constantin. The press was given a lengthy mention and the judges added a personal comment, namely that I had referred to them as 'provincials' in the press. They concluded that in the 'interest of the children', who were now 'scared' of their mother and needed 'peace', visitation would only be in Hans-Peter's house – but, as the court was aware that a mother should have contact with her children, I should see them alone.

The fact that I had not been allowed to present my evidence or defend myself, that what Judge Monkmann and Hans-Peter Volkmann were claiming was treated as undeniable truth, that the judges made a personal note against me (although it was a journalist, not me, who had used the word 'provincial') and that the access time was set at 9 a.m. to increase my expenses (since it meant travelling the day before), no longer surprised me nor my entourage. But now, not only had my constitutional and human rights been flouted, but a court decision effectively stated that I was a child molester!

Effectively I had not been with my sons since 6 July 1994 and whether these minimal access rights would be abided by was doubtful. But Herr Struif's insistence and the media's attention was such that Klaus finally conceded. However, I sensed a trap: I was to walk alone on to the desolate property, be locked in Hans-Peter's house, while next door, Wilfred, Antje, Klaus and Hans-Jorg's wife – all lawyers and a judge – would observe and testify at will. It would be my unwitnessed word against theirs and I knew that this would be the end of the road for me. I sent faxes to embassies, consulates, ministries, politicians . . . Mr Sullivan immediately reacted and kindly suggested that his chauffeur Alan should accompany me. The French authorities appointed Catherine Urban, as delegate for French people living abroad.

We left Hamburg at 7.15 a.m. to be in Verden by nine. I was apprehensive, convinced that something ominous was awaiting us. Yet how could I not go and see my children?

We arrived at the turning into the woods where a new wooden barrier blocked the public path. A red car was parked in front of it. We sighed and proceeded on foot up the icy 600 metres of track. The three of us were silent and tense. Someone had put a barrier across a public road. Would no one dare to protest in Verden? Soon we saw a man walking towards us in the misty distance. It was Hans-Peter's lawyer, Klaus. We passed the abandoned railroad track and reached the 'private property' notice just as Klaus arrived. Mrs Urban stopped so as not to trespass on the property while Alan and I marched on, escorted by Klaus. All was quiet and still except for a German shepherd dog watching our advance. At the top of the drive we turned right towards Hans-Peter's house. A man stood there. He advanced and handed some papers to me. This was a court bailiff.

This was the trap! Hans-Peter and I had married in London and an English divorce petition had been served on him six months ago. Under German law this had established the competence of the English courts. But Hans-Peter had argued for a stay in the English divorce, saying that in our separation agreement (signed before I left Germany in 1992), we had agreed to divorce under German law and that proceedings had started in Germany. The English court thus required a confirmation from the Verden judge that no such proceedings were pending in Germany. Notwithstanding Herr Struif's constant demands, this confirmation had never been transmitted.

I telephoned Herr Struif on the mobile I had brought as protection (which added strain to my finances). There was nothing I could do but take the papers. I felt physically sick. A visit had been granted so that they could corner me. A mother was going to see her sons and she would lose them for ever. It was clear what a divorce in Verden would imply for the three of us. I wondered how much my little boys would despise those people once they grew up and realised how their own mother had been treated and betrayed and how they had been used.

Paper in hand, Klaus led me into the sitting room. To the left was a small sofa, a table and an armchair. My two boys were perched, stiff-necked, straight-backed, side by side, their backs to the large window giving directly on to Monkmann's house. Tall, skinny, her hair pulled back in a bun, Frau Schwarz, the child-minder, sat rigidly in the armchair. No one glanced at me as I walked in. Only Tini lifted his eyes as I came closer. The atmosphere was intense. The room had only the bare essentials. There was not a paper in the litter bin, nor an envelope lying on the desk. It was as if this were a showroom, uninhabited the rest of the time.

'Hello, Alexander. Hello, Tini.'

Alexander answered curtly without lifting his head. Tini looked up quickly and back down. I put my bag on the floor and sat down on the empty chair opposite Frau Schwarz, to the left of Constantin, without another word, conscious of the strain my boys were under. They had not seen me for a very long time and seemed to have been briefed intensively on what they were allowed to do and not to do in my presence. The three of them continued with a game, oblivious of my presence. Frau Schwarz then invited me to participate. Between his dice throws, I noticed Tini looking at me attentively as if he were trying to absorb every detail of my features. I wondered if he had forgotten what I looked like. Slowly I turned my head towards him and smiled but he immediately turned his eyes the other way. Frau Schwarz was talking non-stop, with an irritating enthusiasm. Alexander was silent, still looking down. His expression was sombre and very tense. His face was pale, his features drawn and his eyebrows knitted as they always were when he was stressed or angry. His movements were slow and deliberate. Sixteen months ago I had taken a happy, boisterous child to the airport . . . today I was looking at a lost soul, neither boy nor man. I desperately wanted to take him into my arms and console him: 'Your mummy is here. She will protect you -' but I couldn't.

We continued playing. As usual, Tini won first and he timidly passed the dice to me and advised me on the moves. Tini wanted his mummy to win but there was nothing left in him of the energetic, jovial child he once was.

240

The game was over.

'Frau Schwarz, would you be kind enough to let me be alone with my children?'

'*Nein*,' she said, then she addressed Alexander in an autocratic voice: 'Do you want me to leave?'

'*Nein*,' Alexander answered without lifting his eyes, frowning.

I did not insist, much as I was determined to see my boys whatever the conditions were.

But Frau Schwarz at least agreed to go and sit on the other sofa. She took up a newspaper but never turned a page, monitoring every word my sons and I exchanged.

I said something to Alexander in French, the language we had always used before:

'*Du Musst Deutsch sprechen*!' he ordered me. I presumed this was another command he had received from his father to ensure that Frau Schwarz could interrupt when she felt necessary. Not wishing to add to the tension, I continued in my inadequate German and started to remove from my bag the presents I had brought from London. Both boys sat motionless, hands on their knees, their wrapped presents in front of them. I moved to sit on the sofa next to Tini and began to open them myself. What-free, normal child would react like that?

I felt the nearness of Constantin's body next to mine. This was my son, whom I had carried in my womb, and today he was not free to touch his own mother. I gently stroked his head and felt his body shiver with delight, but he did not dare to move. Alexander's face tightened. The torture was numbing me, but I continued in a jolly voice to unpack the boxes of Ninja Turtles while my sons still sat expressionless. Finally, carried away by the excitement of their new toys, Alexander quickly grabbed his and Constantin followed suit. Their voices lightened until Frau Schwarz turned towards Alexander. At once he put the toy back on the table:

'*Das ist doff*' (that is stupid).

'Will you show me your rooms?' I quickly asked, to distract their attention from this new difficulty. Tini did not answer. Alexander mumbled, staring straight ahead of him: 'We can't. They are locked.'

I was horrified. Hans-Peter obviously did not want me to see the conditions under which my sons were being kept.

Constantin was relaxing a little and ventured: 'Are there any more things in the bag?'

I took out toys from their London bedroom. I had chosen to bring Alexander's Batman, Tini's Robin, their dinosaurs and some Playmobil toys. I laid them on the table. Both looked down like two little trained dogs who had to receive their master's order before being allowed to eat. What would happen to them if Frau Schwarz reported their disobedience?

It is difficult to express how I felt, faced with the horror of my children's existence, faced with my inability to change it, faced with not even being able to take them into my arms. Finally, Alexander took a *Jurassic Park* dinosaur:

'This one's mine. Do you remember, Constantin? Mine had a mark on the back.'

'*Ja*. And this one's mine . . .' Their voices bubbled up again as happy memories flooded back. Frau Schwarz turned once more. Alexander's excitement vanished and Tini stood up. He picked up a ball I had brought and decided to go outside to play with it. Frau Schwarz rushed after him and I overheard her telling him to stay indoors.

'Alexander, tell me about school.'

I picked up a toy and asked him which ones he wanted me to bring next time. He looked so sad. I patted him on the head:

'Alexander, I love you. I haven't abandoned you. I'm your mother and will always love you . . .'

Tears welled in his eyes, his lips trembled, he stood up and rushed out of the room into the entrance hall, past the cloakroom and out on to the lawn. He was running fast, Constantin behind him, and through the window I saw them disappearing into Judge Monkmann's house. We had spent one hour and twenty minutes together, always in the presence of this severe woman. The visit was over.

Frau Schwarz came back into the room.

'What happened?'

'I told my son I love him. When he heard these natural words from his mother, Alexander ran off in a panic.'

I had said it automatically, more to myself than to this woman who had so interfered in our lives.

'Oh, but you know it is much better for your sons to live here in the country than in a big city. I love your sons as if they were my own,' she went on.

It was difficult to control myself but I had to.

'Frau Schwarz, wherever one lives, children need their mother. I would be very grateful if you could ask Alexander and Constantin if they want to come back to say goodbye to their mummy.'

Reluctantly she left the room and I telephoned Alan in his car to ask him to pick me up. Through the window, I saw Alexander and Constantin coming out of the house. Alexander hesitated and ran back. Constantin and Frau Schwarz came back into the room. Tini stood leaning against the wall, looking at me fixedly as if he needed to absorb my features once more. I came up to him and asked him if he wanted to play with me. He did not answer and looked at Frau Schwarz.

'Shall we clear up for your daddy?' I suggested, to distract him again from the hurt of the situation. Tini shot to the table and started packing the toys as quickly as he could. My heart sank at this demonstration of the authoritarian discipline they were subjected to. Klaus walked in with Alexander.

'Say goodbye,' he ordered.

'Bye,' obeyed Alexander and ran off. Tini hesitated. I managed to steal a kiss. Then, he too was gone.

Frau Schwarz and Klaus led me to the door as Alan arrived.

'This visit went very well. The boys need time to trust

their mother again,' Klaus explained to Alan. I signalled to Alan that we should go.

I was very upset as I described to Catherine and Alan the conditions under which the boys and I were 'allowed' to see each other and the depressed state Alexander was in.

'But I thought the Celle decision stipulated you should see them alone.'

'I know. But this is a no-win situation. They will claim again that it is "the children's wish" to see me only in the presence of Frau Schwarz.'

My situation was so hopeless, so depressing that I could not get worked up about it. But the disturbing picture of my sons haunted me day and night. Would anyone be able to help them? The local court had considered that the way they were living was appropriate in Germany.

As I had expected, Klaus's answer to my lawyer's complaint about Frau Schwarz's presence was met with the claim that it was 'the children's wish' since, and I quote, 'Frau Schwarz was the most important person in their lives' – surprising since one would expect their father to be.

Struif's complaint about the road being blocked and our having to walk in freezing temperatures had little effect. The following month the roadblock had been replaced by a permanent metal gate which was bolted when we arrived. Catherine, Alan and I proceeded on foot. Klaus stood in front of the entrance to Hans-Peter's house. He greeted Alan and led Catherine and me through to the sitting room. My children and Frau Schwarz sat in exactly the same position as last month. Klaus left the room, closed the door behind him and returned to Judge Monkmann's house.

I kissed my sons and introduced them in French to Catherine. As there was only one spare chair I went to the dining room to get another one for Catherine. The door was locked. I squeezed myself on to the small sofa beside Tini and could feel his body reacting warmly to the proximity of mine. Alexander, to his right, was tense.

Frau Schwarz and the boys continued their game of Mikado. Constantin was winning and he brightened up, proud to show off his skills to his mummy. Alexander's face was sombre and his features were drawn. He only addressed Frau Schwarz.

When the game was finished I asked Frau Schwarz if she could kindly leave the room with Catherine, reminding her that the court decision said I should be alone. She flatly refused, and asked Alexander.

'*Nein*,' he replied in the same monotonous voice as he had last month. 'The decision says Frau Schwarz should be here,' he added without lifting his eyes from the table, his hands crossed between his legs.

I was stunned. Not only was my ten-year-old son being told about court decisions but he had been lied to in an attempt to make him believe that it was his mother who was defying the law.

Frau Schwarz suggested sitting on the other sofa and invited Catherine to join her. The two women started chatting in German and Alexander relaxed. For a moment the three of us felt unobserved. I moved between them and began reading a French book I had brought from London. The children relaxed.

Suddenly the door opened. Klaus walked in. Immediately Alexander tensed up. He no longer listened to my words and focused on his uncle, as if he was awaiting his order. Klaus addressed the two women and walked back out. Alexander once again became engrossed in the book. Ten minutes later the phone rang. Alexander answered and gave the receiver to Frau Schwarz.

'It's Klaus. He wants to speak to you.'

I overheard Frau Schwarz:

'*Nein. Nein* . . . Everything is going well . . . I am talking to the lady. The mother and the boys are reading a book.'

Again, Alexander had been on the defensive but, realising that Frau Schwarz had confirmed the status quo, his attention was back with me. Tini was happy and as I stroked the back of his neck his shoulders snuggled close to mine. Suddenly, the door flew open and Klaus barged menacingly into the room ordering Catherine to leave the house at once.

'It is unnecessary. Everything is peaceful,' interjected Frau Schwarz.

Klaus ignored her and, pointing at Catherine, repeated his order.

'Then Frau Schwarz should also leave,' Catherine calmly answered. 'The Celle decision stipulates -'

'In that case, I declare this visit over!' Klaus declared, looking at Alexander who had carefully concentrated on his uncle's words. Before I had time to notice, he stood up and ran out of the room at top speed. Tini hesitated for a second then ran out behind him. Klaus followed them into Judge Monkmann's house.

The visit had lasted forty minutes. Frau Schwarz looked genuinely embarrassed.

'I don't understand him. Why did he have to interrupt the visit?' she complained to Catherine. I called Herr Struif and as Klaus returned, Frau Schwarz discreetly slipped out of the house with Catherine. Before leaving I asked Klaus whether I could take the Lego I had brought into the boys' room. Without waiting for his answer, I walked up the stairs. There was a newly built door on the landing.

'It's locked!' I exclaimed.

'Dr Volkmann locks all the doors in the house because he doesn't want the press coming into the rooms.'

Klaus's explanation was so ridiculous that I did not comment.

'I would like to say goodbye to my boys.'

'They don't want to see you.'

Catherine was waiting outside and the two of us walked towards Wilfred Monkmann's house. Tini and Alexander were standing at the entrance.

'Come here,' Klaus ordered Alexander, who came

immediately and let himself be kissed. He then looked at his uncle and ran back into the house. Tini seemed a little less scared and stayed beside me a few seconds longer.

In December though, the gates were open as the Monkmanns were selling Christmas trees and customers needed to be able to drive in. I had come with Alan only, and the visit lasted an hour. Alan had seen Hans-Peter coming from the main house towards the house where I was with the boys, and waving through the glass door to someone inside, obviously Frau Schwarz, at which point the boys ran out. In January, Alan was on holiday and Catherine drove me to Verden. She waited in a temperature of minus 4 degrees in the car. Several cars were parked in front of Monkmann's house and Catherine observed members of the clan coming in and out of the house to assure themselves she was still in the car.

For the January visit, Herr Struif had written to Klaus to inform him that since Frau Schwarz refused to leave the room it would ease the atmosphere if Catherine Urban could also be present. However, as we arrived, Klaus forbade her entry to the house.

'But my lawyer informed you she would be coming!' I exclaimed.

'I sent him a fax yesterday afternoon to tell him this is unacceptable.'

'But I was on the plane from London yesterday.'

Klaus had sent his fax at 5.15 p.m. I had spent another £470 just to be able to look at my little children sitting terrified, unable to talk to them freely in a locked house.

Frau Schwarz's attitude was entirely different this time. She refused even to sit on the other sofa and talked continuously to my boys to counter any conversation I might have with them. Alexander, however, was not as tense as he had been during the previous visits. He looked unbelievably sad and demoralised. His resigned look and the disturbed expression in his eyes worried me greatly.

Alexander had been forced to do the most horrifying thing any child could be asked to do – betray his own mother. As a ten-year-old boy, he had little choice but to abide by what his father had ordered him to say. Children have a loyalty to their parents and do not question them at that age. He had cried in court during his private interview with the judges and had no doubt been terrified. Yet he was undoubtedly conscious that what he had been coerced to say was untrue – for instance when he had said he had no friends in London.

Today, I knew Alexander's mind was in a dilemma and I could see the guilt he was carrying in his eyes – a guilt he could not identify or analyse, but a guilt he could not live with. During the other visits he had withdrawn into himself and had not looked at me. Today, he gaped at me, as if to say: '*Mummy, save me. But I know you can't.*'

Everything about Alexander reminded me of someone who is in deep depression. His placid movements, his empty, defeatist expression. Children do commit suicide. My sons were in danger.

Catherine and I had concluded that Klaus had been acting on his orders during the last visit. He had brought her into the house. Had Judge Monkmann told him off? Had Klaus then come back to carry out his order: 'Get her out. We don't want any witnesses. Who is this woman anyway?'

My children, who had been trilingual, baptised in an Orthodox church then educated in a spirit of freedom and open-mindedness, were being denied what both parents had wanted for them, and had regressed greatly. Constantin no longer knew how to spell my name. Alexander had been incapable of calculating four times four. His school books in London were marked 'excellent'; he had learned history, geography, English. The only knowledge he seemed to have today was about the Bible.

Alexander said they had breakfast at Ute's, Frau Schwarz took care of them in the afternoons, they never left the property and Hans-Peter was away at work. From my past experience of Hans-Peter, lazing around the house, expecting everyone to serve him, I knew it was doubtful that he would be capable of attending to two children's daily needs. Where did my boys live? With Gundel? With Ute? When we had come unexpectedly with the television crew in September they were not here. This house seemed uninhabited and not a single toy was lying around when I arrived for my visits.

This visit was once again interrupted in an ominous way. Suddenly Antje's children were unleashed from Judge Monkmann's house into the yard separating the two houses. And as if a school bell had rung, Alexander shot up and disappeared, Constantin on his tail. As soon as they reached the porch, Klaus came out and all the children disappeared back into Monkmann's house.

In February, Frau Schwarz, 'the most important person in the boys' lives', was not present, but another third party was: Hans-Jorg's wife, a lawyer. The visit lasted one hour exactly. Alexander looked even sadder and more submissive and I was struck particularly when I gave Alexander his favourite London chocolate muffins. He opened the box and looked sadly at them.

'We've already had breakfast,' he said before closing the lid.

Alexander had the biggest 'sweet tooth' I knew; now even this innate instinct had been tempered. Tini was also different. He was cold and uninterested in me as if he had been disappointed that although his mother had finally appeared their situation was unchanged. His mother had failed to protect them. He snubbed me and this time it was he who ran out first after Frau Schwarz told him the time: the visit was over.

A child psychologist I had spoken to believes that they purposely cut the visits after an hour, so as not to run the risk that my sons could 'warm' to their mother. Four weeks separating this one hour per month was enough for them to erase its significance. The boys had no choice, watched over by Frau Schwarz. They knew I would go away and they would be left to carry the consequences of any forbidden words or actions. I dreaded to think what their punishment might be.

The visits were upsetting for me and I am sure for the boys as well. Alexander was growing up and had begun to ask questions. Constantin had realised I had been of no use and his instinct for survival blocked me out of his mind.

German *Panorama* (approached by Ulricke) had filmed its documentary. They were the first to succeed in interviewing Hans-Peter and Klaus. Hans-Peter had admitted that the children were under stress:

'Constantin is very nervous and Alexander has become very unsure of himself and is sometimes aggressive.'

Klaus had commented:

'Of course, what Dr Volkmann has done is at the borders of legality. However, he felt he had no choice . . . If the children had been returned to London, the proceedings [in Verden] could not have gone ahead and the children would not have been heard again by a German court.'

A German lawyer who was interviewed a few months earlier had said that the Volkmanns' case would imply that one should kidnap children, hide them long enough from the police and in time the situation would be resolved. Defy the law in order to win. This cannot be right!

But it was precisely what the Monkmanns and the Volkmanns had done and Klaus proudly stood in front of the camera, leaning against the banister of Hans-Peter's staircase, confirming that it was by defying the law that Hans-Peter had managed to win his case. Hans-Peter had acted illegally so that the proceedings could be held in the German courts where he evidently thought it advantageous: Alexander's statements, *Ich bin doch Deutscher* etc, would secure the non-return of the children, and Hans-Peter's illegal acts would be sanctioned.

Chapter 17
The Ultimate Call

Will I be able to focus people's attention on the injustices you have suffered? Will I be able to reach the hearts of those who may bring Germany to recognise its international obligation and perhaps reform its justice system to ensure the protection of its children? Alexander, Constantin, your mother is calling out for help – powerless before all else.

Klaus was entirely wrong when he presumed that the English court would necessarily protect me, one of its citizens. Hans-Peter's suspension of the English divorce was granted to him until the 'final determination of the proceedings in Germany'. In other words, the English judge gave priority to Verden in determining in which jurisdiction the divorce would be heard.

These proceedings were illustrative of how members of the European Union viewed each other's legal systems. Although the Lower Saxony court had seemingly overlooked our summons, the Lord Chancellor's department had been reluctant to intervene in proceedings abroad, or express its disapproval to its German counterparts.

In turn, the Lower Saxony court had ostensibly expressed its mistrust of any other jurisdiction, in making sure that they would be handling all decisions. Indeed as early as 20 September 1994 the Celle court ordered the children to remain in Germany until the appeal hearing – otherwise it was felt that I could hide them in England. Since then, all my demands for access were rejected on the grounds that I could 'use this opportunity to take my children back to England'. Apparently the Lower Saxony court's determination to keep control of the situation out-weighed the value of respecting children's human rights. The German courts were apparently fit to consider 'the children's interest' (which was the basis upon which each single decision had purportedly been made) – whereas the English courts were evidently not! Klaus had publicly confirmed this perception in the November 1995 *Panorama* interview.

Faced with the Verden court's dogged protection of an abductor, its nationalistic attitude towards me and its defiance of my sons' right to a mother, I was horrified when the English judicial system threw me into the hands of the German one.

An old friend who had accompanied me to the London hearing was outraged when she found out that Hans-Peter had received British 'emergency' legal aid.

'British taxpayers' money is funding a German citizen who had abducted British children, defied English court orders, and denied a British mother access to them!' Incensed, she wrote to the newspapers, and the *Sunday Telegraph* published an article entitled UK PAYS FOR GERMAN TO WREST SONS FROM WIFE.

Germany's position on legal aid however is in stark contrast to the English one. Whereas Hans-Peter's legal expenses were assuredly minimal (with his brother-in-law, his sister and Judge Monkmann as his advisers), I had been ruined financially by mine. Most of our case had been fought in Germany and on top of the exorbitant lawyers' fees I had incurred extortionate travel expenses, phone and fax bills. To date I have spent over £100,000. For nearly a year I had been unemployed and unable to survive on social benefits – yet I had still not been granted German legal aid. The Verden court had still not approved my application.

As a federation, Germany does not have a centralised board that can autonomously examine and determine the validity of each request. It is up to the local courts to decide whether or not they will allocate legal aid. I found this rather surprising since in essence it means that local judges have the power to elect whether claimants will, or will not, succeed in having their cases heard.

My financial situation had become alarming. I was dreading the day when it would prevent me from pursuing my case. I was mortified by the idea that I would be paralysed, while my children's basic human rights were at stake, merely because of lack of material resources. For Verden, needless to say, such an outcome would mean victory, a dream come true: mother would have laid down her weapons, abandoned her children . . . there would be silence at last and, in time, Verden's behaviour would be forgotten.

But for dear, dear Herr Struif's compassion and generosity the pace of legal letters and court applications would have been hampered. Now that the divorce papers had been served on me, the Verden judge declared that its jurisdiction was competent: divorce and final custody would be decided in Germany. Herr Struif immediately wrote to request that the children and both parents be examined by an independent expert from a neutral country. He suggested a world-famous child psychologist from Switzerland who spoke German, French and English. Herr Struif insisted that an opinion could be formulated only if the boys were interviewed in French and/or English since this was the language with which they associated their mother and their lives in London. Furthermore, he argued, I would not be able to express myself adequately in German.

His demand was rejected. The Verden judge estimated that 'since the court's language was German', our right to be interviewed in other languages was uncalled for. Furthermore, the children spoke German fluently and the mother's knowledge was deemed sufficient. So the judge duly appointed a German-speaker from Bremen! Bremen, where Hans-Peter had his practice, and where he was presumably also a member of the Chamber of Doctors.

Bremen, the very place where Hans-Peter had influence and where lawyers had refused to take on my case or to challenge the Volkmanns.

Adding insult to injustice, I discovered that the appointed person was not specifically a child expert but simply a court-registered general psychologist. There was no way a professional report could be established in a context such as this. After almost two years of seclusion and blatant indoctrination, only an independent specialist in children's behaviour, examining them away from their new environment, would be able to determine their true mental state.

Verden had its own way of defining children's interests and human rights. If I was not German bred and German was not my mother tongue, this was my shortcoming and penalising me for it was a matter of course. If my sons only knew how to relate to their mother in a language other than German, they too should be denied this prerogative. The price for leaving Hans-Peter, one of their established community members, was high – it included undermining my children's birthright and leaving them motherless.

This latest decision, however, prompted a radical change in the attitude of the English authorities. If in the past they had viewed my case with reserve and a certain degree of indifference, now they seemed mobilised and prepared to become actively involved. The full attention of the European Community (in particular, members of the English and French governments) became focused on the case – but Verden was recalcitrant and Germany's current government remained unheeding: the Bremen psychologist would examine both the children and the parents.

An appointment for me to meet with the psychologist was set. The psychologist had agreed to interview me in Hamburg where I felt comfortable and secure, but my suggestion that she could see the boys' London environment was discarded.

In my inadequate German, I endeavoured to give a clear picture of our lives. I had brought several photographs with me, in a vague attempt to exhibit proof that my sons had friends in England and had not been clothed from 'cheap shops', as the Celle judgment had claimed (not that cheap shopping would be evidence of a deficient mother, in most people's opinion).

The psychologist was a woman in her sixties, of average height with long hair tied back in a bun. She informed me that she had interviewed Hans-Peter and his parents, had seen the Monkmanns and the boys' school.

'Would you like to talk to my parents?'

'No, that will not be necessary.'

'But what about their London teachers?'

'No. You've shown me their reports. That's sufficient. Next week, I'll pick the children up from their father's property and drive them to the Verden Youth Authority premises to speak to them for a couple of hours.'

'Is this how you'll interview them? Just taking them out for a couple of hours and bringing them back to their father?'

'Yes.'

I did not confront her with the obvious comments which were racing through my mind, too aware that anything I said could be detrimental to me and, consequently, to my sons. I had serious doubts about the neutrality of this woman. She had been chosen by the Verden judge. Furthermore, I was living far away and was inconsequential in her life whereas the Volkmanns and the Monkmanns were firmly entrenched in the Bremen community where she herself lived. Once more, I could do little more than endure in silence what lay ahead. Tomorrow we would meet my boys to see how they reacted to their mother – but of course this meeting would be held at the Youth Authority and considered as my access right for the month of May.

The next morning, Alan and I set off for the thirteenth time. We sat in silence when we reached Verden. Neither of us found it necessary to comment on the day's situation. We both knew what awaited me.

As I entered the building, Frau Kranitz walked towards me and muttered: '*Guten Morgen.*' Her expression was hostile. She remained still until a few minutes later, the psychologist walked up the stairs with a courteous smile. Alexander and Constantin, upright and stern-looking, marched in behind her. As they passed me, they did not raise their eyes. My sons barely greeted me:

'Hello,' they said, then soldiered on into a tiny room Frau Kranitz had pointed us towards.

Both boys were tense and neither of them looked at me as we sat down around a Formica table. Only Alexander ventured a few quick answers to my questions as to how they were. Constantin sat motionless and I could sense how rigid his body was. As the ritual had been during my visits, we began playing a society game. I could sense how bored they were and wondered how Hans-Peter had trained them to sit still and execute this diversion when their mummy was around.

Precisely an hour later, Alexander stood up fidgeting and impatient:

'We must go back. I have to do my homework and Constantin wants to play in the woods.'

And they both rushed out towards Frau Kranitz's office. I tried to explain to the psychologist that these were not the reactions of 'normal' children.

I returned to the car, distraught and filled with fear. 'Hans-Peter was here. I saw him walking in the car park,' Alan reported.

Hans-Peter had remained outside, commanding his puppets with an invisible thread, making sure they would follow his orders.

If Hans-Peter was destroying my sons, manipulating their thoughts, dictating their movements to metamorphose them into automated troopers, I had to stop him. But I knew this was not the way: not by coming here, straight into the wolf's mouth. Every single time I had come to Verden it had been used to distance me further from my son's lives.

As if he had read my thoughts, Alan broke the heavy silence:

'Catherine, you can't go on like this. These visits are destroying you and it is exactly what Hans-Peter wants. Unless you can see your sons in normal circumstances . . .'

Alan was right and I knew it. But would I ever obtain honourable conditions?

Under Article 21 of the Hague Convention, the Berlin central authority had a responsibility to secure me 'effective access rights'. But the London Child Abduction Unit was informed that since the Verden court had granted me *some* access, this issue was no longer in the scope of the Convention. There was nothing further they could do to help. The police could do nothing either. It was up to my lawyer to see that the access rights were abided by. Our only solution was another court application. But, the Verden judge duly cast it aside and requested a report from Frau Kranitz.

By now I knew the tunes by heart and predicting Verden's move was a pushover. Well-formulated reports made by the Youth Authority would justify the court rulings, claiming that they were in the 'children's interest' or according to the 'children's wishes'. Whether Frau Kranitz actually saw my sons or not before dispatching her communiqué was immaterial and once the judicial system had rendered its sentence, Hans-Peter's clan would be sheltered.

Frau Kranitz faithfully announced that the current conditions should be upheld. As is the custom, she provided detailed arguments to support her conclusion – and in her capacity as representative of a public authority, she attested to a blatant untruth. Without even witnessing it, she declared that if Dr Volkmann had had a third party present during the visits, Frau Laylle had also brought in a friend on 'many occasions'. *Once* Catherine Urban had been *led* into the house by Klaus and her presence was then used to slash that particular visit to forty minutes!

Although we now had additional clear evidence of the local authorities' alliance with the Volkmanns I felt this would end up as a whitewash just as before. There had been so many incidents which had fuelled my utter conviction that *this time* they had gone too far, that this time they would be thwarted, that this time their abuse would be stopped . . . but it never was.

Whatever infractions Verden might commit, the distance separating me from my sons had steadily increased over the months; their spirits, as they once were, withdrawing further and further from my reality. I had trained myself not to think about them, and recently my nights had been free of the recurrent nightmares which had haunted them for so long. However, no sooner had I found some calm than I would suddenly feel their little bodies wrapped around mine, feel what it had been like to hold them in my arms. It was a physical sensation and at times I had no control over it.

I tried to settle down, cast out the memories, and turn my attention to what most needed to be done: telephone and fax everyone who needed to be informed. Catherine Urban, who is also the President of French Women Abroad, intensified her campaign to increase the French government's attention to my plight. She is a mother, a professional and a very energetic person. Her brief encounter with my boys had deeply distressed her. No 'normal' child behaves as my children did then. She was certain that they were terrified, manipulated and in psychological danger. In her official capacity, she sent reports to the Quai d'Orsay (the French Foreign Office), the French Ambassador in Bonn, deputies and senators, and publicly addressed Monsieur de Charette, France's Foreign Minister.

In London, Sir John Stanley, co-chairman of the All Party Group on Child Abduction, mobilised the other Members of Parliament who had been involved in my case and together they marshalled the support of the Lord

Chancellor's department. John Taylor had recently been replaced by Gary Streeter. He was a sensitive and compassionate man who was clearly concerned about children's issues. An investigation of the workings of the Hague Convention was under way.

Sir John is an exceptional man whose kindness, compassion and devotion knows no limits. He had been attentive to my case since the very day I had approached him and had fought with a fortitude and resilience that few men possess.

'It is for your children that I am doing this,' he had once told me as I tried to thank him for all the time and effort he had invested in me.

I respected and admired this man enormously as I knew his involvement was exclusively centred on the well-being of children and was truly selfless. If one day, our European children are protected, much will be owed to this one man.

Sir John also instigated another debate in the House of Commons. Further approaches to Germany were made by both France and England. But rather than change its position, review its laws and their applications, Germany's current government remained deaf to all solicitations and indifferent to the German media who were now actively voicing dismay and outrage. The government's answer was to withdraw behind the arguments of the independence of the justice system or the boys' 'wishes' – even though no one (outside Hans-Peter's entourage) had ever been to check on them or investigated the local set-up. Judges had handed down ruthless decisions, affecting two minors' lives and eradicating all their chances of happiness, and they had been condoned.

A school report reached Herr Struif – the first in twenty months. It was a scrap of paper which had a short listing of subjects with marks beside some of them. There were no teachers' comments and the name of the school had been whitened out.

Several weeks later, the first written information on the children reached Herr Struif. There were no words from the boys themselves. Hans-Peter had typed a 'report' summarising his views on how the children were. It was a matter-of-fact account of the boys' activities to illustrate how happy they were in Verden, how they had become friends with the Monkmanns and Uncle Klaus's children. However, Hans-Peter went on to say, both had been 'traumatised' (to such a degree that Constantin had been frightened to walk up the stairs of the house alone!) by the uninvited appearance of their mother and the media campaign she had instigated – although a few sentences earlier Hans-Peter had proudly announced that Alexander had done so well in a football game that his picture had appeared in the local papers.

This report was accompanied by a recent photograph of the boys, dressed in Bavarian grey flannel suits. I showed this photograph to Erica, whom I had recently met through mutual friends. She was appalled:

'This is sheer provocation.'

Erica came from Bremen where she had spent most of her life before moving to France, and recently to England. She had two teenage daughters and six years ago had adopted a Brazilian orphan who 'fell into her arms' and whom she couldn't bear to leave behind in the shocking conditions in which she had found him. Erica was an amazing woman and her love and compassion for children was boundless. When she heard about my case she phoned me, and from then on her attempt to save my sons was unmatched. Erica took up my struggle as if it were her own and restoring to my sons their right to a mother became her mission.

By an extraordinary coincidence, Erica had once had dealings with Ute's pastor and his militant wife. She had not been in touch with the woman since but had no doubt she would remember her. Erica decided to write to Frau Neumann and appeal to her commitment to the children's rights campaign she advocated on television. Frau Neumann lobbied against abortion and crusaded for the necessity of children to remain with their mothers, even in difficult circumstances.

Erica received an answer: Frau Neumann agreed that although children should normally stay with their mothers my sons were much better off living with their father. They had been very unhappy in London and had a bad relationship with their mother. Furthermore, since their mother had 'hired private detectives' and had alerted the press, they now lived in constant fear of her.

'This is fantastic. She is just repeating Hans-Peter's words. How on earth can a woman in her position make statements about someone she does not know and about conditions she has not seen? She herself campaigns on television – yet you shouldn't, for your own children! What do they expect? For you to just lose your children in silence? Will they then deem you a good mother?'

'Oh no. If I didn't fight for them, they would also say I was a bad mother. This has been going on for nearly two years and defaming my character has never been an obstacle to them.'

Erica had not lived through my story since the beginning and she found it impossible to imagine.

'Catherine, I am going to Bremen to speak to her. See if I can make any sense out of those people and try to mediate a solution. I just cannot accept that this is happening. Bremen is my home town.'

Kind, generous and compassionate, Erica set off to Bremen a few weeks later for a round-table meeting between the pastor, his wife and Hans-Peter. The children, of course, had not turned up. She returned to London depressed but even more determined. The Neumanns and Hans-Peter had thrown her into total turmoil and frustration.

'They wouldn't listen. They had closed ranks against you. How can a priest, a representative of God, take sides? And the side of an abductor! Punish children! The

261

fact that Hans-Peter had abducted the children was past and irrelevant. The fact that you had come to Verden uninvited on 13 January last year was given as the absolute reason why your sons should never see you . . .'

Erica began to alert everyone she knew in Germany. As far as she was concerned, such a travesty of justice had to be exposed. Fate had brought her into my life and she was wholeheartedly devoting herself to my cause. Erica was a godsend. Her determination and faith revived mine and for the first time I had the feeling that the wind might be turning; a miracle might yet happen.

Although I found solace in the fact that Germans like Erica were supporting me, I was no longer able to sustain the pressure of the monthly trips to Verden. A week before the visit was due, I would start panicking, overwhelmed with anguish. I would develop stomach cramps that prevented me from eating, and spend my nights tossing and turning. The thought of Verden, the two lone houses, the eerie room, Frau Schwarz's insidious presence, the treachery, were heart-rending. The tension inside me would intensify until I would find myself walking up the lengthy muddy track with Alan in silence, my heart pounding. What would await me this time? Which device would they use to send the boys running off in exactly one hour? What trap would they have set to finally eradicate me from my sons' lives for ever?

And then, with a knot in my heart I would enter this cold, soulless drawing room, find my little sad and frightened angels, and share the agony of their existence. Forced to speak in broken German, confined to a locked space, barred from any intimacy, observed and unable to hold my own sons in my arms. How did he punish them when Frau Schwarz reported any wrongdoing? I was there for one hour but they were the ones who were left behind to face the consequences of any forbidden word or gesture. Observed and commanded, it was not possible for them to disentangle their feelings. How can I ever describe the turmoil, or find the words to capture my

262

agony? How can a mother be expected to witness the suffering of her own children, watch them craving love and freedom, while she is forced to remain utterly powerless to protect them? I felt myself being crushed by the weight of relentless and limitless cruelty. My whole being was crying out in pain.

My father took a firm view.

'Catherine you shouldn't go any more. You can't continue to spend over £600 a month to give Hans-Peter the satisfaction of ruining you. By accepting his terms you are securing exactly what Hans-Peter wants: to demoralise you and destroy Alexander and Constantin's image of their mother. It would be better for them to remember you as you were, a cuddling and free mummy, than see you like this. These conditions are utterly humiliating and abusive. It's not a question of abandoning your children, quite the opposite.'

I knew that my father was right. I had discerned Tini's recent reactions to me. He had been cold and dismissive, probably convinced that his mummy had not tried to alter his existence. Children see their parents as masters of their destiny. Only Alexander had started showing signs of scepticism. But how could he express them once I was gone?

My friends voiced a similar opinion. They too had observed how my trips to Verden profoundly affected me. Two years had gone by. I had forgotten to live, dedicating my whole existence to my fight, incapable of allowing myself any form of distraction. They could see how it was eating away at me. They were concerned:

'Catherine, you've done more than anyone could expect. When they are free to think for themselves your children will realise that you did not abandon them. But now you need your strength – for them – and if you continue at this pace, you'll burn out.'

The thought of what lay ahead of me loomed like an ominous dream. The unimaginable was becoming reality. Hans-Peter was succeeding in excluding me from my sons' lives. He was 'winning' through the use of illegality and evil. He had written in his original letter that he had no intention of 'sabotaging' my relationship with the boys, no intention of 'not letting me see them'! There had been so many lies.

I often wondered how Hans-Peter was able to reconcile his behaviour with his conscience. After all, he must be aware that one day Alexander and Constantin will be adults and feel the need to find out the truth. They will be able to read their father's letters, the court depositions, the press articles . . . Doesn't he realise how betrayed they will feel then? Doesn't he realise that what he has done will hurt his own children most of all? But then, this is what obsessions do – kill judgement, lucidity and freedom of mind. Hans-Peter had become the prey of his own unconditional hatred. He had been spoiled rotten, his mother bending to all his whims, never contradicting him, and consequently he had not learned to control and discipline himself. Why does the German government tarnish its image by blindly supporting him?

I sat at my desk and wrote to my children. Each word had to be carefully chosen to try and convey my message, while not giving Hans-Peter any pretext to attack me. 'Mummy loves you. Mummy has not and will never abandon you . . . These visits are too degrading for the three of us . . . Every child has a mother. Every child is allowed to see her . . . I will go on fighting until we are able to be together again, normally.'

I informed both embassies, and Catherine Urban offered to drive up to Verden to deliver my letter personally on 15 June 1996, the day of my entitled visit. We were all nervous, I most of all.

As has been customary throughout this case, nothing happened the way any of us had predicted. Catherine arrived at exactly 9 a.m. She saw Frau Schwarz's car parked by the house but Klaus was not there to greet her. The door of the house was locked, so she rang the bell. A young girl, sixteen, perhaps seventeen years of age, opened the door. Catherine had never seen her before. She introduced herself and asked whether she could see Klaus.

'Dr Volkmann is not here,' the young girl answered, unsure.

'Ah. I wanted to see Klaus, if it's possible.'

'Who is Klaus?'

Catherine was taken aback by these odd and seemingly staged answers. The conclusion she drew was that Hans-Peter had anticipated I would appear with a court bailiff, hoping to attest to his and Frau Schwarz's presence.

For once we had wrongfooted them and Catherine was able to ask whether she could see the boys and give them a letter from their mother. The girl called out and Alexander slowly walked out of the drawing room and towards Catherine. First she spoke to him in German and, as she recounted to me, Alexander's eyes were glued to the floor. Then she proceeded in French:

'*Ta maman vous aime . . .*' At this point Alexander looked up into her eyes.

'Catherine, I wanted to take him in my arms . . . He looked so sad. It was as if once I had spoken French to him, he could hear your voice instead of mine. His eyes were begging for love, your love.'

Catherine explained to Alexander that I was not abandoning them, quite the opposite, and that I had written them a letter. He took it in his hands and slowly went back to the drawing room. 'I then talked to this girl, as I wanted Alexander to be alone with your words. I really believe he read it but of course we will never know for sure – not until you can see him alone.'

But would I ever see my children again? My sons' and my future together was now entirely at the mercy of a woman who barely knew me and had had no interest in the French grandparents! Final custody and access rights would be determined on the basis of the Breman psychologist's report (which for some reason she would not deliver to the court until August 1996). Until then, there was nothing else. Frau Kranitz had stated that my current

access should not be improved. I couldn't brave these barbaric conditions any longer.

I wondered how many times Hans-Peter and Klaus
would be on the telephone to the psychologist before
August. Would Hans-Peter beg? Make the children phone
her separately? After all, this report was the final solution
to resolve his longed-for goal of eradicating me for ever
and leaving our sons motherless.

His court application aborting any form of access was
boosted by a claim for child maintenance (through the
Youth Authority). Moreover, the amounts requested
from me were backdated to March 1995! At this stage,
everyone supporting me was speechless.

My parents, who had obtained from the High Court of
Justice in Paris a two-week access right per annum (in
French family law grandparents are entitled to visitation
rights), had still hung on to a remote hope that they would
be with the children from 15–30 July 1996 as per the
court order. But predictably Klaus faxed my lawyer at the
last minute to announce that the children would not be
coming 'since this was their wish'. Not only did my sons
supposedly not wish to see their mother, but they were
not interested in seeing their grandparents either! In any
case, Klaus went on, 'The Verden Youth Authority supports the children's opinion and their [Verden Youth
Authority's] view should take priority over any decisions
made by the French High Court of Justice.'

Whereas I may still, one day, see my sons – as adults –
my parents never will. They will die without even having
been able to talk to them. Alexander and Constantin were
the only grandchildren my father had.

At the end of August, the psychologist's report was
finally submitted. This was the first report, made after a
two and a half years' separation from their mother. There
was an introductory résumé of the situation. As usual the
facts that Hans-Peter had abducted the children twice,
been in contempt of court and denied me any form of
access (or contact) with the children were omitted. As

usual, the press campaign I had instigated (once I had realised I would be permanently excluded from my sons' lives) was vigorously and repeatedly used against me.

My 'fight' for my sons was overbearingly interpreted as a negative aspect of my personality. The psychologist considered me 'a woman who was accustomed to succeed in all things' and that when I lost the battle for my children, I had formed an *idée fixe*: the need to fight that battle at the expense of adopting a reasonable attitude and leaving my children be. She even quoted passages of the letter Catherine Urban delivered to my sons to reinforce her point, implying that being their 'biological' mother should not entitle me to have any particular claims on them. Without having observed the circumstances of my life in London, nor talked to anyone in my surroundings (including the children's maternal grandparents) the psychologist decided I was a 'bad' mother who never loved, cared nor had any time for her sons. Working (without which I would have been unable to support the boys) was a proof of my lack of interest in the children.

On the other hand, she viewed Hans-Peter as an oversensitive person who was highly concerned about his children. Later though, she stated that his inability to keep his feelings under control was affecting the children and deeply impaired the restoration of normal relations with their mother. The psychologist described Gundel as a very 'dominating woman who prevented the children from articulating, or even being allowed to articulate, their own feelings where they did not agree with the grandmother's ideas'. Furthermore, she constantly said bad things about me to the boys and openly made derogatory comments about foreigners. Her parochialism was such that she had told Hans-Peter 'that under no circumstances should he find himself a foreign wife' before he set off on the holiday where he met me.

We learned that Hans-Peter had a girlfriend whom he had known for several years. They worked and lived together. Although some twenty years his junior, she was the dominant partner in the relationship and would often have to remind Hans-Peter to do some work rather than sit down and talk. She was viewed as a very positive influence on him, whereas I had been over-demanding in my expectations.

It may be questionable whether a man who had acted unlawfully and was in a 'constant state of anguish' would exert the best influence on a child's education and instil a sense of morality in them, but the Verden-appointed psychologist did not even entertain this point. The children's whole environment was favourable in Verden with their father and unfavourable in London with their mother. Final custody should be transferred to Hans-Peter.

The psychologist described one of the tests she had carried out. The children had to draw a castle. Alexander initially refused to draw the picture. He asked why he had to do it and what was to be gleaned from it. Alexander then expressed an inner resistance and 'was attempting to convey a specific picture of his feelings', exhibiting fears that the psychologist's conclusions might not tie in with his consciously adopted attitudes.

Constantin drew the castle and when she asked him if his mother should have a room, he immediately said 'Yes'. But when she enquired which would be her room, Constantin became conscious of what he had spontaneously said and frantically corrected himself, insisting that his mother was not 'allowed' and asked the psychologist if she could delete his 'Yes'. He then repeated several times that he had made a mistake. When she brought him home later on, the first thing he told his father was that there had been a misunderstanding. In her conclusion, however, the psychologist insisted that the boys had not been 'manipulated' and – at least with Alexander – it had been his 'will' to remain with his father.

Surprisingly enough, the psychologist did state that Constantin still had a strong bond with his mother and that Alexander has positive feelings on his 'subconscious level' and that he had loved his mother in 'earlier times'.

This did not seem to represent a major dilemma for her when she drew the conclusion that 'now their relations have been seriously disturbed' and this was the 'current condition'. And if they had a 'disturbed relationship with their mother' this was 'the result of her own behaviour'. The fact that I had not really been in touch with my sons since they left London in 1994 was overlooked throughout the report.

The report was full of contradictions and I found it extraordinarily biased. Many of my quotes were twisted to become detrimental, and I did not recognise some of my supposed statements. Everything about me was unremittingly negative. Having a babysitter minding them for one and a half hours (until 5.30 p.m.) confirmed that I had disregarded my sons. On the other hand, she made no comment on Hans-Peter's returning home at 6.30 p.m., nor on the children spending all afternoons in the care of their paternal grandmother – even though she later considered Gundel's 'authoritarian character' and prejudices a very harmful influence on the boys.

The report also confirmed that Frau Kranitz (whose official role was the protection of children and who was not of one of their parents) had offered Hans-Peter her support as early as the summer 1994 holidays – although I had custody and she had never spoken to me. There were no additional comments.

The Bremen psychologist's report was essentially as I had expected, bar one very clever technicality: she would examine access rights only *after* the decision on custody was made. Since under German law, it 'is not possible to go against the wish of the parent who has custody', (according to a letter from Bundeskanzleramt) this could give the Verden court the opportunity to exhibit a sign of 'good will' by granting me decent access rights – which Hans-Peter would then be empowered to deny me.

The set for the final act was now completed. Verden would soon be at peace, backed by an irreversible final judicial decision. No one would be able to interfere. 'In the interest of the children' and according to the 'children's will', every illegality, demeaning treatment, inhumanity and prejudice had been condoned. No outside psychologist would ever examine the boys, they would lose their mother, probably for ever, they would never be able to travel freely . . . but Verden had succeeded in its ploy.

I had fought for my sons as best I knew. Most saw my plight as a fairly normal reaction for a mother whose children had been snatched away from her for no reason. But Verden had characterised it as 'evidence' of my uncaring nature and used it against me. But had I not fought for my sons, wouldn't Verden have proclaimed the same? Except then, they would have been able to close the case and rest in peace long ago.

Had I run my course? Should I turn the page and ignore the fact that I have two children; forget I am a mother and find a magician to cast a spell on me to obliterate my eternal concern for my boys? There was nothing left to creed for. The road was blocked and it was dark. There was no single ray of hope to light it any more.

I had fought for over two years, with determination, will and strength in the name of humanity, of justice and of all I believed in – but above all for my sons' rights. I had always held on to the belief that justice would prevail – one day – that it was only a matter of endurance. Now, I no longer knew what life was about and how I should go on living it . . . There was so little left I could believe in, so little I could reconcile myself with. My friends tried to comfort me. 'The boys will be back,' they would say. I do not doubt this. One day, in many years to come, they will know what it is to find their mother. But how can anyone understand that it is not I who suffer most, it is they and that this is the real source of my agony? How can anyone understand how harsh it is to endorse Man's injustice? If only I could sleep for ever and forget. But I am a mother, and because of this I have no right to sleep. Not for them, not for all the other children

270

who suffer the same injustices.

On 16 September 1996 the Lord Chancellor's department released its report on the workings of the Hague Convention and articles appeared the next day in several newspapers. The *Times* article was the largest and its headline read: GOVERNMENT ACCUSES GERMANY OF FAILING TO OBSERVE INTERNATIONAL ACCORD. My case was cited as being a key to the government's strong response. I was ecstatic and regained some of my faith in life. Our government had taken an official position, showing that it cared for children and that it was determined to ensure their protection. Gary Streeter, Parliamentary Secretary at the Lord Chancellor's department, pledged that Britain would take the lead at the Hague Convention meeting in March 1997 (the first in years) to ensure a review of the procedures on child abduction. Britain will be there and I am proud to be a citizen of a country that shows such fortitude. In France, the Minister of Justice, M. Jacques Toubon, who has taken a personal interest in my case has also ordered an investigation of Germany's adherence to the Hague Convention. His compassion and his support have been unequalled. Now, I can only pray that the German government will respond and realise that a small community deep in the forest should not be allowed to manipulate the law, get away with nationalism or give. whoops of joy at the sight of their destruction of others. A small community should not be allowed to negate fifty years of harmony and express regressive views. If we are to live in peace and harmony, if we can deem our society to be 'civilised', how can we allow such inhumanity towards our children? How can the notion of the child's 'wishes' be used in such matters – leaving the door open for the abductor to manipulate his child through fear and propaganda in order to legalise his actions? No child in the world would wish to be denied the love, care and comfort of one of his parents. No child could grow up into a stable, self-confident individual after living through such an experience, after being stripped of what is essential.

Shouldn't our society protect children instead of allowing them to be used as a legal loophole to satisfy criminals? Most children's 'wish' would be to play rather than go to school – yet the law makes it compulsory for them to receive an education. How then can the law use the notion of a child's 'wishes', expressed in such circumstances, to steal away what is half of him and one of his only true and natural rights?

I often wonder how Hans-Peter feels. Is he proud that he has been so successful in his planned destruction of others? Proud that he has managed to manipulate his sons? Proud that they are now in his command and dependent on his mercy? From what I see of his behaviour, he acts more like a hunted animal than someone who is at peace with himself, wishing to deny his sons all that is theirs – extending his claim over them to deny them even their right to multi-nationality. On 21 October 1996 Hans-Peter wrote to the French Embassy in Bonn asking for the cancellation of their French nationality.

Alexander and Constantin, like all children, began life loving both their parents. This has now been forbidden to them. They are trapped behind a wall of lies, deceit and corruption. But I am their mother, the very essence of their lives – and no legal system, no manipulation, no coercion, will ever alter this fact.

But this is no consolation to me now. On the contrary, it only increases my worry that the longer my darling sons are held prisoners the more their minds will be damaged and confused. I have dedicated every single minute of my day to the fight to protect them and save them.

Over and over again, I ask myself why I allowed them to go on holiday. Why was I so naive? Why didn't I see the warning signs? Why did I trust a legal system that has taken them further and further away from me? At night I stay awake, dreaming of the days I used to cuddle them, hearing their laughter and feeling their caresses. The days go by, and they are growing up alone, away from their mother, who is unable to share their fears, to alleviate their pain . . . And I cannot help asking myself: will they ever forgive me for having been weak, for having been blind to the hatred that exists in our world?

Epilogue: A Letter to my Children

Alexander and Constantin,

I have nothing left but my love and my life to give to you. My letters are censored, my phone calls blocked, my words twisted . . . This book is for you – it is the only way I have left to communicate my indestructible, boundless love for you. One day, when you grow up and are free again, maybe then you will read these words.

But for now, it is for others to read them, while you remain unaware of their existence. My loves, I am your mother and I do not know why life has burdened us with such a fate. I only know that, even in my helplessness, I will never abandon you and will continue to fight to give you back your self-respect and your freedom to be loved by your own mother. As strong and determined as I am, I cannot succeed alone – but maybe with the kindness of others who will read this book and help me to make this a national and international issue, your human rights will finally be restored to you, so that you, and other children like you, will be protected against human evil.

Alexander, Constantin – my darling children, I have always loved you more than life itself. Whatever happens, I will always love you and I pray to God to keep you and preserve you. My every working hour is devoted to you and at night I cry for you. I ache to hold you, to comfort you, to love you – as only a mother can. I will always, always, be there for you, my darlings. I will not – cannot

– ever give up. You are part of me: without you I cannot live, I can only exist. But we *will* be together again – one day.

Till then, sleep well at night and let us meet in our dreams. In the dark our thoughts are our own. No one can take them away. They are ours to hold and to cherish, then we can laugh again, hold each other, love each other and be happy as we once were. And when morning comes, wake up brave and strong, and look forward to the day when we will finally be free to be together again. My darling boys, that day will come: whether on this earth or beyond, that day will come . . .

> Sleep well, my darlings.
> When darkness falls and all is still,
> Find refuge in the solitude of night,
> And in the secret of your hearts,
> Enjoy a temporary truce.
> You who inhabit my endless dreams,
> Night after night, you are in my arms,
> My eternal loves.

For ever yours,
Mummy,
July 1996

Appendix

My case, outrageous though it is, is not unique. Child abduction within the EU is much more common than one may think. Increased mobility means that there are more marriages between citizens of different countries. Inevitably, many end in divorce, and one of the parties (usually the wife as she follows her husband abroad) then returns to her country of origin. In most cases couples treat each other with a certain amount of regard and avoid bitter legal disputes. Others, however, take the law into their own hands. The Hague Convention of 1980 was set up to curtail such excesses. The result should have been a model of co-operation between states. This is not the case.

While some countries abide by the letter of the Convention, others interpret it according to their own internal values. Germany, the loudest advocate of a European Union, is the worst offender, as official figures in Britain show: thirty-six abduction cases were reported in the last three years – no children have been returned from Germany. Many more abductions were recorded from France (due to the larger number of Franco-German marriages) and the return rate is similar.

The basic aim of the Convention is 'to secure the prompt return of the children'. Article 13 is the only exception, and the German courts have used this exception consistently to keep illegally retained or abducted children in Germany. Although the minimum age is not stipulated, the Convention clearly specifies that the child should have 'attained an age and degree of maturity at which it is appropriate to take account of his view' for Article 13, paragraph 2 to be considered. An example: Mr Pascal Holdry's children were three and a half and five and a half when they were interviewed by the German court.

The Convention further adds that the views expressed should be genuinely those of the child, and not the result of pressure or indoctrination, and that the 'judicial and administrative authorities shall take into account the information relating to the social background of the child's habitual residence'. But in none of the cases I have seen had this been done. In fact, court decisions were backed by the testimonies of local social welfare representatives, most of whom had no contact with the foreign parent, nor any knowledge of the child's habitual environment.

The decisions were different in form, but similar in essence. The child's 'wish' was always to remain in Germany. When the child was abducted by a mother, the court had an additional argument to substantiate its sentence, namely that children should not be separated from their mothers (hence the large numbers of fathers who contacted me when my case was publicised). When abducted by a father, nationalistic justifications came into play. Another example: 'in Germany [the six-year-old girl] learnt to trust her father, whereas in England, nasty things were always said about Germany.' In another, the claim by the social welfare representative that the five-year-old child had been telling her classmate that she had two fathers, one in London and one in Germany but she prefers the German one, was used by the court. An article listing these examples appeared in the English press. Entitled: 'In the name of the Fatherland', it was critical of Germany's obtrusive attitude towards children. German articles followed suit, denouncing the inhumanity of the legal system.

German family law seems to be the basis of these heartless decisions. The legal reform of the early 1960s had not amended all the laws dating from the Third Reich, which is rather astounding in the European context. Under German family law, for instance, a child's surname may be changed without going to court and without the other parent's agreement.

In the majority of the cross-country cases I have seen, parents were granted minimal access rights (under supervision); some none at all, allegedly in accordance to the child's 'wishes' and the 'risk' of re-abduction. This was how Pascal Auldry saw his daughters (under supervision) for two hours in four years. Charles Bruder had not seen his son in eight years . . . One French father does not even know where his child is, since the German grandmother abducted him several years ago. Another, who also had no contacts, discovered that his wife had changed his son's surname (another 'ex-parte' decision possible under German law).

All these parents' lives were being utterly destroyed but each reacted differently to these harrowing circumstances. Franco Haffner, a US citizen who has been in touch with me, had to sell his business to sustain the legal costs and his move to France (to be closer to his daughter whom he saw for only a few hours in four years). In August 1994 his proposed contact visit was again rejected. He became frantic, killed his wife and committed suicide. His daughter, then just eleven years old, was the only witness. She is now mute and an orphan.

I do not think anyone can judge or know how they will themselves react. If someone had told me my sons would be abducted and I would never be with them, I honestly believe I would have said that I could never live on. I did, and I found a strength I never knew I had – but my strength is geared in a certain way: to fighting a cause. This has become my only objective and I will never abandon it; not until our laws change and our European children can be protected.

My case, like so many others, illustrates a serious problem which needs urgent attention. Most people do not abduct children. Most divorced couples, even if they are living in different countries, arrive at civilised arrangements for their children's sake – conscious that the ultimate cost of their disagreement can only be borne by their children. A man like Hans-Peter, who has abducted his children cannot have done it for their good. I do not believe that a man who truly loves his children would take their mother away from them. A true judicial system cannot connive at abductions, a true judicial system cannot shelter the one who damages his own children's stability and right to happiness. This system cannot be labelled 'Justice'. Children have a right to know, love and spend time with both parents. Children have a right to love and be free, and because they are children, they have to be protected against those who deny them this human right.

Acknowledgements

Above all, I would like to thank my parents, but also my friends. They have given me the most amazing support, love and attention throughout my ordeal and still continue to do so. Without them, I would never have summoned the courage and belief in myself to go on as I have:

Maurice and Olga Laylle,

Claudine Ward, Sandra Menzies, Amelie Knecht, Brigitte Pahl, Debbie Hodges, Viscountess Caroline Windsor-Clive, Valerie Woodmansey, Ginette Hiait, Charlotte Stratos, Lila Rachidian . . .

and particularly

Nicolette Narten, Leonard Louloudis, Joachim von Bonin, and Erica Thoma.

Also,

Catherine Urban, au Conseil Supérieur des Français l'Etranger

Philippe Perrier, Consul de France, Londres

Michael Sullivan, British Consul-General in Hamburg

The Rt. Hon. Sir John Stanley, Member of Parliament

Sénateur Xavier de Villepin, Président Commission des Affaires Etrangéres au Sénat

Gerard Castex, Quai d'Orsay

Alan Kingston and my German lawyer, Herr Struif.

All consistently helped me and have a very special place in my heart.

Everyone who has supported my cause and shown me such kindness.

And my deepest gratitude to: Monsieur Jacques Chirac, Président de la République Française; Monsieur Jacques Toubon, Ministre de la Justice, Garde des Sceaux; Monsieur Edouard Balladur, Ancien Premier Ministre; Monsieur Hervé de Charette, Ministre des Affaires Etrangères; Mr. Gary Streeter, M.P., Lord Chancellor's Department; The R. Hon. Sir Jeremy Hanley, Member of Parliament, Foreign Office; Sir Nigel Bloomfield, British Ambassador in Bonn; Monsieur Francois Sheer, French Ambassador in Bonn; Monsieur Jean Gueguinou, French Ambassador in London; Baroness Chalker of Wallasey, Foreign Office; Madame Arnoud, French Embassy, Bonn; Alex Brown, Vice Consul, British Consulate in Hamburg; Mr. Michael Nicholls, Lord Chancellor's Department; Allison McPherson, Consular Department, Foreign Office; Lord Bruce of Donnington; Kate Hoey, Member of Parliament; Bill Cash, Member of Parliament; The Hon. Bernard Jenkin, Member of Parliament; Mr. Ian Duncan Smith, Member of Parliament; Mr. Bill Olner, Member of Parliament; Dr. Wolfgang Schauble, Bundestag member; Willie Wimmer, Bundestag member; Monsieur Pierre Mesmain, Depute Paris 16; Mr. Newman, The Chairman, Committee on Petitions, Luxembourg; Mary Bonotti, MEP; Mrs. Anne Hennon, Luxembourg; Ray O'Rourke, Assistant to Mary Banotti; David Newans, Assistant to Stan Newens, MEP; Denise Carter; Reunite; Sir Tim Bell, Lowe Bell Communication; Mr. John Craven, Investment banker.

And to all those journalists who believe in exposing social injustice, wherever they find it – I offer my thanks, but even more, my admiration of their profession.

The British and French governments

My friend Philippa Leslie who has spent many evenings editing this text.
Gary Lux, Clintons Solicitors

Hans Marcus, Edmonds Bowen & Co.
Madame Joelle Parmart, lawyer in Paris
Mrs Moira Andrews, who did much to assist me in Germany.